"Truly, it's just a little cut."

"Best to be safe." Eli carefully extended Sadie's hand over the sink, filled a dipper with water, then looked up. "Ready?"

Seeing reassurance instead of disapproval in those cool gray eyes of his was a new experience for Sadie, one she found she rather enjoyed. "Ready," she answered.

He slowly poured the water over the cut. It was strange to feel him holding her hand like this. His own hand was smoother than those of the ranch hands she was used to. She sensed strength there and an unexpected protectiveness.

"Looks like there's a sliver embedded in your palm. This might hurt a bit."

She nodded. His expression shifted and she saw the flicker of concern as he caught hold of the offending sliver, then the small spurt of triumph mixed with relief as he pulled it free.

"Sorry."

"I hardly felt a thing." Which was the absolute truth as far as the cut was concerned.

Books by Winnie Griggs

Love Inspired Historical

The Hand-Me-Down Family
The Christmas Journey
The Proper Wife

Love Inspired

The Heart's Song

WINNIE GRIGGS

is a city girl born and raised in southeast Louisiana's Cajun Country who grew up to marry a country boy from the hills of northwest Louisiana. Though her Prince Charming (who often wears the guise of a cattle rancher) is more comfortable riding a tractor than a white steed, the two of them have been living their own happily-ever-after for more than thirty years. During that time they raised four proud-to-call-them-mine children and a too-numerous-to-count assortment of dogs, cats, fish, hamsters, turtles and 4-H sheep.

Winnie has held a job at a utility company since she graduated from college, and saw her first novel hit bookstores in 2001. In addition to her day job and writing career, Winnie serves on committees within her church, on the executive boards and committees of several writing organizations and is active in local civic organizations—she truly believes the adage that you reap in proportion to what you sow.

In addition to writing and reading, Winnie enjoys spending time with her family, cooking and exploring flea markets. Readers can contact Winnie at P.O. Box 14, Plain Dealing, LA 71064, or email her at winnie@winniegriggs.com.

WINNIE GRIGGS

The Proper Wife

Steeple
Hill®

Published by Steeple Hill Books™

STEEPLE HILL BOOKS

Steeple
Hill®

Recycling programs
for this product may
not exist in your area.

ISBN-13: 978-0-373-82861-6

THE PROPER WIFE

Copyright © 2011 by Winnie Griggs

www.SteepleHill.com

Printed in U.S.A.

And let us consider how we may spur one another on toward love and good deeds.

—*Hebrews* 10:24

To my dear friends Connie Cox and Amy Talley who helped me brainstorm, provided critiques and generally listened to me moan when I got stuck or needed to talk through the sticky parts.

Chapter One

May 1893
Knotty Pine, Texas

He needed a wife and he needed one soon.

Eli Reynolds strode through town, ignoring the intermittent drizzle as he pondered his current situation. According to the workmen he'd hired, the renovations to his newly acquired home would be ready by the end of next week. Once that was done he and Penny would no longer have a legitimate reason to remain at the boardinghouse.

Which meant his time was running out.

Because no matter what the cost, he was determined to be married, or at least have wedding plans, before he moved himself and his nine-year-old half sister into that house. Mrs. Collins, the widow who ran the boardinghouse where he and Penny were staying, was doing a good job of watching over his sister for the time being. But leaving an impressionable young girl like Penny in the care of a housekeeper or governess every day while he went to his office at the bank was an unacceptable option for the long-term.

Trusting a servant with such a precious duty had already resulted in one tragedy. He wouldn't make such a costly mistake twice.

This business of finding a proper wife should have already been settled, *would have already been settled,* if he hadn't so badly misjudged his field of candidates. He thought he'd found the right woman in Myra Willows. She appeared intelligent, mature, of good character, competent in the domestic arts—all the characteristics he was looking for. He'd actually been on the point of declaring his intentions yesterday when he'd been pulled up short by a bit of gossip.

He'd overheard a couple of bank clerks speculating that Miss Willows might possibly be the person behind that ridiculous pseudonym of Temperance Trulove, the very woman who penned the ridiculous and highly melo-dramatic bit of drivel titled *The Amazing Adventures of Annabel Adams* for *The Weekly Gazette.*

Eli didn't quite credit that the rumor could be true—Miss Willows seemed much too reserved and sensible a female to indulge in such nonsense. But at this point he wasn't willing to risk being wrong, not with his sister's upbringing hanging in the balance.

So he'd been forced to regroup, to review the remaining names on his list and chose another bride.

Eli turned his collar up against the weather as a spurt of water fell on him from the eaves of the nearby store-front. What a day! He wasn't just damp, he was beat. Bone-deep, soul-achingly beat.

Truth to tell, the turn his life had taken two months ago, and the nonstop effort he'd put into building a new life for himself and Penny since then, was beginning to wear on him. But soon it would be done and he could relax a bit. Until then, he would continue pressing on toward his goal.

"Looks like you could use yourself a rain slicker." Sheriff Hammond lounged against the doorpost of his office, whittling on a stick.

Eli moved closer to the building to take advantage of the meager shelter from the shower. "A bit of rain never hurt anyone." He winced as he felt a trickle of water make its way down his back. "Then again, I may have to look into getting myself one of those slickers if this weather continues."

The sheriff grinned in sympathy. "Spring showers tend to be unpredictable in these parts." Then he went back to whittling. "How's Mrs. Collins's arm doing?"

The boardinghouse proprietress had fallen and hurt her arm about a week ago. She seemed to be bearing her injury well, but having her out of commission had put the entire boardinghouse in disarray. And the arrival of her friend, purportedly to 'help out', had only served to add to the problem rather than alleviate it. Sadie Lassiter had breezed in from whatever distant cattle ranch she called home with all the grace and finesse of a brown-eyed, auburn-haired dust devil.

He pulled his thoughts back to the sheriff's question. "The doctor says she should refrain from using it for another week or so. But she seems impatient to be back at work."

Sheriff Hammond nodded. "That's Cora Beth for you. The woman can't stand to sit idle." He tipped his hat back with the point of his blade. "How's Miss Lassiter working out?"

It would be ungentlemanly of him to speak his true feelings on the matter. "She is trying," he temporized. "And I'm sure she's good company for Mrs. Collins."

Sheriff Hammond grinned. "As bad as all that, is she?"

Eli merely spread his hands.

"Ah well, Cora Beth's shoes would be hard for anyone to fill." He shaved another curl of wood from his stick. "By the way, mind giving Mrs. Collins a message for me?"

"Be glad to."

"Tell her I'm heading out to the Martins' place in the morning and I'll be happy to carry a food basket for the Ladies' Auxiliary if she still wants me to."

"Will do." Apparently part of the sheriff's duty in these parts was to periodically look in on the various families on the outlying farms and ranches.

With a wave, Eli moved along the wet sidewalk again, eager to reach the boardinghouse where he could dry out and get something filling to eat. Too bad it wouldn't be one of Mrs. Collins's always excellent meals. If he was lucky it would be more edible than the scorched roast Miss Lassiter had served last night.

Eli had barely taken a half dozen steps, however, when he found himself hailed again. One of the benefits—and hazards—of small town life he supposed.

Mrs. Danvers, who ran the mercantile with her husband, stood in the doorway of her store. Swallowing the urge to keep walking, he tipped his hat. "Good day, ma'am. Is there something I can help you with?"

"It's such a dreary day that I thought you might want to come in out of the weather for a bit." She gave him an ingratiating smile. "I'm sure Imogene would be happy to fix you a hot cup of tea while you dry off by the stove."

The woman would be better served to focus her matchmaking schemes elsewhere. Eli had scratched

Imogene Danvers off his potential-bride-list early on. She was too timid, too much under her mother's thumb to provide the kind of oversight he wanted for his sister. And having an overbearing, meddlesome woman for a mother-in-law was not something he was inclined to look favorably on either. "That's very kind of you, but the weather doesn't show signs of letting up any time soon and I need to see to my sister."

A flicker of disappointment flashed in her eyes and then she rallied. "Such a thoughtful brother you are. Perhaps another time."

"Perhaps." He tipped his hat again and moved on.

And yet another reason for him to find a wife soon. He was well aware that his wealth and newcomer-to-the-area status had made him the target of every matchmaking momma and marriage-minded female in the area. Time to take himself off the market.

Which brought him back to making his selection. He'd given the matter careful consideration most of the day and had decided that the widow Collins was now the obvious choice. The only reason she hadn't been his first choice was the fact that she had three children of her own and a younger brother to raise. But while this meant Penny wouldn't have her undivided attention, perhaps it would be offset by the fact that Penny would have other children in the house to play with.

As for appearance, she wasn't an eye-catching beauty, but with her light brown hair, bright green eyes and ready smile there was a sweetness to her appearance that was quite pleasant.

Yes, this might work out for the best after all.

Eli finally reached the boardinghouse and sprinted up the steps, pausing under the shelter of the front porch roof to shed his wet hat and brush the drops of water from his coat.

After stomping his boots on the porch, he stepped inside and hung his hat on the hat tree in the entry. His attention was almost immediately caught by the sound of unruly giggles coming from the dining room.

Apparently the weather-confined children had found some sort of amusement indoors. There were five other youngsters besides Penny currently in residence here. Mrs. Collins's three girls, Audrey, Pippa and Lottie, and her young brother Danny were, of course, permanent residents.

The other child, Mrs. Collins's niece Viola, had moved in just last week. The child's parents were currently on a trip out of the country. Viola, it turns out, was also Miss Lassiter's niece since Miss Lassiter's brother Ry was married to Mrs. Collins's sister Josie. From what he could tell, that nebulous relationship was the only thing the two women had in common.

It seemed odd that a woman who professed to have grown up on a cattle ranch would be so inept at cooking and housework. Since Miss Lassiter's arrival, routines had gone out the window, the meals had been barely palatable and housework seemed to be handled with a less-than-impressive 'lick and a promise' approach.

About the best one could say for her in the way of domestic skills was that she had a way with children. In fact, his normally reticent sister had taken a keen liking to the flibbertigibbet of a woman. Then again, Miss Lassiter acted as if she were little more than an overgrown child herself. It was probably just as well he'd be moving Penny away from her unfortunate influence soon.

Speaking of which, was that Miss Lassiter's voice mingled in with the children's laughter?

* * *

Sadie, blinded by the cloth wrapped around her head, felt a half dozen hands turning her this way and that, leaving her completely disoriented. The sound of laughter blended with that of the rain pattering against the windows.

"Enough, enough," she protested, "I'm getting dizzy." *Please, Heavenly Father, help me get through this without showing signs of panic.*

"One more turn," replied one of her tormenters. It sounded like Audrey, who, though only seven, was often the ringleader of any mischief the group got into.

Finally the hands fell away and Sadie was left standing with no point of reference to tell her which direction she faced. She took a deep breath, keeping the smile planted firmly on her face. "All right, you little imps, look out 'cause here I come."

Because of her fear of small, dark spaces, blindman's bluff had never been one of her favorite games. She'd promised Cora Beth to keep the restless children occupied for an hour or two, though, and she'd made the mistake of letting the children pick the activity.

Really, this wasn't so bad. Even though she was blindfolded, there was lots of room to move around. It wasn't like her nightmare of being trapped in a closet or chest.

Muffled giggles, from Pippa and Lottie this time, cued her that the five-year-old twins were located to her left. She already felt a touch of anxiety thudding in her chest at the prolonged darkness, but she resisted the urge to go after the two youngest and instead turned to her right.

Holding her hands out in front of her at chest level reassured her that there was lots of room to move around and Sadie took a couple of tentative steps before she made contact with the sideboard. Ah-ha! A point of reference. The sound of footsteps scampering away to her left brought a smile to her face.

"Remember, you can't leave the dining room," she warned with mock sternness.

Something brushed against her ankle, startling a squeak from her. A moment later her heart returned to normal rhythm as she realized who the culprit was. "Does it count if I catch Daffy?" she called out.

"Cats can't play."

So, Viola was straight ahead. Her eight-year-old niece hadn't been 'it' yet. Sadie took a couple of confident steps, straining to catch any sound that might indicate her target was on the move.

Then she caught the sound of a heavier footstep, coming from the direction of what she judged to be the hallway. It wasn't Cora Beth. Uncle Grover, then. *Thank you, Father.*

All she had to do was tempt the good-humored older gentleman to enter the room and she'd have an easy capture. And the sooner she could remove this blindfold, the easier she'd breathe.

Moving as quickly as she dared under the circumstances, Sadie headed in the direction of the hallway. "Would you step in the dining room for a moment," she called out in her sweetest tone.

Sadie's hand connected with a sleeve and she latched onto her quarry's arm with an iron grip. "Gotcha!" She smiled in relief. "Sorry, Uncle Grover, but I caught you fair and square."

Why was his sleeve wet?

"Not exactly."

Uh-oh. She recognized that stern tone at about the

same time she realized the arm beneath her grip was much too firm and muscled to be Uncle Grover's.

Sadie released his arm as if it were a snake, then yanked off her blindfold. She looked up into the disapproving gray eyes of the much too proper Mr. Eli Reynolds. His censuring stare made her feel smaller than her five-foot-three height.

The man disapproved of her—for the life of her she couldn't figure out why—but this was no doubt going to add another entry to his list of her shortcomings. "I'm so sorry." The heat climbed in her cheeks. "I thought you were Cora Beth's Uncle Grover."

"So I gathered." He didn't raise his voice and his tone was conversational. So why did she feel as if she were being scolded?

"You've obviously found an enjoyable way to pass the afternoon," he continued. "Much more enjoyable than, say, chores would be."

Oh yes, there was definitely a barb buried in that smooth-as-corn silk tone. "Most of the chores are done," she said. "The kids and I were just having a bit of fun while supper simmers on the stove."

"How pleasant." He gave her a pointed look. "I wonder how Mrs. Collins is faring? Perhaps I should send Penny to check on her."

And to think she'd thought him interesting and in need of a friend when she'd first met him a week ago. "Cora Beth is resting at the moment." Not that she owed him an explanation.

Then a smile twitched her lips as an impudent idea took root. "But it *is* time for me to check on things in the kitchen." She handed the blindfold to Audrey. "Looks like Mr. Reynolds is 'it' now. Y'all have fun."

With that, she swished past the suddenly disconcerted gentleman and headed toward the kitchen.

That should give the too-stuffy-for-his-own-good Eli Reynolds something new to frown over.

Chapter Two

Sadie felt quite pleased with herself—for all of about five seconds. Putting him on the spot that way had been a petty move on her part. No matter what his demeanor, she was convinced his intentions were good and he didn't deserve such treatment. But the man really did have a way of getting her back up. Did he even know *how* to have fun?

Poor Penny. What would that little girl's life be like once she moved out of the boardinghouse and had only her brother for company?

Shaking off that thought, Sadie pushed open the kitchen door and immediately forgot the Reynolds siblings.

"Goodness, Cora Beth, what do you think you're doing? You're supposed to be resting." Sadie had come here a week ago to lend a hand while her brother's sister-in-law recuperated. Though she'd only met Cora Beth twice before, she'd jumped at the opportunity to do this. Not because she'd felt charitable, but because she'd been feeling restless and purposeless of late. Coming here and pitching in was supposed to make her feel useful, but so far things hadn't exactly worked out as planned.

Cora Beth was too polite to say anything, but Sadie

knew her domestic skills had not lived up to the challenge of running a boardinghouse. Rather than trying to lend a hand herself, she would have done better to have hired some competent help. In fact, Sadie was beginning to wonder if she'd ever find a place where she served a real purpose.

Cora Beth smiled over her shoulder. "I'm tired of resting. Thought I'd check on the stew."

Sadie pushed her much-too-maudlin thoughts aside and marched across the room, glad Eli Reynolds wasn't here to see that his fears were well-founded. "Dr. Whitman said you weren't to use that hand any more than you had to for another week."

"It only takes one hand to stir a pot."

"Still, that's my job for the time being. I may not be able to cook as well as you, but I can make do. And I didn't travel eighty miles just to watch you defy doctor's orders." Sadie held her hand out for the spoon. When Cora Beth hesitated, she added "We may not know each other well, but you should've learned enough about me by now to understand I can be downright stubborn when I've a mind to have my way." Having been raised on a cattle ranch in a mainly masculine household, Sadie had spent most of her life surrounded by folks who tended to either underestimate her abilities or treat her as if she were still a child.

One thing this trip had accomplished was to give her an opportunity to show her mettle among these relative strangers and she aimed to take full advantage of that.

Cora Beth held onto the spoon a moment longer but Sadie stood firm.

"Oh, very well." Cora Beth surrendered the spoon and moved away from the stove. She gave Sadie an exasperated look. "And there's nothing wrong with your cooking."

Sadie gave her an unconcerned smile, deciding to be gracious in victory. "There's no need for you to sugarcoat things—I know my shortcomings as well as my talents. Out at Hawk's Creek the kitchen has always been Inez's domain and I'm happy to leave her to it. About the best you can say for my cooking is that it's edible. But we'll all muddle through for the next few days while you take care of yourself."

Heavenly Father, please let me do well enough not to embarrass Cora Beth in front of her boarders again. I'm asking not for myself, You understand, but for the folks who have to eat my cooking. Sadie struggled with her conscience a moment, then added a postscript to her silent prayer. *All right, it would also save me a bit of embarrassment, as well.*

"A commendable attitude."

It took Sadie a moment to realize Cora Beth was responding to her comment—not her silent prayer.

"Did I hear Mr. Reynolds come in?" Cora Beth added.

Sadie tried to keep her tone light. "Yep. Walked smack-dab into the middle of our blindman's bluff game." Funny, though, that even when she was irritated with the man she could notice how the rain had darkened his pecan-brown hair a couple of shades and caused it to curl up slightly at the ends.

"Oh dear." Cora Beth gave a rueful smile. "I take it he didn't approve."

An understatement. Sadie sighed. "I don't know what I did to curdle that man's cream but it's plain to see he doesn't think much of me." It was a shame, really. *Her* first impression of *him* had been positive, and it wasn't just because she liked the lean, broad-shouldered look of him. He was a bit too somber, perhaps, but he had a certain air of quiet confidence mixed with respect for others that she admired. What had really drawn her to him, though, was the hint of suppressed sadness she thought she'd sensed in him.

Of course, she'd been known to be wrong before.

"I'm sure it's not as bad as all that." Cora Beth's words drew her back to the present. "He just needs to get to know you a little better is all. He's really a very nice man."

Nice, yes—he just didn't approve of her. Which was a new experience for Sadie. She might still be treated as something of a child at home, but folks tended to like her. And as one of the Lassiter siblings and part owner of the Hawk's Creek Ranch, Sadie was used to her name, at least, commanding a certain degree of respect.

"You have to agree, though," Cora Beth said, "a man who takes such good care of a younger sister the way Mr. Reynolds does must have a lot to recommend him."

Sadie refrained from comment. Was Cora Beth forming an interest in the newest resident of the boarding-house? She wouldn't blame her if she had—still, for some reason, that thought didn't sit well.

Best to change the subject. "Now, get yourself on out of here. If you don't want to lie down, why don't you find a book to read or something quiet to do with the kids?"

"Don't you want some company?"

Sadie knew if Cora Beth stayed she'd try to lend a hand. The woman just didn't know how to take it easy. "That's not—"

The door eased open just then, and Penny stood there, hesitating as if unsure of her welcome.

Sadie smiled at the young girl. "Hi there, princess, come on in." Then she arched a brow Cora Beth's way. "Seems I have someone to keep me company, after all. And since I intend to teach her all my kitchen secrets, you'll just have to run along."

Cora Beth looked from one to the other of them, then smiled. "Very well. I think I'll see what Uncle Grover's been up to today."

As soon as she'd left, Penny looked up at Sadie. "Are you really going to teach me secrets?"

Sadie tapped the little girl on the nose. "Actually, my biggest secret is that I'm not very good in the kitchen. But if you'd like to help, maybe between the two of us we can pull off something acceptable. What do you say?"

Penny's buckskin-colored pigtails danced as she nodded.

"Good. Now, let's find you an apron." Sadie hummed as she bustled around the kitchen, glad of the girl's company. She'd taken a real liking to the quiet nine-year-old this past week. And it really warmed her heart to see that the feeling was returned. With Penny she never felt judged or that she had to prove herself. The little girl just seemed to enjoy being with her.

Once she'd tied the oversized apron on Penny, Sadie put a finger to her chin. "Now, let's see. The stew is doing fine and the bread is already done." She'd even managed not to overcook or undercook it this time. "I guess we're ready to work on dessert."

Penny smiled, luring forth the rare appearance of her dimple. "I like dessert."

"So do I. Cora Beth helped me with a pound cake this morning, but I thought we might try to make a sauce to pour over it. Inez, the cook over at our ranch, makes a really scrumptious honey sauce that I think I can duplicate." At least she hoped she could. "Why don't you get the honey from the pantry while I get the butter and the cream?"

Penny nodded and headed off to do just that.

Sadie placed the butter and cream on the table then paused when she spied a neatly folded copy of this week's *Gazette* on the counter. At least one thing had gone right since her trip here. Mr. Chalmers had agreed to run her story and it had met with gratifying success. She might not be a good cook, but it seemed she could spin a fine yarn. The thought of accomplishing something like this entirely on her own boosted her spirits again.

"Here's the honey."

Sadie glanced at the crock in the girl's hands and gave her an apologetic smile. "Sorry, princess, that's the wrong container." Cora Beth had taken pains to explain to her that *that* particular jar contained a special honey that she used exclusively for her fruitcakes. Apparently it took on a special flavor because of the flowers that grew near the hard-to-find hive. "There's a blue crock on the same shelf where you found that one—it has the store-bought honey."

Penny nodded and turned back. But before she'd taken more than a step, she dropped the crock.

Sadie gazed down in horrified fascination at the sticky shards of crockery and gooey splatters. Cora Beth was not going to be happy.

"I'm so sorry. I didn't mean to—"

Penny's cracked-voice apology snapped Sadie out of her thoughts and she gave the girl a bright smile. "That's okay, princess, it was an accident. Don't you worry any more about it. Goodness knows I've had more than my fair share the past few days."

"Is Mrs. Collins going to be very upset?"

Sadie flipped her hand dismissively. "Oh, not at all. I'll just get her some fresh honey and she'll be happy as a hog in a wallow."

Penny wrinkled her nose as she smiled. "You say the funniest things."

"That I do." She gave the girl's shoulder a pat. "Now, you fetch the mop while I get a pail of water to clean this up. And watch your step."

Worried that the little girl might cut herself on the shards, Sadie fetched the other crock of honey and placed it on the table with the butter and cream. "Do you mind working on the honey sauce while I clean the floor? It would really be a big help."

Penny's shoulders drew back and her chest puffed out a bit, obviously proud of being given such a 'big girl' responsibility. "I can do that."

Hiding a smile, Sadie got her started, pouring the ingredients into a large bowl in what looked to be the correct proportions. "Now you just stir that up until it's all mixed together and the lumps are gone." She gave the girl a challenging look. "It may take a while to get it just right. Think you're up to it?"

"Oh yes. You can count on me."

Sadie gave her a big smile. "I know I can. You and I make a pretty good team."

Rolling up her sleeves, Sadie stepped over to the splatter and got down on her knees. At least *this* chore was one she was confident she could accomplish well.

A few minutes later she dropped the last of the larger shards into the trash pail and wiped the back of her hand across her forehead. "How's it coming?" she asked Penny.

"There's still a few lumps, but I'm getting close."

"Good. Guess I'd better check on the stew before

I finish up here." She certainly didn't want to scorch supper the way she had last night. Who knew a roast could go from pink to charred so fast?

She put her hands on her thighs, prepared to stand. But her shoe caught on the hem of her skirt and she came down hard, landing on her backside with a jarring thud.

"Oh!" Penny's exclamation rang with anxiety.

But before Sadie could tell her she was okay, the door pushed open and Eli Reynolds stepped through. Sadie groaned inwardly. Of all times for her biggest critic to show up.

"Have you seen—" Penny's brother halted mid-sentence, his expression turning to a mix of surprise and something else she couldn't quite identify from this distance.

Then he crossed the room, bearing down on her with long, quick strides that took her aback.

"Sadie fell," Penny proclaimed worriedly. "I don't know if she's hurt."

"I'm fine." Even if she hadn't been, Sadie would never have hinted otherwise. She ignored the urge to rub her now-tender backside. If only he would just go away and leave her to recover her wounded dignity in private.

She stared up from her less-than-dignified position as he knelt beside her, waiting for the inevitable censure. Instead, he met her gaze with a concern that took her completely by surprise. "Are you sure you're not hurt?"

She blinked, not quite certain how to react to this softer side of the man. "Yes, I mean, there's no need—"

Why in the world was she stammering? She took a deep breath then offered a self-mocking smile. "The only thing smarting at the moment is my pride."

He studied her a moment longer, then offered a hand. "In that case, here, let me help you up."

She allowed him to take her elbow, liking the feel of his strong, protective grip. When he placed his other hand at her back to steady her, she decided, that yes, she liked this very much indeed.

"You're bleeding!"

Penny, her complexion ashen, was pointing to Sadie's hand.

Sadie stared at the thin ribbon of blood running from her palm as if it belonged to someone else. Then she turned back to Penny. "It's all right, princess. I must have put my hand on a bit of crockery when I fell. But it doesn't hurt. Truly."

Mr. Reynolds intervened. "Just to be certain, let's clean it up and have a look."

"Oh, that's not necess—"

He caught her gaze and tilted his head ever so slightly toward Penny. "I think everyone will feel better if I do."

Penny nodded. "You don't have to worry, Aunt Sadie. Eli's real good at making boo-boos feel better."

She saw his brow go up at Penny's use of 'Aunt Sadie' but he let it pass without comment. Warmed by the thought that he took time to address his sister's 'boo-boos', she allowed him to steer her towards the sink.

Even as she followed docilely along, though, Sadie again tried to make light of her injury. "Truly, it's just a little cut."

"Best to be safe." He carefully extended her hand over the sink, filled a dipper with water, then looked up. "Ready?"

Seeing reassurance instead of disapproval in those cool gray eyes of his was a new experience for Sadie, one she found she rather enjoyed. Then she realized he was waiting for her response. "Ready," she answered.

He gave her an approving smile, then slowly poured the water over the cut. It was strange to feel him holding her hand like this. His own hand was smoother than those of the ranch hands she was used to, but not soft in a namby-pamby way. She sensed strength there and an unexpected protectiveness.

"Looks like there's a sliver embedded in your palm." He glanced up and met her gaze again. "This might hurt a bit. I'll make it quick."

She nodded. Staring at his bent head, she noticed the way his hair tended to curl around his ear, how his brow wrinkled slightly when he was concentrating. His expression shifted and she saw the flicker of concern as he caught hold of the offending sliver, then the small spurt of triumph mixed with relief as he pulled it free.

"Sorry."

She blinked and it took her moment to realize he was apologizing for any discomfort his actions had caused her. "I hardly felt a thing." Which was the absolute truth as far as the cut was concerned.

Penny held out a bit of cloth. Sadie had been so riveted by Eli that she hadn't noticed Penny had crossed the room. "You can use this for a bandage," she said to her brother.

"Of course." He took the cloth from her and again his touch was gentle and sure as he wrapped her palm in the makeshift bandage.

"Thank you." Was that soft voice hers?

He cradled her hand a moment longer as his gaze caught on hers.

And held.

For several long, breath-stealing moments.

Chapter Three

"**W**ild wiggly worms, what happened in here?"

At the sound of Danny's horrified question, Eli abruptly released Miss Lassiter's hand and they both spun around.

He straightened his cuffs, trying to regain his composure. Surely Cora Beth's brother didn't think—

A heartbeat later he realized Danny was staring, not at the two of them, but at the mess on the floor.

"Just a little accident with the honey crock," Miss Lassiter explained. "Nothing to get all excited about."

"Who—"

"It doesn't really matter who dropped it. What's done is done."

Eli raised a brow at her hasty interruption. Did she have trouble admitting when she'd made a mistake?

Danny didn't seem inclined to let the matter drop. "But that was the last of Cora Beth's fruitcake honey."

Fruitcake honey? What was that?

Miss Lassiter, however, seemed to have no trouble understanding the significance. "I know, and that's unfortunate. But don't worry, I'll make it up to her."

Eli took himself in hand while Danny and Miss

Lassiter babbled on about the honey. No doubt his uncomfortable, off balance feeling of a moment ago was caused by sympathy for Miss Lassiter's injury, nothing more. After all, it was quite natural for a gentleman to feel some concern for a lady in distress. Especially a petite little thing like Miss Lassiter.

It was time he set his mind to more important matters. Like pressing his suit with Mrs. Collins. He'd set a few pieces in motion this evening and then lay his case before her tomorrow.

No doubt she would think his proposal sudden, but Mrs. Collins struck him as a sensible woman, one not given to fanciful notions. And since his offer of marriage would afford her an opportunity to finally shed the onerous workload she bore as proprietress of this boardinghouse, he was confident she would view his suit most favorably.

He spared a glance for Miss Lassiter. She'd moved back to the table with Penny and the two of them were stirring something in a large bowl. They looked so comfortable together, as if they were old friends. How did she manage to coax that sweet smile from his sister so often?

He shook his head to clear it from those stray thoughts. This waffling was unlike him—he preferred an orderly, calculated approach to decision making. Cora Beth Collins was the logical choice and she would make a wonderful mother figure for Penny.

And after tomorrow it would be settled.

The evening meal passed pleasantly enough. The food, while not up to Mrs. Collins's standards, was passable. And Miss Lassiter made a point of giving credit to Penny for making the dessert sauce. While his sister reddened under the attention, she also seemed pleased by it, as well. He would have to remember to thank Miss Lassiter for her consideration.

He was also pleased with the progress he'd made with Mrs. Collins. Earlier he'd sought her out and asked for her help with the selection of a cook-housekeeper for his new home. He'd solicited her opinion on what qualities he should look for, then asked for suggestions on which local women might be suitable. He'd been impressed with her thought processes—another signal that he'd selected the right woman. In the end, he'd convinced her to allow each of the three women she'd recommended to take a day and cook the meals here at the boardinghouse so she could help him evaluate their performances.

He'd dropped a few hints about how dearly he valued her opinion and how he hoped to find a woman 'just like her' to preside in his home. He'd been subtle, as propriety dictated, but he was confident she would not be completely surprised when he proposed tomorrow.

Once the meal ended, Eli stood, ready to make his exit with the other boarders so the family would have the freedom to clear the dining room, but Mrs. Collins detained him with a comment. "I understand the work is almost complete on your new home," she stated.

Eli nodded, taking it as a positive sign that she had singled him out. "Yes. Unfortunately that means we'll soon have to say good-bye to the wonderful hospitality we've enjoyed here at your fine establishment." Of course, if things worked according to plan, she would soon be enjoying the relative ease that came with presiding over *his* household.

"As pleased as we've been to have you and Penny with us," she replied, "I'm certain you'll be happy to be settled into your own home."

Eli found himself momentarily distracted by the sound of Miss Lassiter's laughter. It was a sound he'd heard quite a bit during the past week, though rarely when he was in her immediate presence. Not a polite titter or girlish giggle, hers tended to be a robust laugh, full of merriment and outright enjoyment. Hard to believe all of that exuberance could be contained in such a petite frame. A second later he had to school his expression as he realized he'd smiled in response.

"At any rate," Mrs. Collins continued, "it's good to see the old Thompson place all spruced up. It was so sad the way it got so run down after Mrs. Thompson passed away last winter."

Audrey approached them with Viola and Penny in tow. "Momma, is it true we have to wait until next week to find out what happens to Annabel Adams?"

"Afraid so, girls."

Audrey's lower lip poked out. "But that's such a long time."

"Which means you'll have an opportunity to practice patience. Now back to clearing the table."

Audrey didn't seem at all happy with that answer, but she nodded and moved toward the table.

Eli, however, was more focused on his sister. "Penny, am I to understand you've actually read this nonsense?"

She responded with a guilty smile. "Aunt Sadie read it to us this afternoon." Her expression turned earnest. "And it's not nonsense, Eli. Annabel Adams is so brave and good-hearted."

Miss Lassiter, was it? He should have known. He'd have a word with her on the subject, but he wasn't such an oaf that he'd dress her down in front of her friends.

As Penny moved away, Mrs. Collins offered him

a smile. "It really is quite harmless and entertaining, you know. Everyone's been talking about *The Amazing Adventures of Annabel Adams* ever since it appeared in the *Gazette* this week. Printing it was certainly a smart move on Fred Chalmers' part. I reckon there'll be a whole lot more folks than usual lined up for his paper next week."

Eli supposed from a business perspective it did make sense. But that didn't mean he approved of his sister reading such drivel. "Any idea who this Temperance Trulove really is?"

"No and Fred Chalmers isn't talking."

Why should he? Keeping the author's identity a secret only piqued the subscribers' interest all the more.

Time to change the subject. "I'm in the market for a carriage and a horse. Do you know where I might find something of quality?"

"Danny would be more able to help you with that than me." They moved toward the boy, who was gathering up an armload of dirty dishes.

Once Eli explained what he needed, Danny nodded. "There's a couple of rigs whose owners would likely part with them for the right price. What kind are you looking for?"

Eli was surprised at how grown up the eleven-year-old suddenly appeared. Apparently he was all business when it came to the livery stable. "Something suitable for getting around town and for short excursions. With enough room to seat three or four comfortably."

"Mr. Anderson's buggy is your best bet then. It's extra roomy and still in fine shape, but now that his kids are moved on he wants to replace it with something that has less seating and more room to haul goods. As for horses—"

"My brother runs Kestrel Stables," Miss Lassiter interjected. "He raises the finest horses in these parts. He and Josie are away right now, but I'd be glad to show you his stock."

That's right, Miss Lassiter's brother was married to Mrs. Collins's sister—that's how the two came to know each other. He'd met Ryland and Josie Lassiter once when they'd visited Mrs. Collins. Ryland seemed like a fine man, much more levelheaded and grounded than his sister.

"She's right," Danny offered. "Ry and Josie raise some mighty fine mounts. It's where I'd go if I was looking to make a purchase."

Eli met Miss Lassiter's gaze. "And can you make deals on his behalf?"

She lifted her chin as if taking offense. "Of course. Ry was the one who taught me most of what I know about horses, so he trusts me. And Henry, Ry's foreman, will know which animals are for sale and which are not."

Something flashed in her expression, there and gone so quickly he didn't quite make it out. "In fact, since Cora Beth mentioned that we'll have someone else in to do the cooking tomorrow, I was thinking I might take a trip out to the ranch. You're welcome to accompany me to look over the stock if you like."

Eli hesitated. Something about her smile made him a trifle uneasy. On the other hand, a horse was an important purchase and he wasn't inclined to wait the month or so until her brother returned from his trip.

Besides, if she was up to something, he was certain he could handle it. "Thank you for your kind offer. Just let me know what time you wish to depart."

Sadie placed the hamper next to the sack Mr. Reynolds had already loaded in the back of the buggy for her. As she stepped back she noticed him eyeing her suspiciously.

"Are you making deliveries to the ranch?"

She allowed him to take her hand and help her up. "You could say that. Kestrel is Viola's home, remember? She wanted to send gifts to her friends there and Cora Beth let her raid the pantry. There are a couple of pears to feed to her pony, a few jars of preserves for the cook, a jug of apple cider for Henry—that sort of thing." No point mentioning the items she herself had packed just yet.

She cast around for a change of subject as he climbed up beside her and decided the weather was as good a topic as any. She waved a hand to draw his attention to the clouds scattered against the dark blue field of sky. "Looks like we're in luck weather-wise. If we *are* in for more rain today, it's several hours out."

He nodded as he picked up the reins. "I agree. We should be back in town well before any foul weather sets in."

After that the conversation lagged. Sadie tried not to fidget as she wondered when and how she should broach her plans for her little side trip with him.

Dear Father above, help me find the right words. This all felt like the right thing to do last night when I planned it, but I'm just not certain he's going to see it that way.

After about five minutes, Mr. Reynolds finally broke the silence. "There is something I wish to speak to you about."

"Oh?" From his tone, this did *not* sound like a conversation she was likely to enjoy.

"In case it has escaped your notice, my sister is young and very impressionable. As are the other children in

Mrs. Collins's household. I think it would be best if you refrain from reading that weekly serial to them in the future."

His words took her completely by surprise. "Why ever not? The children enjoy it and it seems harmless enough."

He raised a brow at that. "Do you truly think it appropriate reading material for children?"

"I wouldn't have read it to them if I didn't." Did he think her so irresponsible? And what would he think if he knew *she* was the author? "The heroine exhibits high morals, healthy curiosity and steadfast courage. Have you even *read* the story?"

He brushed her question aside. "I didn't need to. I've seen its ilk before. It's a frivolous piece of work, one that is liable to put notions in innocent young minds that are at best nonsensical, and at worse dangerous."

How dare he! She shifted in her seat to face him more fully. Did the man realize how pompous he sounded? "Dangerous? That's a bit melodramatic, don't you think? I suppose you'd prefer that I read to them from school books or perhaps morality plays."

He didn't seem at all ruffled by her sarcasm. "If you must read to them at all I will be happy to furnish you with copies of suitable material." He glanced her way with a stern look. "Penny is my sister, and I must insist that you accede to my wishes in this matter."

Sadie took a deep breath. As much as his criticisms stung, and as much as she disagreed with his perspective, he *was* Penny's brother and guardian. It was not her place to argue with him about her upbringing.

I'll trust in You to look out for the girl, Father. Goodness knows she'll need some sort of intervention if she's to be allowed any fun at all in her brother's household.

"Very well." Sadie was proud of the calm tone she managed. "I won't read to her about Annabel Adams's adventures without your permission." Besides, it wasn't as if she'd have much opportunity anyway. The installments came out once a week and he'd be moved into his new home soon. And she'd be headed back to Hawk's Creek before long, putting even more distance between them.

Hoping to lighten the mood, she changed the subject. "So tell me about where you and Penny come from. That's definitely not a Texas accent you speak with."

"We come from Almega, New York, a city about thirty miles southeast of Albany. It's much bigger than Knotty Pine with a nice variety of theaters, museums, fine restaurants, and even a hospital. All of the latest modern conveniences are available there and you can find more shops on one street than there are houses in Knotty Pine."

She supposed she should be impressed, but it all sounded terribly crowded to her. "So what made you leave such a fine place to come out here?"

A muscle in his jaw twitched. She was probably being too nosy again.

"I thought the change would be good for Penny," he finally said. "And the bank here was a good investment opportunity."

He'd done all this for his sister? He must care a great deal for her. "Penny sure is a sweet girl and bright as all get-out. I know Cora Beth's kids and Viola are all quite taken with her. She seems a mite shy, though."

He stiffened. "She's just naturally quiet."

Sadie heard the note of defensiveness in his voice.

"Of course. I didn't mean to imply I thought there was anything wrong with her." She smiled. "Any more than there's anything wrong with Audrey for her natural chattiness."

He seemed to relax at that, and his lips twitched in a smile. "True—no one would ever accuse Audrey of being a wallflower."

Oh my, he really should smile more often. Then she caught site of an oak with a double trunk and a twisted branch. "You need to turn on that road off to the left up ahead."

When he followed her directions without question, Sadie felt a twinge of guilt. She'd wait just a few minutes more, she told herself. Once they were off the main road a piece, she'd fill him in.

She kept up a stream of chatter hoping to keep him distracted from his surroundings as she watched for the milestones Danny had told her about.

Fifteen minutes later, he interrupted her mid-sentence. "Miss Lassiter, are you certain this is the right way? I haven't seen any farmhouse or other sign of civilization for a while."

"Oh, we're going in the right direction—I'm sure of it."

"Your brother's ranch is out this way?"

Okay, time to come clean. "Not exactly."

That brought the expected frown. "Explain, please."

She winced at the frostiness of his tone. Perhaps she really should have let him in on her plans sooner. "I have an errand to run for Cora Beth and thought we'd handle that bit of business first."

"An errand?"

Did she detect a note of suspicion in his question? "Yes. I need to fetch something she needs." Oh dear, was he slowing the horse? "I assure you it's important. We just need to go a little further down this road."

He pursed his lips as if unhappy with the unplanned detour, so she quickly added, "And I promise you, Cora Beth will be *very* grateful."

Finally he nodded, and to her relief he allowed the horse to resume its earlier pace. "I suppose, if Mrs. Collins asked you to do this, it's the least we could do. But I hadn't expected to be gone all day."

"You won't be."

A few minutes later he cut her another sideways glance. "I'm beginning to feel like we took a wrong turn. Are you certain you know where we're going?"

"Absolutely. I asked Danny to run through the directions twice and I've seen several of the landmarks he gave me. It should be just a little farther along."

He didn't seem reassured. "Exactly what is the nature of this errand you are running for Mrs. Collins?"

Sadie took a deep breath and then offered him her brightest smile.

He was *not* going to like the answer to that question.

Chapter Four

"Actually, I'm looking for Josie's honey tree."

Eli thought for a moment he'd misheard. "You're what?"

"Looking for Josie's honey tree." She made the statement as if it were nothing out of the ordinary. "I want to replace the honey that spilled out on the floor yesterday."

He pulled the buggy to a stop and set the brake. He couldn't believe he'd gone all this way down a rutted-pig's-trail-of-a-road on such a fool's errand. When he turned to speak to her again it was all he could do not to growl. "And Mrs. Collins asked you to do this?"

"Actually, I intended it as a surprise." Before he could say anything she rushed on. "I never said Cora Beth asked me. I just said we were fetching something for her. Which we are." She grimaced, then sat up straighter. "I'm sorry. I *do* know that a lie by omission is still a lie. You're right to be angry. I should have been more up-front with you."

Her honesty was disarming but it still didn't make him any fonder of the current situation. "If you felt the need to replace the honey you ruined, why couldn't you just purchase a jar at the mercantile?"

A flash of some strong emotion crossed her face, but then she shook it off. "Because that honey was special." Her tone was earnest but he noticed the way she clasped and unclasped her hands in her lap. "It was the last of a batch of wild honey that has a unique flavor. Cora Beth uses it to make those wonderful fruitcakes that she sells. She didn't say anything but I know she's worried about missing some of her regular delivery dates, what with her hurt arm. And now this. She counts on the income from those cakes to help her make ends meet."

Something she would have no need to do once she became his wife. Not that he could say that to Miss Lassiter.

"The location of the hive is supposed to be secret," she continued, her voice a nervous babble, "but I had a suspicion Danny would know where it might be." Her expression turned smug. "I grew up with two brothers of my own and they weren't likely to let a secret like that get the better of them. Sure enough, when I questioned Danny he admitted he followed Josie, all sneaky-like, on one of her trips. He couldn't get real close—seems he swells up something awful when he gets stung, but he got close enough to spot the general vicinity."

That was it? That was what she'd based this ill thought-out expedition on? "I'm going to find a place to turn this buggy around and we're going to head right back to the main road."

Dismay clouded her expression. "You can't, not when we've already come this far. Look, right over there is the turtle back rock Danny told me about. We're close, I know it."

"Miss Lassiter, I don't—"

She placed a hand on his arm. "Please. If not for me, do it for Cora Beth. This would mean a great deal to her."

Her action, as well as the touch of desperation in her tone, startled him.

As if seeing him weaken, she pressed her case. "Give it just ten more minutes. If we haven't found the hive by then, I'll go without complaint." She gave him a cajoling smile. "Besides, who doesn't like the idea of a treasure hunt?"

He had to bite back a smile at that—the woman really was incorrigible. "Oh very well—ten minutes." He hoped he didn't regret the decision. "What's the next landmark we're looking for?"

She released his arm and settled back into her seat. "Thank you. There should be a small cabin of some sort just a little way farther along. Then we'll need to go the rest of the way by foot."

Of course they would. But he absolutely drew the line at wondering through the woods. If it wasn't in easy sight of the trail he would most definitely put an end to her quest. "If Danny didn't set eyes on the hive itself, how do you know you can find it?"

"He says he got close enough to hear her working. Don't worry, I'll find it."

The small cabin turned out to be a one room building that looked as if it would topple over with the next good wind that blew by.

Eli tied the horse to a bit of brush, then paused as he considered a possible flaw in her plan. "Do you even know how to collect honey?"

But she nodded confidently. "I've done it a time or two—remember, I have two brothers and I grew up on a ranch." She smiled as he took her hand to help her down. "How about you?"

"I have not yet had that pleasure."

His sarcasm seemed lost on her. "Don't worry, I'll show you how. I have some netting and gloves for the two of us so we shouldn't have to worry much about getting stung. And I also have some oil-soaked rags for smoking the little critters, along with a bucket to collect the honey comb in."

He'd wondered why she'd packed so many provisions to deliver to her brother's ranch. "Sounds like you came prepared."

"Of course. Actually, I don't know how Josie managed it on her own. I've always thought of this as a two-person job. Come to think of it, it'll be interesting to see how she managed to not destroy the hive while she was at it."

He stepped forward to assist as she reached behind the seat of the buggy to collect her supplies. He was irritated with her, yes, but he was still a gentleman.

Miss Lassiter studied the brush beside the road and finally pointed toward a narrow space between two scraggly saplings. "There's a trail here, just like Danny said. But it's overgrown and looks to be marshy in spots, so watch your step."

He stepped forward. "I'd better take the lead." He wasn't going to risk her getting them lost or wandering too far afield.

Saying the trail was overgrown was an understatement. Within minutes Eli began to wonder if this was actually a trail at all. When his left shoe sunk into a muddy patch a few moments later, he was ready to call the whole thing off. "I'm sorry, Miss Lassiter, but I think—"

"Look, there it is."

Eli glanced to his left where she was pointing and sure enough the brush gave way to a small flower-bedecked clearing. And right at the edge of it was a crudely constructed man-made hive.

Without waiting for his lead, she moved toward the clearing. "Why Josie, you clever girl. So this is how you were able to harvest honey from the same hive time after time." She glanced over her shoulder at Eli. "Normally, when you harvest honey from a natural hive, you end up destroying the hive itself or killing the queen. But Josie's created a cleverly designed artificial hive using this log. This way, you can get at the honey with minimal disruption to the bees." Then she looked around. "Oh my—no wonder the honey has such a distinctive flavor. I see honeysuckle vines, wild roses and larkspur, but I don't even know what half of these other flowers are."

Eli was struck by the way her face fairly glowed with pleasure as she took it all in. That simple joy made her look even more childlike than usual.

Then she turned back to him and her expression immediately sobered. "Sorry. I know you're in a hurry to get this over with."

Oddly moved by the loss of her smile, he almost felt as if he should apologize to her for having dampened her mood.

She waved toward the bag he carried. "You can set that here." As soon as he'd set it down, she dug around inside and withdrew two pair of gloves and netting.

She turned and handed him a large piece of the netting. "Place this around your head and tuck it securely into the collar of your shirt. It'll keep the bees from getting to your face and neck. Then put these gloves on to protect your hands."

Eli studied the material uncertainly. He hadn't really expected them to find the hive, hadn't considered that he might actually have to assist in the harvesting. Where was his backup plan when he needed one?

But it seemed he was committed to this project now. With a mental sigh he did as she'd instructed.

Despite his misgivings, he actually found himself intrigued by the whole honey-gathering experience. Miss Lassiter spent some time exploring the setup of the hive and the implements Mrs. Collins's sister had left on site, all carefully wrapped in oilcloth and stored off the ground to keep them from rotting or rusting. His companion seemed delighted with each new discovery and her explanations were filled with superlatives. When she finally set to work, she patiently explained everything she did and everything she needed him to do in great detail, from how to gently waft the smoke into the hive to how to slice the comb as she lifted the frames.

Her bubbly enthusiasm and childlike pleasure in the task puzzled him. The woman seemed to tackle every job she undertook as an adventure to be savored. Which, while naive and inefficient, was also an intriguing novelty. One, he was certain, would become tiresome over time. And surprisingly she seemed much more confidant and capable than she had with her duties at the boardinghouse.

Once they'd finally collected enough honey to satisfy her they moved a safe distance from the hive with their treasure. She set her burdens down and removed the netting from her head, losing a few hairpins in the process. "Now aren't you glad we came?" she asked as she tucked the cloth into the sack. "You had a chance to experience something new, and Cora Beth will be so pleased with the honey."

He added his netting and gloves to the sack and then glanced up at the sky as he picked it up. "Let's just try to make it to your brother's ranch before that rain starts."

She seemed disappointed with his staid response, but nodded. "You have the sack, so I'll take—"

They both reached for the bucket of honey at the same time, their hands overlapping on the handle. He studied her small, delicate hand next to his larger, coarser one and felt that same something strange that had jangled through him in the boarding-house kitchen yesterday.

He forced his gaze up to meet hers and was surprised by the soft warmth in those sorrel-brown depths. Shaking off his momentary disquiet, Eli released the bucket and straightened. "We'd best hurry."

He preceded her as they marched toward the road, wondering what had gotten into him lately. Perhaps all the events of the past few months were finally starting to have an effect on him. He—

A movement on the ground in front of him caught his attention and he halted mid-step. His pulse quickened as he recognized the coiled form. He *hated* snakes!

His companion bumped into him and he took firm hold of her arm. "I don't want to alarm you, but there's a snake directly in our path. Move back." He tried to keep his voice calm, to ignore the sweat trickling down his back. She would no doubt count on him to keep her safe.

The snake lifted its head and flicked its tongue in their direction. Fighting his own visceral reaction, Eli tried to tug Miss Lassiter back with him. Problem was, she didn't seem to feel the same sense of urgency.

Blabbering some nonsense about the snake being harmless, she tried to pull away from him. Concerned for her safety he held onto her all the harder and tried to pull her away from the snake's proximity.

And then it happened. He caught his left foot on something and a sharp pain in the vicinity of his ankle drove him to his knees.

Chapter Five

Sadie's heart thudded in her chest as she dropped to her knees beside him. "What's wrong? Are you all right?" *Please God, let it just be a stumble.*

His expression was contorted, a sure sign he was in pain, but he still tried to get up. "The snake. Where—"

"Gone." She placed a hand on his shoulder to keep him down. "But like I tried to tell you, it was just a harmless king snake."

He went very still, his expression closing off. Then he nodded stiffly. "My apologies for the overreaction. It seems I made a bit of a fool of myself."

Sounded like it was his pride that was injured. Growing up with two older brothers, she'd dealt with her fair share of *that* ailment over the years and knew how prickly it could make a fella. "I'm sure the snakes in this part of the country look different than those do where you come from." She offered a reassuring smile. "And when in doubt it's always wise to give the critters a wide berth."

Her words didn't seem to ease his stiffness any. Ah

well, he'd get over his wounded pride soon enough. Right now they had other things to worry about.

"Can you walk? 'Cause we probably ought to get a move on. Collecting that honey took a little longer than I expected and from the looks of those clouds up there the rain is going to come in sooner than we expected."

He glanced up toward the sky and nodded.

Sadie bit her lip as she studied him. He seemed to be okay but the fact that he'd made no move yet to stand was making her uneasy.

She could almost see him gather his strength before he started to push himself up, and her stomach knotted.

"You *are* hurt." It wasn't a question.

"I think I twisted my ankle," he admitted. "I'll be fine once I get back to the buggy. If you can find me a stout stick to use for leverage—"

"Take my arm and I'll help you up."

His look was dismissive. "I appreciate the offer, but you can't support my weight."

Now he *did* sound like her brothers. "I'm stronger than I look."

She saw the stubborn glint in his eye—probably that pride thing again. Before he could protest further she gave him a stern look of her own. "Look, I don't see any stout sticks nearby and I sure don't intend to waste time looking for one while we wait for the bottom to fall out of those clouds. So just take my arm."

His irritation was plain, but after a second he nodded. "Very well." He took the arm she offered and gingerly stood, while carefully avoiding putting any weight on his left foot.

She gave him a minute to steady himself. "Okay. Now put your arm around my shoulder and we'll get you to the buggy."

Without a word, Mr. Reynolds set his hand gingerly on her nearest shoulder.

The man was exasperating. "That'll never work. I assure you I won't break and I won't swoon. For the next few minutes I will simply think of you as one of my brothers and you are free to think of me as a sister. Now, put your arm around me to my other shoulder so you can get proper support and we can get out of here."

His lips compressed, but he did as she'd commanded.

As they picked their way along the overgrown trail, Sadie was acutely aware of his arm around her, of his weight against her—warm, heavy, vital.

So much for thinking of him like a brother.

By the time they finally made it back to the road, the first drops of rain had begun to fall. It was intermittent, but the fat drops, suddenly darkened sky and oppressive air promised worse to come.

Once at the wagon, he released her and used the frame of the buggy to leverage himself up onto the seat. At least they'd made it to the relative shelter of the buggy before the worst of the weather blew in.

"I apologize for not being able to hand you up," he said as he settled in, "but—"

"Don't give it another thought." She resisted the urge to rub away the tingle that lingered where his arm had been.

"If I can impose on you to untether the horse, we'll get on our way."

She could tell that simple request had not been easy for him. "Of course. Just as soon as I fetch that pail of honey."

"But the rain—"

"Oh, a little rain never hurt anyone. After all the

trouble we put into collecting it, I don't intend to leave even a drop behind if I can help it."

Before he could protest further, she hiked her skirts up to her ankles and dashed back into the thicket. She grabbed both the honey and the supplies just as the rain began to fall in earnest. Encumbered by her bulky burdens, she made slower progress on the return trip and by the time she was ready to scramble onto the seat beside him she was more than a little damp.

But it had been worth it.

She ignored Mr. Reynolds's censoring glance and laughed as she tried to shake some of the water from her skirts. "I haven't played in the rain since I was a schoolgirl—I'd forgotten how fun it was."

Of course, it would be a lot more fun if her companion wasn't so stodgy. She wished there was some way she could get him to relax and see the joy in the little things.

Eli resisted the urge to roll his eyes. How could she make light of her sodden state? She had to be uncomfortable. And even on this warm May day, there was a real chance of her catching a cold if she didn't find something dry to change into soon. He had to get her back to town.

Then she sat up straighter. "Would you like me to take the reins?"

Some of his sympathy evaporated as he gritted his teeth and released the brake. "It's my ankle that's hurt, not my hands." Just because he'd overreacted when he spied the snake was no reason for her to try to mollycoddle him.

Using the small clearing in front of the ramshackle

cabin, he turned the wagon around and headed back the way they'd come.

There, that should show her he could still handle the buggy. He gave her a sideways glance. "Given the weather and the condition of my ankle, I think it best we return to town rather than proceed to your brother's ranch."

"Yes, of course. We need to get the doctor to look at your ankle as soon as possible." She rubbed her hand over her arm as she stared out at the downpour.

Had she already taken a chill? He shrugged out of his relatively dry jacket. "Here, put this on."

"But—"

"No arguments. You're soaked through and the last thing we need is for you to get sick." He tried gentling his tone. "After all, Mrs. Collins is counting on you."

She chewed her lip a moment as he held her gaze and slowly nodded. "Thank you."

His coat swallowed her up, making her appear even smaller than normal. Several tendrils had escaped the confines of their pins and hung, damp and forlorn, down her neck. His hand moved, almost of its own accord, to brush her cheek in reassurance. At the last moment he came to his senses and flicked the reins instead, hoping she hadn't noticed his lapse of control.

They rode along in silence for a while as he tried to maneuver the overgrown trail in the rain. The throbbing in his ankle was getting worse and his mood was going downhill with it as a bright flash of lightning lit the sky just then, almost immediately followed by a much-too-close clap of thunder. His companion jumped, but Eli had no time to reassure her. It took all of his focus to steady the horse. Even so, he couldn't help but notice how tightly she grabbed the seat.

"That sounded like it was close." She didn't sound quite so carefree now.

"It was probably further away than it seemed." Why this sudden urge to comfort her?

A moment later they rounded a corner in the trail and Eli pulled back on the reins. "Whoa."

Up ahead, a tree was down, completely blocking the road. The char marks on the trunk left no doubt as to what had happened.

Miss Lassiter leaned forward, trying to get a better view through the driving rain. "Do you see any way around it?"

He could tell from her tone that she already knew the answer. "Afraid not."

She sighed as she settled back in her seat. "What now?"

What now indeed? Under other circumstances he might have tried to find a way to hitch the horse to the trunk and move the blamed thing, at least enough to allow the buggy through. Or left the carriage behind and rode out on the horse alone to find help. But between the worsening storm and his throbbing ankle there was no way he could make the attempt now. They needed a fallback plan. And there was only one option.

"Now we go back to that cabin and wait out the storm." He used his most decisive tone. "Once the weather clears I'll find a way to get us out of here." To add to their problems, he had no idea what kind of shelter that miserable looking cabin was going to afford them when they arrived. He fervently hoped it was more solid than it appeared, but with the luck he was having lately he wouldn't be surprised if it leaked like a sieve.

It took a bit of maneuvering to get the buggy turned around on the narrow, overgrown road. By the time they were headed back toward the cabin, Eli could feel the tenseness in his shoulders and jaw. Hearing her sneeze only added to his worries about what the rest of this day might hold. What a mess!

She shifted on the seat, glancing his way from the corner of her eye. "I'm sorry I got us into this fix. I suppose I should have thought this whole thing through a little better."

He agreed, but it would be churlish to say so. Besides, he could have put an end to this as soon as he discovered what she was about. He'd examine his reasons for not doing so later. "I don't think there is any value to be had in either assigning or assuming blame." He tried to ease his foot into a more comfortable position. "Our efforts would be better focused on trying to find shelter from this rain."

It didn't take long to make their way back to the cabin, but this time they were headed against the wind. Spray from the rain peppered their faces, dampened their clothes. Eli pulled the buggy up as close to the door as possible. Not that it mattered. A person could only get so wet.

Before he could even set the brake, Miss Lassiter had scrambled down and raced around to his side of the buggy.

The woman was already soaking wet.

"Come along, let me help you inside."

He held onto the frame of the buggy again as he climbed down, but then gingerly placed his arm around her shoulder. There was no time for another argument over the proprieties.

He did his best to help her open the door of the cabin, taking out some of his frustration on the stubborn hinges. Once inside, it took a few minutes for his eyes to adjust.

There were four windows with shutters, one set on each wall. Since most of the shutters were broken or askew, enough daylight had pushed through so that it wasn't entirely gloomy.

It might have been better had it not revealed quite so much.

A thick coat of dust covered everything. 'Everything' being a generous term. Very little furniture remained. And it wasn't just dust—leaves and other debris from outside had made their way inside, as well.

The cabin consisted of one large open area, with an alcove to their right—probably for sleeping—and a fireplace to their left. Fortunately, the roof seemed relatively sound. There was one steady drip in the alcove area and one near what must be the back door. Other than that, the place appeared dry.

He glanced his companion's way, expecting to see dismay, and perhaps something stronger. Instead she was looking around with interest, seeming pleased by what she saw. "God was definitely looking out for us," she said cheerily. "We ought to be able to wait out the storm in relative comfort here."

A sudden rustling from across the room snagged his attention. Before he could do more than stiffen, a squirrel shot out of a far corner. His companion, who'd merely shrugged her shoulders at the sight of that snake earlier, jumped. The animal, tail flickering in agitation, disappeared through a half-shuttered window, apparently preferring the rain to their company.

Miss Lassiter gave him a sheepish look. "Sorry. Hope I didn't jar you. The squirrel startled me."

"I'm fine." He released her shoulder and braced his arm against the wall. To be honest her reaction made him feel slightly better about his own reaction to the snake.

A few other skittering noises came from the vicinity of the alcove, but he told himself they were caused by the wind coming in, not mice or other vermin.

Besides, there were more pressing things to worry about at the moment. Like, was that a working fireplace? A fire would go a long way to helping them dry out.

"Will you be all right for a few minutes?" she asked, reclaiming his attention.

Eli eyed her suspiciously. "Of course. But where do you think you're going?"

"I need to unhitch and tether the horse. And while I'm out there I intend to fetch whatever I can find in the buggy that we can use to make us more comfortable in here."

All things *he* should be taking care of. "That can all wait until the storm—

She held a hand up, palm out. "I can't get any wetter than I already am. And it would be cruel to leave the horse standing out there for who knows how long hitched to the buggy. Besides, we can't risk him getting spooked by the storm and running off."

She was right, of course. But that didn't make him like it any better. "At least take this." He pulled his hat off. "That scrap you've got on your head is no protection in this weather." And from the looks of it, it probably wouldn't ever be fit for use again.

She nodded and untied the ribbon that secured the soggy bit of frippery. He placed his more sensible hat on her head and found himself brushing the hair off her forehead to tuck it under the brim. The wisps tickled his fingers, as if even her hair was prone to playfulness.

He moved back and studied the picture she made in his too-big-for-her coat and hat. They swallowed her up, making her look like a child playing dress up. But she was covered except for the bottom half of her skirt.

As if reading his thoughts she gave him a reassuring smile. "Thanks, this is much better. And don't worry, I shouldn't be long."

He watched her head back out into the weather, feeling frustrated at his enforced uselessness. Then he looked around, taking stock of their temporary shelter. The least he could do was get to work doing what he could to make the place as comfortable as possible. Even though he was certain that thanks to Miss Lassiter, this would be one of the most uncomfortable afternoons he'd spent in quite some time.

Arms full, Sadie shoved the door of the cabin open with her shoulder. The load was bulky and awkward to manage but she hadn't cared for the idea of making a second trip to the buggy in this weather.

Stepping inside, she found Mr. Reynolds sitting on the low hearth, working on cleaning out the fireplace. Even with damp clothes and smudges on his sleeve, the always-dapper banker was still quite handsome.

He looked up and caught her staring so she looked away, setting the hamper and the covered bucket of honey just inside the door.

"I feel sorry for the mare," she said to cover her embarrassment. "She's a good horse and deserves a nice dry barn to wait out the storm in."

"Hopefully this will blow over soon."

Sadie refrained from comment, but she'd seen this kind of storm before. She doubted it would be over "soon."

"So what did you find in the buggy?" He eyed the hamper with interest. "Any food?"

"Hungry, are you?" She grinned as she folded the blanket into a smaller square. Then she set it down on top of the hamper and bucket, taking care to not let it touch the dirty floor.

"Not starving," he answered. "But I wouldn't turn down a bite to eat." He gave her a challenging smile. "Not that I'm worried we'll starve. There's always that honey you have there."

"Bite your tongue—that's for Cora Beth." She doffed the hat he'd loaned her and bumped it against her skirts to shake some of the water off. "Besides, I don't think it'll come to that." She removed the coat and gave it the same treatment. No point trailing water all through the place—all this dirt and dust would turn into a muddy mess. "The hamper has all of the stuff Cora Beth helped Viola pack for the folks at the ranch. I think they'll forgive us if we help ourselves." She tried to jab a few stray hairpins more securely on her head. "I know it's nothing fancy but we can always pretend we're on a picnic."

"Picnic fare sounds good. Given the situation, I'd say we're lucky to have it."

"I'd say, rather, that the Good Lord was looking out for us." She opened the sack and began digging around. "As far as other supplies, I found an old picnic blanket under the wagon seat, and I also have this sack of honey-gathering tools, including—" she straightened "this flint."

His eyes lit up at that. "Good. Because as far as I can tell the chimney is clear, and I think the first order of business should be to get a fire started so we can try to dry out."

"I agree." She looked around as she crossed the room. "And there certainly seems to be a lot of material laying around that we can use for firewood. That old stool and those rickety benches both seem to be fit for nothing else. And the shutter on that window is already hanging by one rusty hinge."

He nodded, only glancing up briefly before resuming his work at the fireplace. "There's a few pieces of actual firewood the last squatters left behind in the hearth. But we could really use some kindling. If you see any twigs or other bits of debris that would serve the purpose gather them up."

She took in the layers of dirt and debris surrounding them and wrinkled her nose. "That shouldn't be a problem."

Once he took the flint from her, she hung his hat and coat on two of the half dozen nails jutting from the mantel. The garments would fare much better there than on any of the dusty surfaces the cabin had to offer.

In short order she had collected a goodly number of twigs, pecan husks and other flammable-looking bits and carried them to the hearth.

She tamped down the urge to offer to lend a hand as she watched him arrange the kindling and bits of wood. Instead, she stood and surveyed the cabin. "If we're going to be stuck here for a while, we might as well try to make it more comfortable. I don't suppose you saw a broom anywhere?"

He glanced up with a surprised expression, then shrugged. "Afraid not." He looked at the floor with a grimace. "Too bad."

"Then I'll just have to improvise. A leafy branch or bit of brush will work just about as well—bound to be lots of those handy. If you'll loan me your pocketknife I'll see what I can find."

He paused and frowned up at her. "You're *not* going back out in that storm."

His commanding tone took her aback, but she kept her own tone light. "Don't worry. I figure with the way things are grown up around here, there'll be something right out the back door."

"Distance won't matter in this downpour. You'll be soaked as soon as you step outside."

So he was worried about her. Why did everyone think she couldn't fend for herself? She spread her arms. "Can't get much wetter than I already am. And you'll have that fire going soon so I can dry out when I get back." She shrugged and added a touch of firmness to her voice. "Besides, I've got to do something to keep busy."

He gave her a long, considering look, then apparently decided to let it go. "At least put the hat and coat back on."

"Of course."

It took some time, and quite a bit of shoving to get the back door opened, but when she looked at the rain-shrouded grounds behind the cabin Sadie gave a little crow of pleasure.

"What is it?"

She smiled over her shoulder. "I've found a real treasure back here. There's a whole tangle of dewberry vines growing right up against the wall, and they're ripe for the picking."

He sat up straighter. "Need some help?"

"No, I can get them. Besides, you have your hands full getting that fire going and I plan to take full advantage of it when I get done."

Sadie snaked a hand toward the nearest vine. "I love dewberries." She plucked two of the plump berries and popped them one after the other into her mouth. Savoring the way the juice exploded between her teeth, she scanned the overgrown patch of ground, trying to spy a likely bit of brush to use as her makeshift broom. No point heading into the weather until she had her quarry in sight.

There! That one should work. She sprinted out into the rain and made quick work of breaking off the targeted bit of brush. In the process she caught sight of a stout stick on the ground. Scooping it up, she headed back to the house. Leaning her brush-broom against the inside wall, she shook out her skirts, then reached back to pluck a few more berries.

Crossing the room with her two offerings, she smiled at the sight of the crackling flames. "Oh good, you've got the fire going."

"The chimney is clear enough to draw the smoke, thank goodness."

She held out the stout branch. "Look what I found. I thought you might be able to use it as a walking stick."

The relief and approval on his face sent an answering warmth through her.

"Thanks." He took the stick and used it to leverage himself up. Placing his weight on it, he took a couple of hobbling steps to test it out. "Perfect."

"Good. Now here, try some of these."

He stared at the berries she held out but didn't make a move to take them. "You picked them, you eat them."

She waved away his concern. "Oh, don't be silly—I've already had a handful." From the look on his face she reckoned he didn't get called silly often. "There are lots more on those vines. This is just a little snack to keep our strength up. I plan to pick a whole passel more once I've gotten some of the cleanup done." She raised her hand a bit closer to his face and slid the berries back and forth under his nose.

After rolling his eyes, he took half of the berries and popped one into his mouth. "Delicious."

"Nothing like berries fresh from the vine. Here take the rest so I can get to work." She held up her other hand, palm out.

With a nod and a thank you, he accepted the rest of her offering.

That was better. The man just needed someone to stand up to him occasionally. And this afternoon was as good a time as any.

Chapter Six

Eli watched Sadie energetically swish her rustic but surprisingly effective broom across the floor, chafing at the fact that he couldn't be of more help. Thank goodness she'd found the walking stick for him, at least he could get around a little better now. Even though his foot throbbed enough to make his teeth ache, the renewed mobility made him feel a little more in control of the situation.

While she swept and cleaned he hobbled around, determined to do what he could. He shoved the heavier bits out of her way, gathered up whatever scraps of wood he could find to stack by the fireplace and tossed some of the rest of the junk in a far corner. The woodpile grew surprisingly large and while he hoped they wouldn't be here long enough to need it all, his gut told him that there was a good chance they would be.

Not that he had any intention of letting Miss Lassiter see his concern. He wasn't sure how she would feel about being trapped out here for an extended period and he didn't relish the idea of having a hysterical female on his hands on top of everything else.

As the minutes ticked away, however, her energy and

continued positive attitude surprised him. He hadn't noticed her being this industrious back at the boardinghouse. Her fervor with the broom coupled with the sodden, muddy hem of her skirt and damp, disheveled hair should have given her the appearance of a scullery maid.

But somehow it didn't.

He wasn't sure if it was the cheery smile she wore, or her soft humming as she worked or something that went deeper, but she looked both softer and more competent than before.

She kicked up enough dust with her efforts to set them both to sneezing, but she maintained her good humor, treating it more as a game than a chore. In short order she had the area in front of the hearth as clean as she could make it given the tools on hand.

Finally setting aside her broom, she fetched the blanket and spread it in front of the fireplace. "There now, why don't you sit and rest that foot of yours?"

That did sound good. "Ladies first."

Rather than showing appreciation for his manners, she looked exasperated. "Oh for goodness sake, this isn't Cora Beth's parlor. Given the situation, I think we can put those sort of niceties aside."

He clenched his jaw. Didn't she realize that, "given the situation," they should make every effort to maintain whatever decorum they could? "Good manners are always in order, no matter the circumstances."

She waved a hand dismissively. "You know what I mean. You're hurt and I've got berries to collect. Now, do you need help getting situated before I head back out?"

Her question set his teeth on edge. He wasn't entirely helpless. "I'll manage."

She studied him uncertainly. "Your foot—"

"Is better off inside my boot where the pressure will keep the swelling down."

"But what if it's a break?"

"It's not." And even if it was, there was nothing she could do about it.

She nodded, then looked around. "Now, what can I put the berries in?"

"Are you sure you want to do that now? The rain hasn't slacked off yet."

She shrugged and gave him a playful smile. "I'd rather be wet than hungry."

He started to point out that they had other things to eat, but then decided there was no point. Her mind seemed to be made up. "In that case I think the hamper is probably our best bet."

"Of course." She knelt and quickly emptied the contents. Reaching for the hat and coat, she nodded toward the blanket. "Set yourself down and I'll be back in no time."

"I'm coming with you."

She paused with one arm in a coat sleeve and one not. "I can handle this. You should get off that foot—"

He ignored her protest. "It doesn't take legs to pick berries. And, since I'll be sharing in the fruits, literally, I should also share in the labor." He grabbed up the hamper, tightened his grip on his cane and headed for the door. She could follow or not as she liked.

A heartbeat later he heard her scurrying to catch up. "You are one of the stubbornest men I've ever come across. And if you'd met my brothers you'd know that was saying something." She flounced past him, pushed the door open, then turned back to face him. "You stand here with the hamper and I'll pick the berries." Before he could argue she held up a hand. "You're almost dry so no point in getting yourself soaked again. Besides, if you insist on going out there I'll feel obliged to give you back your coat and hat and how gentlemanly of you would that be?"

Speak of stubborn! He stared at the downpour. "Perhaps we should just wait to see if this lets up soon."

"It's not coming down quite as hard as it was earlier. And what if it doesn't stop? I'd just as soon get to it while I'm still wet. Once I get dry I'm not going to be quite so eager to step outside again."

He supposed that made sense. But the woman was never going to dry out at this rate.

Without waiting for his response, she drew the collar of his jacket up higher and stepped out into the storm.

Several minutes later, as she dumped yet another handful of berries in the hamper, he took her wrist and drew her out of the rain. "Time to come back inside. We have plenty enough to hold us for a while."

As if not quite trusting him, she peered into the hamper. "I suppose that'll do for now."

Eli turned, glad that he could finally get off his feet. He hadn't taken more than two steps, though, when he realized she'd stepped back out in the rain. What was she up to now?

Ignoring the throbbing in his foot, he set the hamper on the floor and limped back toward the door. "Miss Lassiter?"

"I'll be there in a minute." Her voice was muffled but he could tell she hadn't gone far.

It was several long minutes later before she reappeared inside the doorway. Not surprisingly, she wasn't empty-handed.

"Look what I found," she said nodding to the four

large pieces of firewood and two stout sticks in her arms. "There's a chopping block out back. There's more but the other pieces hadn't been split yet and they were too heavy to carry. Anyway, I thought these might come in handy for the fire."

Hadn't she seen the small pile he'd stacked by the fireplace? Or, like him, was she worried about how long they'd be stranded here? "It was a good thought, but these pieces are soaking wet."

"I know, but if we place the pieces just inside the fireplace around the fire, they'll dry out faster. Then if we get down to where we need them, we'll have a better shot at getting them to burn."

While she crossed the room with her burden, he followed more slowly with the hamper. The woman had a sensible head on her shoulders after all, it seemed. Had he been wrong about her in other ways?

Once she'd arranged the damp wood to her satisfaction, Miss Lassiter stood and rolled her shoulders. Then she shed the garments he'd loaned her and hung them back on the make-do coat pegs.

"Thanks for the use of your hat and coat." She studied them with a wince. "I'm afraid they're showing signs of what I put them through."

He shrugged. "They can be replaced."

She made no move to approach the blanket and her face wore a slightly embarrassed look. Surely she wasn't worried that he would—

"I've got water in my shoes," she blurted out. "I was thinking I'd take them and my stockings off and set them by the fire to dry. If it won't offend you, that is."

Was that all? "Of course."

She nodded and hesitated. Realizing her dilemma, he busied himself with studying the items she'd pulled from the hamper earlier, keeping his gaze averted to allow her what privacy he could while she removed her footgear.

A few moments later she carefully arranged her shoes and stockings on the uneven hearth.

"Ready to eat?" Wanting to put her at ease, he kept his tone conversational.

She nodded. "As soon as we give thanks."

Give thanks? She saw something in this situation to be thankful for? But he supposed keeping to normal rituals in such an otherwise unusual situation gave her comfort and perhaps some sense of normalcy. So he would go along with her request. And since she seemed to be waiting for him to lead the blessing, he dutifully bowed his head. "For the food we have before us, Lord, we give You thanks and ask that You continue to bless our respective families and our endeavors. Amen."

Miss Lassiter echoed his "Amen", then nodded toward the cluster of food items. "I'll take one of those pears if you don't mind."

He nodded and reached for the fruit. To his surprise, she remained standing as he handed it up to her. What now?

As she accepted the pear from him, he noticed the red marks on her wrist and frowned. "What happened?"

She followed the direction of his gaze, then gave a sheepish smile. "I got a little careless. Dewberry vines have lots of nasty little thorns and I tangled with a few when reaching for the plumper berries." Before he could offer sympathy, she shrugged. "Don't worry, though, I've gotten much worse on other berry-picking expeditions."

She took a bite out of the pear, and his gaze was captured by a little dribble of juice that found its way to her chin. He couldn't seem to look away, until she used her sleeve to wipe it away.

Giving his head a mental shake, he turned his focus to the food, grabbing the jug of apple cider to moisten his unaccountably dry throat.

Miss Lassiter appeared not to have noticed anything out of the ordinary. She was staring at one of the windows, her head cocked to the side. "Sounds like the rain's coming down even harder now. Good thing we picked those berries when we did. We may be in for a long afternoon."

Eli merely nodded. No point in adding to her worries. Fact was, even if the rain stopped in the next few minutes, he had no idea how in the world they were going to get around that fallen tree. His only hope right now was that they'd be missed before long and someone would be out looking for them.

"Did you tell Danny you were planning to come out here?" He kept his tone casual.

"Not specifically. It was supposed to be a surprise."

So much for that idea. No one would know where to look even if they realized the two of them were missing. Miss Lassiter had definitely not thought things through this morning.

"You might as well sit," he said. "There's plenty of room here."

She shook her head. "My skirts are soaked." She wrinkled her nose. "Sitting would be uncomfortable right now. I thought I'd stand in front of the fire for just a bit to try to speed the drying process."

Which was sensible but it put him in the position of lounging on the floor while she remained standing. He wasn't doing very well in the gentleman department.

They ate in silence for a while, Eli trying hard not to

stare at her bare feet and trim ankles peeking out from the hem of her skirt.

An explosive sneeze, quickly followed by a second, jerked his gaze up to her face. "Are you okay?" Had she caught a chill?

But she dismissed his worries. "I'm fine. I think it's just all the dust we kicked up when we were cleaning earlier."

Eli grabbed the jug of cider. "Would you care for some of this?"

She nodded and set the core of the pear in the fireplace. Wiping her hands on her gown with the indifference of a child, she took the proffered cider.

"I'm afraid you'll have to drink straight from the jug—I didn't see any drinking glasses."

The caveat didn't seem to bother her. "I'll manage."

As Miss Lassiter drank, Eli studied her closely for other signs that she might be taking ill, but she seemed remarkably robust.

After a couple of deep swallows, she absently handed the jug back to him while she studied the room. "I wonder what kind of history this place has. I mean, I know it's not much to look at today, but now that we've cleaned it up a bit, I can picture how it might have looked back when it was new. It would have made a cozy little home for some farmer and his wife."

Eli looked around skeptically. Even though it was mid-afternoon, the dark-lidded sky and semi-shuttered windows left the one room cabin in shadow except for the area here by the fireplace. No matter how hard he tried, he couldn't picture this place as anything but a hovel.

"Whatever its history, apparently it didn't suit," he

said diplomatically. "It appears to have been abandoned for some time."

"Yes, but aren't you at all curious about why? Maybe there was some great tragedy, where the farmer or his wife died and the one left behind could no longer bear to be here. Or maybe they headed farther west looking for adventure. Or maybe the farmer who lived here married a woman who preferred life in a big city." She had a faraway, dreamy look. "There are so many stories a place like this could tell."

What in the world was she going on about? "Speculating over such things seems like a pointless exercise."

She studied him as if he had somehow disappointed her. "Don't you like imagining things? I mean, don't you ever do things like make up stories to tell Penny?"

He shifted, feeling her opinion of him had just dropped a few points. "I read to her from time to time." It was hard to keep the defensiveness from his tone.

"Not quite the same, but it's a start."

A start? A start on what?

She bent down and scooped up some of the berries. "I think my back is dry enough." She fanned her skirt out with her free hand. "Time to dry the front." And with that she turned to face the fire.

Eli placed his palms behind him on the blanket and leaned back as he studied her back. She was definitely a puzzle to him. How could a woman be so sensible one moment and so fanciful the next? And why was Penny so taken with her? His half sister had been so quiet and withdrawn since the tragedy. But around Miss Lassiter she seemed more lighthearted than she had since he'd assumed guardianship.

Truth be known, while he'd hoped it was just a matter of giving Penny time to grieve, he'd worried that she'd been permanently scarred by everything that had happened. Yet she seemed to really come alive around Miss Lassiter. And while he was relieved to see the old Penny come back, he couldn't help but be curious as to the reason.

He studied the coiled tendrils that had escaped his companion's pins, listened to her soft humming as she held her skirt out to the fire. And wondered again if perhaps he'd misjudged her.

Sadie studied the flames as she absently munched on the berries. How very sad and lonely to live without the occasional daydream, without letting the imagination have reign from time to time. Had he always been that way? Or had something in his life hardened him? Maybe he just needed someone to teach him how.

For Penny's sake, of course.

She wiped her hands together as she finished the berries. Her skirts were still damp, but they were dry enough to sit now.

Sadie turned and knelt down across from him on the quilt and reached for the sack.

"What are you looking for?"

"Just seeing what we have to work with." She emptied the sack, dumping the contents between them. There were the gloves and large pieces of net they'd used to protect themselves from the bees. Some rags. A ball of twine she'd brought just in case.

Mr. Reynolds didn't appear impressed. "Doesn't look like there's much that'll be of any use to us."

His lack of imagination was showing again. "All depends on how long we'll be stuck out here."

"Hopefully it won't be longer than another hour or so."

Sadie nodded, but she wasn't feeling very confident. The rain was still pounding pretty hard and not showing any signs of letting up. "So, what do we do now?"

"What do you mean?"

"Well, we can't just sit here staring at each other all afternoon."

He raised a brow. "I'm open to suggestions."

Was he now? "Do you know any games?"

There went that eyebrow again. "You mean like chess?"

She grinned and shifted to a sitting position. "Afraid we don't have a board and pieces handy. How's your memory?"

"Better than average."

"Then let's put it to the test with a word game called *I Packed My Suitcase*. The rules are pretty simple."

For the next hour they occupied themselves with simple word and memory games. It took a while, but once Mr. Reynolds relaxed, he seemed to get into the spirit of the challenge. He turned out to be quite competitive, but no more so than her brothers.

But unlike her brothers, he didn't tease or throw the occasional game her way. It was refreshing to know he considered her a proper opponent.

Finally, he reached for his makeshift cane. "I'd better feed the fire again before it goes out."

She popped up to a kneeling position. "You should stay off that foot. I can take care of it."

He gave her a reproving look. "I'll manage."

Sadie sat back down on her heels. So much for the easy camaraderie they'd shared a moment ago.

She watched him stir the coals and lay additional chunks of wood just so. "You're pretty good with a fire. Have you ever been out camping?"

"No, but I've tended my share of fireplaces."

"Too bad. There's nothing like sleeping out under the stars on a clear night." Not that she expected him to understand such a simple pleasure.

Eli frowned, not certain he'd understood her properly. "I would imagine it would be uncomfortable, what with having to deal with the hard ground and the elements and the insects." Sort of like what they would be faced with if the rain continued for much longer.

"Oh but if you've got a proper bedroll the ground doesn't feel so hard and if by the elements you mean the fresh air, the stars and moonlight, the scent of trees and grass and saddle leather, then it's really quite pleasant. As for the insects, I like the sound of their nightly chirping but yes, the mosquitoes and such can be a problem. A bit like the thorns on a rose, you put up with taking a little extra care in order to enjoy the beauty of the flower."

The woman was an incurable romantic. She always seemed to try to paint things in the most positive light. Why couldn't she accept that not every cloud had a silver lining?

He pushed himself up, leaning heavily on his makeshift cane. "Well, to each his own, I suppose."

She tried to brush a stray tendril off her forehead. "So, what shall we do now? I can come up with another word game if you like."

He was tired of word games. "Why don't you tell me about your family."

"All right." She gave him a cheeky grin. "I like to think we're a pretty special lot, but I suppose I'm a bit biased. My father comes from a long line of cattle ranchers. His grandfather built Hawk's Creek and it's grown to be one of the biggest and most respected cattle ranches in northeast Texas. Mother came from a prominent Philadelphia family, a real socialite. But when she met my dad she was ready to give up everything to be with him, just like in a fairy tale. She married him and settled quite happily into life as a cattle rancher's wife. Unfortunately, she died when I was eight, so for most of my life it's been me and my two brothers and my dad. I spent a good part of my growing up years trying to keep up with my brothers, while they spent theirs trying to treat me like a baby sister."

Something about the way she said that last part caught his attention. Almost as if she had mixed feelings about the role they'd cast her in. His curiosity got the better of him. "Tell me about your brothers."

She smiled in obvious affection. "Ry and Griff are the best brothers a girl could ask for, bar none. But they're as different from each other as the moon is from the sun."

"How so?"

"Ry is five years older than me. He's the one who taught me to ride a horse, how to climb a tree and how to fish. But over the past dozen years he's spent as much time in Philadelphia as he has at Hawk's Creek—maybe more. He got himself some big city polish and a college education and eventually became a lawyer."

"Actually, I met him just before he and Mrs. Collins's sister set out on their trip. I didn't spend much time with him but he seemed to have a well thought-out approach to things."

"Yep, that's Ry. He seemed a little lost for a while— sort of torn between his life in Philadelphia and his life on the ranch. But he met Josie last year and Viola became his ward about the same time. Those two were the saving of him. He's settled down and found a way to make his west-meets-east background work for him."

"And your other brother?"

"Griff's three years older than me and there's not a lick of ambivalence in him. Just like our pa, Griff's a cattle rancher through and through. His life is tied to Hawk's Creek like a tree to the earth. He seems to know just about everything there is to know about cattle, and a lot of it he got on his own." Her smile took on a reminiscent quality. "When I was still in pigtails he taught me to throw a rope and to build a fire and skip stones." She stared into the fire. "Since our dad died three years ago it's been just him and me running the ranch."

"Sounds to me like they haven't babied you at all. On the contrary it seems they've taken pains to teach you to be much more independent than is normal in a young lady." Perhaps her hoydenish tendencies were a result of her upbringing in an all male household.

She laughed. "Oh they taught me all kinds of useful skills. It's just…"

"Just what?" he prompted.

"They never stopped seeing me as the baby sister. Someone to be humored, teased and then patted on the head while the menfolk took care of things. They still call me 'Sadie girl', same as they did when I was six."

"Sounds more of an endearment than a judgment."

She laughed self-consciously. "Oh, you're probably right. I don't know why I even mentioned it. My brothers love and respect me. Same as I do them."

He eased himself back down on the blanket. "So, your brother Ry likes to work with horses and do a bit of lawyering on the side, and your brother Griff has ranching in his blood. What do you want out of life?"

She seemed uncomfortable with that question. "I'm still trying to figure that out."

Then she brushed her hands and hugged her knees. "My turn. What about you? Do you have any family besides Penny?"

Eli shifted. He shouldn't have started this line of talk. "It's just Penny and me now."

Before he could turn the subject to something less personal, she made an observation. "Penny's so much younger than you—I guess you were really an only child growing up."

He nodded. He'd been on his own for what seemed most of his life. But not any longer. He hesitated a moment, then decided it wouldn't hurt to share just a little of his history. After all, she probably was hungry for a bit of a distraction from their current situation. "Like you, my mother passed on when I was young— six in my case—and it was just me and Father until he remarried when I was seventeen. Penny was born a few years later. I'd moved out shortly after so I'm afraid I didn't know her as well as a brother should until I recently became her guardian." He hadn't done all those things for his sister that her brothers had done for her.

"I can tell you care for her a great deal. She's lucky to have you."

Penny probably didn't share that sentiment. But he fully intended to make up for that lack, as well. With the proper wife by his side, his little sister would get the attention and discipline she needed to grow into a confident, genteel young lady.

Afraid he'd revealed too much, Eli cast around for another kind of distraction. "You know, I imagine I can use my knife to scratch a checkerboard into the floor. If I pull the tacks out from some of those old shutters waiting for the fire that'll give us one set of pieces and we can break some of twigs into bits to make the other set. I think we can actually try to make a game of it."

She nodded agreement and moved to the woodpile. Eli studied her for a moment, wondering how she could say with such authority that Penny was lucky to have him for a brother. She barely knew either him or his sister so her feelings on the matter were meaningless. So it was altogether strange that he'd felt that uncharacteristic shot of pleasure at her declaration and smile of approval.

Not that he was seeking her approval. No, it was more likely just a sign of how tired he was.

Eli sat on the uneven hearth, staring moodily into the night-darkened room. If pressed he'd guess it was probably sometime around midnight, but he wasn't curious enough to pull out his pocket watch. He shifted, trying to get comfortable. Not easy since his foot was throbbing unmercifully.

Sadie slept nearby, her soft breathing keeping a steady rhythm that seemed to be in tune with his own pulse beat. He'd insisted she place his folded coat inside the sack and use it for a pillow, so hopefully she was relatively comfortable. Perhaps not quite as comfortable as she would be if she'd had one of those proper bedrolls she'd mentioned earlier.

He studied her in the faint light afforded by the glow from the fireplace. Curled up on her side, with her bare feet and ankles peeking out from her modestly arranged skirts, she looked both peaceful and oddly vulnerable. She was such a petite thing—he really couldn't blame her brothers for wanting to coddle and protect her.

But if they still considered her a child they were off the mark. She'd surprised him today. There'd been no hand-wringing, no hysterics, no sitting back while she waited to be rescued. All things he would have expected from most of the well brought up women of his acquaintance.

In fact, Miss Lassiter had proven herself to be both resilient and industrious. She'd tended to the horses, cleaned, picked berries in the rain, collected firewood, and when insects became a problem as the light began to fade, she was the one who'd come up with the idea of using the netting to cover the windows. And she'd done all of that without any prompting or expectations from him.

Just as surprising, however, was her generosity of spirit. She'd been quick to share the bounty of the berries, making sure he had some before she ate her fill. And she'd gone out of her way to find him the walking stick in the pouring rain. He absently picked up the stick, resting his hands on the knobby end. She probably didn't realize how having this had made him feel a bit more useful, a bit more in control.

Or had she?

He listened to the sound of frogs and insects playing counterpoint to the occasional drip-drip-drip of water falling from the eaves. The rain had finally tapered off to an intermittent drizzle about forty minutes ago—with luck it would be entirely gone by morning.

Then what? Hopefully he could use the harness to hook the horse to the tree and drag it far enough for the buggy to squeeze by. If that didn't work he could always ride out on the horse and go for help.

But it wouldn't change any of the facts regarding their

current situation. He stared again at her peacefully slumbering form.

Somehow he didn't think she'd realized yet that both of their lives were about to change.

Chapter Seven

Sadie stretched, wincing at the stiffness of her muscles. A moment later she remembered where she was and sat bolt upright.

Eli—hard to think of him as Mr. Reynolds after what they'd shared the last twenty hours—was over by the fireplace, placing another chunk of wood on the embers.

"Good morning."

He glanced over his shoulder. "Good morning."

The lines on his face seemed more deeply etched this morning. "Did you get any sleep at all?"

"Some."

Liar. Then she realized how quiet it was. "The rain stopped."

"So it seems." The thought didn't seem to cheer him up any. He nodded toward the hamper. "I prepared breakfast." His voice held a hint of dry humor.

She scooted over and peeked inside. "You picked more berries. But your foot—"

"I managed."

"Thanks." She studied his profile. Something was bothering him. Was it his foot? Or was he concerned about how they were going to move that tree? Or was it something else?

Whatever was on his mind, the least she could do was try not to add to his worries. She got to her feet with as much dignity as she could muster. "I think I'll step outside for a few moments before I eat."

"Of course."

She pulled her stockings and shoes back on, noticing he kept his gaze averted. As she headed out the back door, she thought again about what a meticulous gentleman he was, despite his brusqueness. He knew how to make her feel comfortable and safe without being obvious or condescending about it. Such consideration was both comforting and refreshing.

Sadie found herself humming as she stepped outside into the fresh morning air. *Heavenly Father, thank You for this glorious day. And thank You for getting us through all the trials of yesterday relatively unscathed. Help me to remember, at least for this day, to think before I speak and act, to not be so impulsive.*

When she returned several minutes later, Eli was poking at the fire with a stick—one that looked suspiciously like the remnants of her makeshift broom. He glanced up but almost immediately went back to studying the fire. She rubbed her arm as gooseflesh pebbled her skin. What had put that somber look on his face?

Sadie finger combed her hair as best she could, then twisted it in a bun at the back of her head. She had no illusions that it looked even remotely smooth and stylish, but at least it was out of her face.

She knelt beside the hamper and scooped up a half dozen or so berries. "Aren't you going to eat, too?"

"I ate while I was picking them."

Still not feeling particularly talkative it seemed. This

time she let the silence draw out as she munched on the berries. But she watched him closely from the corner of her eye.

Soon this little adventure of theirs would be at an end. In a strange way she was kind of sorry. She was surprised to realize she'd actually enjoyed spending time with him, especially since he'd lost that disapproving frown somewhere along the way.

After her second handful of berries she decided to try to draw him out. "So what's the plan for this morning?"

For a moment it appeared he was going to ignore her question. But he finally turned and settled on the hearth, facing her. "We need to talk."

She slowly placed the stopper back in the jug of apple cider and folded her hands in her lap, steeling herself for whatever bad news he wanted to impart. "All right. What about?"

He raked a hand through his hair, as if trying to gather his thoughts.

"If you're worried about that tree across the road," she offered, "I'm pretty sure we'll be able to move it. And even if we can't, we've likely been missed and folks will be looking."

If anything, his expression grew more sober.

He leaned forward, giving her a probing stare. "I'm not worried about the tree." He waved a hand dismissively. "Or at least that's not what I want to discuss with you at the moment."

Now she was *really* getting worried.

He rubbed the stubble on his jaw. "I've been debating with myself since first light about whether to have this discussion now or after we get back to town. And I've come to the conclusion that it's better to discuss this while we have a bit of privacy."

All this hemming and hawing was starting to irritate her. "Then out with it."

"What you said a moment ago, about us having been missed by now—"

When he paused she clasped her hand around her knees. "I know you're concerned that Penny's been worried to distraction about you. But I've been thinking on that. Since no one knew we were making this little side trip, Cora Beth probably figured we decided to hole up at Ry's place to wait the storm out. Course, that means they probably won't send anyone to look for us for a while yet. But—"

He made an impatient movement with his hand. "That's not the point I was trying to make."

"Oh." This time she decided to keep quiet until he had his say. No matter how long he took getting to the point.

"There's no way to broach this without being indelicate, so I'll just be direct."

About time.

"We spent the night alone here last night. And we're not going to be able to hide that fact."

Sadie felt the heat rise in her face. What was he saying? "But—" She swallowed then tried again. "But nothing happened. I mean, you were the perfect gentleman—" She couldn't finish that sentence.

He gave her a sympathetic look. "I want you to know that you're not to worry about any of this. I'm prepared to do the right thing by you. As soon as we get back to town we can announce our intention to get married."

Married! She scrambled to her feet—hang dignity. "Mr. Reynolds! You're making too much of this."

But his expression never wavered. "I know this is not ideal, not for either of us, but I see no other option."

If she wasn't so angry at his high-handedness she'd be mortified by his obvious lack of enthusiasm for what he was proposing. "Then you aren't looking hard enough because *I* sure see other options." Her mind scrambled to come up with something. "For one, we can just go about our lives as if nothing happened—because *nothing did*. And I'll be heading back to Hawk's Creek in a week or two anyway."

"Miss Lassiter, I refuse to believe you care so little for your reputation." He stood and clasped his hands behind his back. "You're in shock I suppose. Understandable. I've had a little more time to reconcile myself to the inevitable, but you haven't had that luxury. Once you've had an opportunity to think things through, you'll see that marriage is the only possible option—for either of us. Believe me I've given this considerable thought."

The fact that he seemed so reluctantly resigned didn't do much to warm her to his plan. She'd be hanged if she'd marry some man who not only proposed to her out of a sense of duty, but who had, up until yesterday, shown such disregard for her as a person.

She tilted up her chin. "I think it says something about your upbringing that you'd regard the townsfolk with such cynicism. I don't know about where you come from, but the people around here are not such self-righteous, judgmental gossips that we should be shamed into marrying just to appease them."

He'd stiffened. "It has been my observation that people are pretty much the same wherever you go. But be that as it may, it's not so much that people will gossip—which they will—but that there are certain conventions within civilized society that we are expected to meet. These conventions are there for a reason and to flout them is to risk ostracism and criticism. Not to mention the sorry example this would set for Penny."

"Penny is nine years old. She won't even notice any improprieties unless we make an issue of it."

He looked like a man who was having trouble controlling his temper. "Miss Lassiter—"

She held up a hand to interrupt whatever other argument he was prepared to deliver. "Save your breath. Nothing you can say will change my mind. Perhaps we should concentrate on getting back to town."

His lips tightened. "Very well. But this conversation is *not* over."

She repented slightly as she noted the way he was favoring his hurt foot. In the heat of their argument she'd forgotten about his ankle. "You're still limping. Maybe we should just wait here until help comes."

"There's nothing that guarantees help is coming anytime soon. Or at all, as you noted a few moments ago. And I'd prefer not to spend yet another night in this cabin. I'll manage."

"But Danny will figure it out—"

"I'm sure he will—eventually. I just don't intend to sit here and twiddle my thumbs hoping it's sooner rather than later. That storm will have washed away any sign of our passing and the searchers might not bother to go past that tree until they've checked out the easier-to-get-to places. Besides," he gave her a crooked grin, "it'll be better than just sitting here and continuing this conversation."

Good point. She gave a short nod. "Agreed. If you think you can get started packing up our stuff, I'll go hitch the horse to the buggy."

She had another reason for wanting to get back to

town as soon as possible. She was worried about his ankle. The sooner Dr. Whitman had a look at it, the better she'd feel.

As she stepped outside, though, some of her assurance slipped away. Surely he was making too much of their situation? He had to be wrong about the sort of reception they'd receive when they got back to town. Oh, she didn't doubt that a few loose tongues would wag, but it would blow over soon enough. There was absolutely no need to do anything so rash as rush to the altar as if they were guilty of something.

By the time she returned inside, Eli had all the supplies packed and the fire damped. She suspected it had been a matter of pride for him to not have to ask for help.

She picked up the honey and the sack while he grabbed the hamper and the blanket. Without a word they exited the cabin. At the doorway she turned and took a final look back. Even with all that had happened, she'd enjoyed their time here yesterday. The two of them had worked together well. Sure, she'd had to overcome his initial tendency to underestimate her, but once she'd elbowed her way past that, she'd felt like a true partner in their adventure, felt her contributions were worthwhile and valued. In fact, it said something for how far they'd come that he hadn't tried to talk her out of tending to the horse and buggy.

Realizing Eli had continued on to the buggy, Sadie hurried after him. He seemed to be leaning heavily on the walking stick, but otherwise fine. If she wasn't so annoyed with him, she could almost wish he would lean on her shoulder again.

Sadie told herself it was concern over his safety on

the uneven ground that prompted the thought, not the miss of his touch on her shoulder.

As he set the hamper in the back of the buggy, she watched him for signs of pain and fatigue. He should have looked a sorry sight—his clothes were wrinkled and covered with smudges from the dirt and ashes, he needed a shave and his limp was pronounced. Not to mention her suspicion that he hadn't gotten much, if any, sleep last night.

So why did he look so appealing, so heroic?

On the other hand, she had no illusions that, with her muddy skirt, hair that hadn't seen a brush in over twenty-four hours and thorn-scratched hands and wrists, she looked like anything more presentable than a scruffy ragamuffin.

Sometimes, life just didn't seem fair. *I know, Lord, I shouldn't be so self-centered and vain. But this man sure knows how to scramble my thinking.*

Once she had settled into the buggy, Eli gave the reins a flick to get the horse moving. Sadie didn't even bother to offer to take the reins this time. She understood him much better now than she had when they set out on this trip—was it really less than twenty-four hours ago?

But this whole issue of marriage had spoiled things. The air practically thrummed with the tension between them and she didn't know how to ease it. How could he believe she would seriously contemplate marriage—they hardly knew each other.

Was he right about the reception they would receive? Would people really think they had, well, had been… indiscreet?

No! And even if they did, it didn't matter what everyone thought. Marriage was a sacred institution, instituted and blessed by God. She refused to marry simply because he couldn't face a bunch of gossips. He might be ready to buckle under but her faith was stronger than that. Besides, she'd always expected to marry someone she loved and who loved her in return. The kind of marriage her parents had had. The kind of marriage her brother Ry had found. She refused to settle for anything less.

And, no matter how much the oh-so-proper Mr. Reynolds postured and argued, he couldn't force her. Because she knew deep down that he didn't really *want* to marry her—his tone and his choice of words had made that abundantly, humiliatingly clear.

Still, she couldn't stop her mind from wondering what it would be like to have him propose to her under other circumstances…

Dear God, I freely admit to being confused. Please help me to discern Your will in this and please give me the strength to follow wherever that might lead.

Eli kept going over this morning's conversation in his mind, wondering if he could have handled things differently, could have presented his case more persuasively. She was undoubtedly one of those females with romantic sensibilities when it came to marriage—he should have realized that. But there seemed to be a sensible streak in her, too. Surely she understood that, under the circumstances, there hadn't been time for flowery speeches and heartfelt declarations—not that he was given to such things anyway.

And regardless of how much she protested, he found it hard to believe she cared so little for what other people thought of her. Most other females faced with such public censure would have been relieved to have him step up with such alacrity. She just needed more time to accept the inevitable, as he had. She would come around, and the sooner the better.

But it would cause less talk if they were of one accord from the outset. There would be enough tawdry gossip as it was, no point adding additional fuel to the fire. He had to make her see reason before they reached town.

Eli halted the buggy a few feet from the fallen tree. Miss Lassiter hopped down almost before he'd tied off the reins. She went to work unhitching the horse without a word, her silence after her chattiness of the day before an obvious testament to her high emotions.

He stepped down from the wagon as well, though much more deliberately. He might not be able to do the entire job himself, but he'd be hanged if he'd sit by and watch her do it alone.

Before he'd joined her, however, Eli heard a rider approaching.

"Someone's coming," Sadie said, echoing his own thoughts. "I knew Cora Beth would send help."

The relief in her voice stiffened his shoulders. Didn't she think him capable of getting them out of this fix?

They both moved toward the tree to get a better look and a second later the rider came into view.

"Sheriff Hammond!" Miss Lassiter's hail sounded like that of a long-marooned sailor who'd spied a sail.

The new arrival reined in his horse just short of the tree. "You folks okay?"

"We are now." She pushed the hair back off her face. "You sure are a sight for sore eyes."

Eli felt a flash of annoyance. Did she really think so little of his ability to get them out of this?

The sheriff's gaze came to rest on Eli's cane. "What happened to you?"

"Twisted my ankle. I'll be okay."

The new arrival leaned back in the saddle, one arm draped casually over the pommel. "I reckon you don't look too much the worse for wear."

"How'd you find us?" Miss Lassiter asked.

"Cora Beth asked me to make sure you'd weathered the storm over at Ry and Josie's place and hadn't got caught out in it." Sheriff Hammond dismounted. "I'll admit I got a mite worried when Miss Dotty told me you never showed up."

"Sorry you had to make a trip all the way out there for nothing." She waved an arm to encompass the scene. "As you can see we took a little detour. How did you know where to find us?"

"Danny pulled me aside and told me about you questioning him on the location of the beehive. He thought you might have been tempted to try to find it."

"He told you where it was?"

The lawman grinned. "Only after swearing me to secrecy."

"We found the hive and gathered the honey, sort of as a surprise for Cora Beth. But then Mr. Reynolds hurt his ankle, and the storm came and the tree fell blocking the road. It was all quite dramatic—a real-life adventure."

Was that a grin the sheriff was trying to hide? "Looks like y'all managed to find a dry place to hole up."

Sadie nodded. "There's a cabin back there a way. Kept us from the worst of the storm and we even managed to get a fire going in the fireplace."

"Oh, the old Dubberly place. Still standing is it?"

"Just barely."

Sheriff Hammond finally turned his focus to Eli. "Glad y'all had a safe place to spend the night."

Eli didn't miss the look or the question behind it.

Should he announce the wedding plans now to set the man's mind at ease?

But Sadie reclaimed the sheriff's attention, chattering on about the honey and lightning strike and the dewberries. He was relieved that she glossed over the episode with the snake.

The sheriff finally tipped his hat back. "Well it sounds like you two had quite an adventure. Miss Lassiter, why don't you get back in the buggy and off this muddy road while Mr. Reynolds and I take care of moving the tree?"

Eli was not surprised to see her forehead wrinkle in protest.

"But I can help—"

"I'm sure you can," Sheriff Hammond's tone was genial, "but I'm also sure you wouldn't want to deprive us menfolk of the opportunity to show off our hero potential for a pretty lady such as yourself. Besides, Cora Beth would have my hide if she knew I allowed you to lend a hand with this."

Eli was impressed, and just a tiny bit jealous, of how easily the man maneuvered Sadie into returning to the buggy without wiping the smile from her face. But, at least now he wouldn't have to watch her do what should be his job.

As the two men tied the horse to the fallen tree, Eli felt Sheriff Hammond's assessing gaze on him once more.

"I want you to know, sheriff, that I'm quite aware of my duty. I have every intention of doing what I can to protect Miss Lassiter's reputation. To that end, we will be announcing our engagement very soon."

The sheriff's expression relaxed a bit. "Then I suppose congratulations are in order."

"I'll ask that you don't extend any felicitations to

Miss Lassiter just yet. She's not taking to the idea very well."

"I see." He glanced her way then back at Eli. "Then of course I'll wait until the more public announcement is made." He was silent for a moment as he worked with the traces. He glanced back up. "I assume I won't have long to wait."

Eli certainly hoped not. "We'll make the announcement as soon as Miss Lassiter gives me leave."

That seemed to satisfy the man and he turned his focus back on the job at hand.

Thirty minutes later the tree had been moved just enough to allow the buggy to slip by. Once Eli maneuvered the buggy around the obstacle, Sheriff Hammond remounted and they set off, with the sheriff riding alongside the buggy.

For a while, Sadie kept the conversation going with light, inconsequential talk. Not that she fooled him for a minute. Was the sheriff as aware of the strained undercurrents as he was?

Finally Miss Lassiter turned to the sheriff. "Would you mind riding on ahead and letting Dr. Whitman know about Mr. Reynolds' injury? I think it's important that he have it tended to as soon as possible."

"Of course." Sheriff Hammond gave Eli a sympathetically amused look, then tipped his hat to Sadie and rode off.

Sadie turned to Eli with an 'I told you so' look. "Sheriff Hammond didn't seem at all inclined to think poorly of us. I knew you were worried for nothing. And I'm sure the other folks in Knotty Pine will be just as understanding, just you wait and see."

"You're wrong." He kept his tone even. "Sheriff Hammond was quite aware of the situation, he was just too much of a gentleman to let it show in front of you. The only reason he seemed so equitable is because I assured him we would be announcing our engagement soon."

"You did *what?*" Her voice rose several octaves. "You had no right—"

"Please compose yourself. I did what was necessary to make certain your reputation did not suffer further damage."

His explanation did not seem to appease her. If anything her chin tilted higher. "My reputation is my business. You don't—"

"Miss Lassiter, just because you speak with such conviction doesn't make what you're saying fact."

She clamped her lips shut at that and tossed her head. The rest of the trip was accomplished in prickly silence.

When they arrived in town, Danny was waiting for them. "Cora Beth said y'all are to head straight for the boardinghouse. I'm gonna fetch Doc Whitman to meet you there and then I'll bring the buggy back to the livery for you."

Eli nodded and turned the buggy toward the boardinghouse. It seemed Cora Beth had already figured out that Sadie needed to be protected from prying eyes. Why couldn't Sadie herself see that?

A few women stood outside the mercantile, watching as they made their way toward the boardinghouse. From the corner of his eye he saw one of them lean over to whisper in her companion's ear.

So it begins, he thought.

Chapter Eight

Sadie tried to ignore the looks cast their way, tried to convince herself that the glances signified nothing more than idle curiosity. Still, the back of her neck prickled uncomfortably.

When they arrived at the boardinghouse, even before the buggy came to a halt, Cora Beth came rushing down the front steps to meet them, closely followed by Uncle Grover. "Sheriff Hammond told me what happened," she said. "I've been worried to no end about you since that storm rolled in yesterday."

Sadie scrambled down from the buggy. "I'm so sorry to have worried everyone like this. It was all my fault." Still feeling the weight of those glances, she felt compelled to add, "But Mr. Reynolds was a perfect gentleman the whole time."

Cora Beth gave her a quick one-armed hug, patting her back at the same time. "I'm sure he was." Then she pushed away and studied Sadie's face. "Are you sure you're all right? You look so pale."

"I'm fine, truly. Mr. Reynolds is the one who's hurt."

Cora Beth turned back to Eli as if just remembering

him. "Oh my, yes, of course. Bless your heart, Sheriff Hammond told me about your foot. Let Uncle Grover help you down and then we'll get you into the downstairs chamber and make you comfortable while you wait for Dr. Whitman."

Sadie wondered if she was the only one who saw the flicker of annoyance on Mr. Reynolds's face. No doubt about it, the man did *not* like to be thought of as weak in any way.

"No need to worry over me." His tone was mild, reflecting no hint of the annoyance she knew he was feeling. "I'll manage fine with the use of this walking stick."

"No need to be stubborn, my boy," Uncle Grover observed. "There's no shame in allowing others to help you now and then." He held the walking stick while Eli climbed down, then handed it back to him. "Sturdy piece of oak you've got there but it's a bit rough. I'll fetch you one of my own to use as soon as we get you settled in."

The words had barely left the older man's lips when Dr. Whitman came strolling up the walk.

Ten minutes later, Cora Beth stepped out into the hallway and turned to Sadie. "We'll just leave him in Dr. Whitman's capable hands for the time being. Uncle Grover can assist if need be. Now, you come along with me and I'll prepare you a nice bath."

Sadie nodded. "Actually, that sounds wonderful."

"You go find a change of clothes and I'll fetch the kettle of water that's been heating on the stove."

Sadie halted and turned back. "Oh no, don't you be trying to fill that tub on your own—I'll be back down in a minute." She placed a fist on her hip. "Promise me."

Cora Beth rolled her eyes but nodded and made a cross-my-heart sign over her chest.

Satisfied, Sadie plodded up the stairs. Her limbs felt heavy and there was an uncomfortable throbbing at her temples. She was suddenly so very, very weary. How could the events of one day have so completely turned her world upside down?

When she stepped inside her bedchamber she glanced in the mirror and gaped at her appearance. No wonder Cora Beth was in such a hurry to get her into a bath. And no wonder those folks in town had been staring. She looked a bedraggled mess. Her mud-splattered and forlornly wrinkled dress, her mussed hair, her smudged hands and face—she definitely didn't look like a lady who'd waited out the storm in the comfort of her brother's home.

Turning her back on the much-too-revealing mirror, she quickly gathered up a fresh change of clothes and a few other necessities, then headed back downstairs. When she stepped into the bathing room, Cora Beth was pouring something into an already full bathtub. An empty kettle sat on the floor next to her.

She glanced up with a smile. "There you are. I hope you don't mind but I added some of the fancy bath salts Josie got for me when she was in Philadelphia this past winter. I thought you could use some pampering after what you've been through."

Just what did Cora Beth think had happened while they were gone? She pushed that thought aside. "I thought you promised not to fool with that kettle on your own."

"I didn't. Nettie Dauber is cooking for us today—interviewing to be Mr. Reynolds's new cook—and she very kindly took care of it for me."

"Oh." So there was an outsider in the house. Would the woman go carrying tales as to what went on here today? Better not think about that for now either. "And thank you for the bath salts, but it wasn't necessary."

Cora Beth waved off her comment. "Don't you worry about that—I wanted to do it. Now, I've laid out several thick towels for you to use and the water is nice and steamy, so you can soak as long as you like."

"Thank you. For everything." Sadie set her clean clothes on a nearby bench and started pulling pins from her hair—what few pins remained, that was. "Any word from Dr. Whitman on Mr. Reynolds' condition?"

"Not yet." Cora Beth moved toward the folding screen that was pushed against the far wall. "As soon as Doc's done with the examination I'll let you know."

"Here, let me do that." Sadie took one end of the screen and the two of them arranged it in front of the tub. When it was placed to their satisfaction Sadie stood uncertainly for a moment. She felt the need to explain. Problem was, she wasn't sure just *what* she wanted to explain. "Cora Beth, I feel just awful for putting you through all this trouble and worry."

"Pish-posh. I'm just relieved you're both okay."

Sadie chewed at her lip for a moment then tried again. "Mr. Reynolds is concerned that there might be some talk around town."

"Is he now?"

Cora Beth's tone was carefully neutral and Sadie wasn't having much luck reading her expression either. "Yes. I told him he was overreacting."

"And how did he respond?"

Still no hint of how she felt. "He asked me to marry him." The words hung in the air between them, almost as a living thing. Sadie hurried to take away some of their power. "Isn't that the silliest thing you ever heard?"

But Cora Beth shook her head. "I don't see anything silly about it at all."

Not the response she'd hoped for. "Oh, for goodness' sake. To marry simply to avoid gossip—it's ridiculous."

"People have married for less compelling reasons."

Did Cora Beth really believe what she was implying? "Compelling? Aren't you giving too much influence to idle gossip?"

"Perception and appearances can be very powerful forces."

"So can the truth and self-assurance."

Cora Beth smiled. "You're right, of course. And I will support you no matter what you decide. You just need to think seriously about the long-term implications of whatever decision you *do* make." Cora Beth kept a steady hold on her gaze.

"But nothing improper happened." The words came out almost as a wail.

"Oh Sadie, I don't doubt that for a minute. But that doesn't change the fact that the two of you *did* spend the night alone together in an isolated cabin. The folks here in Knotty Pine are good, fair-minded people for the most part, but the rules of acceptable conduct among *any* Christian community are very unforgiving in such matters."

Sadie couldn't dredge up a direct response to Cora Beth's logic, so fell back on her own emotions. "But marriage is a sacred institution. No matter what the circumstances, I could never make those vows lightly."

Cora Beth straightened and made a shooing motion, indicating Sadie should step behind the screen. "For goodness' sake, here we go nattering on while your bath is getting cold. Get out of those dirty clothes so I can wash them and you can get your soak."

As Sadie complied, Cora Beth continued. "I wouldn't expect you to make this decision lightly. Nor does Mr. Reynolds strike me as a man who would enter into marriage frivolously."

"Then you understand my position." Sadie tossed her skirt over the screen.

"I truly admire your scruples," Cora Beth continued after a moment, "But there are times when we must set our personal wishes aside. Do you think you can face the whispers and stares?"

Sadie tossed the remainder of her clothing over the screen. "I'm not so fainthearted that I can't face down a gaggle of gossipers."

"When it comes down to it," Cora Beth continued, "would marrying Mr. Reynolds be such a terrible fate?"

Sadie was glad she was behind the screen so Cora Beth couldn't see the heat rising in her cheeks. Sure, Mr. Reynolds was a nice-looking man, and there was something about him that tugged at her more than she cared to admit. But looks and honorable intentions weren't everything. And when she'd daydreamed about the man she might one day marry, he wasn't some straightlaced city fella and he sure wasn't some dour banker. No, she was looking for a rancher, someone who wasn't afraid to get his hands dirty and who would want to set down roots at Hawk's Creek, to help her turn her share of the place into something they could manage and take pleasure in together.

Realizing she'd been silent for far too long, Sadie covered her lack of response by making a bit of noise and she eased herself into the still-warm water of the tub.

Cora Beth cleared her throat. "Well, you just clear your mind of all of this for now and have a nice long soak before your water gets cold. There'll be time enough to think and pray over this after you're rested."

Once Cora Beth was gone Sadie settled herself more comfortably, letting the water envelope her. It felt wonderful.

But the niggling thought that this was the last moment of peace she would have for quite some time wouldn't allow her to totally relax.

Alone at last. Eli lay in the unfamiliar room they'd ushered him into and stared at the ceiling. First, his unexpected role as guardian, then the tragedy with his stepsister, Susan, and now this. It seemed that for the past year, no matter how meticulously he planned, no matter how good his intentions, no matter how certain his path, some unseen force had been playing fruit basket turnover with his life.

He had to get a better handle on things, had to put himself more firmly in control of his future, of Penny's future.

But for now, he needed to get this matter under control. If he didn't, all of his careful planning to ensure that his and Penny's new life here was above reproach would be for naught. Somehow he had to gain Miss Lassiter's cooperation. Because he wasn't about to let himself be defeated by the vagaries of circumstance. He'd just get busy figuring out how to turn this set of circumstances to his advantage.

The first order of business, of course, was making certain Miss Lassiter came to her senses and accepted the inevitable outcome, just as he had. Since he knew his strengths as a negotiator, he was confident he could make that happen in the next day or two. Once he had her agreement in hand, he'd salvage a portion of his original plan, with a few adjustments for the woman now irrevocably cast as the leading lady.

At least picking Miss Lassiter for a wife provided the advantage of his knowing from the outset that Penny would approve.

She wasn't the woman he would have chosen for the role, of course. He'd been looking for someone with more maturity and decorum. But he was willing to set aside his own preferences given the situation. Besides, though he still had some reservations about her suitability to take on the role of Penny's caregiver, perhaps Miss Lassiter wasn't as big a flibbertigibbet as he'd first thought.

Yes, she undoubtedly was spontaneous and unortho-dox—two characteristics he had little appreciation for. But she'd shown surprising spirit during their ordeal. The fact that she hadn't uttered a word of complaint, fallen apart or given much thought to her appearance spoke well of her.

Perhaps she was one of those people who was at her best in a crisis. Which had both its good and bad points. Good in that she wouldn't fall apart when faced with problems. Bad in that, since they wouldn't be in a con-stant state of crisis, would she revert back to her flighty ways?

He let his mind dwell on the idea of being married to Sadie Lassiter. Surprisingly, he wasn't as upset by that thought as he would have been just twenty-four hours ago. With the right man to teach her the proper way to go about things, she could be the proper sort of wife he was looking for. And the idea of being the one to teach her, of taming her spirit just enough to take her place beside him, was actually quite intriguing.

Growing up without a mother, being raised by her father and brothers and a bunch of ranch hands—it was no wonder she was more than a little hoydenish. She had it in her to be level-headed and responsible, he could see that now. She just needed the right person to draw that out, to help her emphasize her better qualities and tame the less desirable ones.

And he was just the man for the job.

The next day was Sunday and Sadie carefully studied the dresses she'd brought with her to Knotty Pine. She usually wasn't one to fuss over her clothes overmuch, but what she wore for her first appearance in public since her and Mr. Reynolds's return to town yesterday somehow seemed a matter of great importance this morning. After much consideration, she settled on her simplest, most modest dress.

Cora Beth had kept her busy inside the boardinghouse with simple tasks all day yesterday, but there was no way she was going to remain indoors today. *Father, I'm determined to visit Your house this morning, no matter what—I truly need to show Cora Beth's neighbors that I don't feel the need to cower in private as if I'm guilty of something. But I'd take it kindly if You could keep the townsfolk's stares and whispers to a minimum.*

She hadn't seen much of Mr. Reynolds since they'd arrived back at the boardinghouse yesterday. According to Cora Beth, Dr. Whitman had verified that his foot wasn't broken, thank goodness. But the physician had also made it clear the ankle would need several days to heal.

It was strange, but she was both looking forward to

seeing him this morning and dreading it. The warring emotions were making her jittery, leaving her with an off balance feeling that she didn't much care for.

Would he be joining them for the church service or would he stay in his room with his foot carefully propped up on pillows? She wasn't even sure which she hoped for more.

When she headed downstairs, Cora Beth stood at the foot of the stairs, almost as if she'd been waiting for her to come down. "Are you sure you don't want to stay here and rest this morning?" she asked. "I know everyone would understand, what with the ordeal you had—"

"I'm perfectly okay—not the least bit tired." There was no way she would cower in her room. The best way to show everyone that her conscience was clear was to walk into church with her head high. "This is a fine Sunday morning and I need to be in the Lord's house giving thanks that He watched over me and Mr. Reynolds during that storm."

Cora Beth touched the locket at her throat. "You know you don't need to be in the Lord's house to give Him thanks. Still, if you've set your mind on going then I won't try to talk you out of it."

Mr. Reynolds stepped into the hallway just then and Sadie felt her pulse kick up a notch. His gaze locked onto hers with a determined glint. Would he bring up that silly notion of their need to marry?

But he broke eye contact and glanced around at the others who had started to gather downstairs. Sadie took in his Sunday-best garb and realized he was planning to go to church service this morning, as well. His foot must be better.

She noticed he was still using the stout branch she'd found for him even though she'd heard Uncle Grover offer one of his own. It probably didn't mean anything, but it still gave her a warm feeling inside.

Cora Beth greeted him as he approached and Sadie dropped her gaze, guiltily aware that she'd been staring.

"I hope you don't mind," Cora Beth said, "but I took the liberty of asking Danny to fetch the buggy for you. I figured you'd want to ride to church this morning rather than walk."

Sadie saw that telltale twitch near the corner of his mouth and thought he was going to protest, then something seemed to flash between him and Cora Beth. To her surprise, he nodded, gave Cora Beth a "thank you," then turned to her. "Miss Lassiter, would you do me the honor of accompanying me and my sister in the carriage?"

Being alone with him would definitely *not* be a good idea, not with her emotions all swirling chaotically and this marriage business between them. "Thank you, but—"

Cora Beth stepped forward. "Go along now, Sadie. I'm sure Mr. Reynolds could use the company and the support."

Before she could protest again, Mr. Reynolds cleared his throat. "I would be most grateful."

She narrowed her eyes. It wasn't like him to sound so humble. But to refuse now in front of the others would seem churlish. Feeling outmaneuvered, she nodded and moved toward the front door.

A little later, as they rode through town, Sadie was grateful that Penny was seated between them. She served as a much needed buffer.

Yesterday, once Penny had assured herself that Sadie and Eli were okay, she'd begun comparing the whole

misadventure to the exploits of Annabel Adams. While
Sadie had been amused, Eli most definitely had not. And
she supposed she could understand his viewpoint in this
particular case.

As the carriage slowed to a halt in front of the church,
Sadie felt the prickles of dozens of eyes studying the two
of them, saw the speculative glances and knowing nods
rippling through the clusters of townsfolk. She thought
she'd been prepared, but she could feel the heat climbing
up in her cheeks.

Sheriff Hammond stepped forward to hand her and
Penny down. "Good morning, ladies. You're both look-
ing mighty fine this morning." He glanced Eli's way.
"Glad to see your ankle isn't keeping you down."

Eli carefully descended from the buggy. "Dr. Whitman is of the opinion I should be as good as new in a
few days."

"I believe he said a week or two," Sadie corrected,
ignoring his frown. "And that was assuming you stay
off it."

The group from the boardinghouse strolled up just
then.

"Hello, sheriff," Cora Beth greeted him with a friend-
ly smile. "I want to apologize again for imposing on you
yesterday."

The sheriff tipped his hat. "No problem, ma'am. All
part of the job."

Somehow, as they prepared to enter the church, Sadie
found herself flanked by Cora Beth on one side and the
sheriff on the other. Eli was right behind them, surrounded by the children and Uncle Grover.

When they slid into the pew, however, Sadie somehow
ended up seated between Penny and her brother. All
through the service, Sadie kept her eyes focused forward,

not daring to meet anyone's gaze but the preacher's. His sermon, one based on Jeremiah 29:11, touched her. It was comforting to be reminded that God had plans for each of them and that those plans were for their good. Still, when she stood at the end of the service she realized she'd heard very little of the sermon itself.

Forgive me, Father, for being so self-centered. Sometimes I need reminding that the only being whose opinion of me really matters is You.

As they exited the church, Reverend Ludlow clasped one of her hands between both of his. "I heard about the ordeal you and Mr. Reynolds endured during our recent storm. I'm thankful that the Good Lord saw fit to keep you both safe."

She was pleased to see there was no trace of censure on the man's face. "Thank you, Reverend. And you're right, God was definitely watching out for us."

She moved on to make way for others exiting the church, and found herself without a companion for the first time this morning. Strange that instead of relief she felt suddenly vulnerable.

"Good morning, Sadie dear."

She turned to find one of the older ladies of the community at her elbow. The face was familiar, but who was she? Oh yes—the lady who ran the mercantile with her husband. "Mrs. Danvers, good morning. It's a beautiful day, isn't it."

"Oh yes. It must be especially refreshing after that ordeal you went through during Friday's storm. I must say I admire how calm you are considering what you've been through. I confess I would be prostrate with hysteria."

Sadie gave a half smile, unsure of how that was meant. "Thank you for your concern, ma'am, but I assure you I am quite well—comes from having a clear conscience, I suppose. Since I suffered nothing more than some minor inconveniences, there's nothing heroic about my current calm."

"Minor inconveniences." There was a note of incredulity in the woman's tone. "How admirable of you to put such a brave face on it. Still, a less…*adventurous* lady would undoubtedly be more strongly affected."

Sadie got the distinct impression that Mrs. Danvers did not think being adventurous was something to be proud of. But she kept her smile firmly in place, refusing to let the woman's words rattle her.

Eli took one look at Miss Lassiter and realized immediately that something was amiss. Not that she gave any overt signs. But still, he saw something in her stance…

He took a closer look, identifying her companion. Ah, Mrs. Danvers—so that explained it. Undoubtedly the less-than-subtle matchmaker was not happy to find her hopes for landing her daughter a match with this particular well-to-do bachelor had been so soundly crushed.

He excused himself from Sheriff Hammond and moved to Sadie's side. "Good day, Mrs. Danvers. Reverend Ludlow gave a mighty fine sermon this morning, don't you think?" He didn't miss the flash of relief that crossed Sadie's face. So, she was not as immune to censure as she had tried to have him believe.

The old biddy, however, gave him a decidedly frosty smile. "Quite fine, yes. I was just complimenting Miss Lassiter on how well she weathered that little adventure the other day."

"Yes, she is a remarkable woman, isn't she? Now, I do hope you will excuse us but I have strict orders from Dr. Whitman to stay off this foot as much as possible."

"Of course. Good day to you."

Eli saw Myra Willows stroll past. Was it just this past Thursday that he'd scratched her off his potential-bride list because of the mere possibility that she could have been the woman hiding behind the name Temperance Trulove? That seemed such a trivial thing compared to his current situation.

As he handed first Penny and then Sadie up into the buggy, he took note of the whispers exchanged behind hands and the eyes that were quickly averted.

He had to convince Sadie it was time to put an end to the gossip and speculation before both of their reputations were beyond salvaging. For Penny's sake, if not their own.

As Eli escorted Sadie into the boardinghouse, the rest of their party strolled up the walk.

Viola skipped up to them ahead of the others and looked up at his companion. "Aunt Sadie, what's a reputation?"

Eli sensed the sudden tension in Sadie, felt an echo of it in himself. The mere fact that the child was raising the issue could only mean she'd overheard some talk.

"It's the way other people think of you," she said. He was surprised at how calm her tone and demeanor were. "For instance," she continued, "your daddy has a reputation for being a good horse breeder and an honest person, your aunt Cora Beth is known for making the best fruitcakes in the county, and Mr. Reynolds here has the reputation for being an honest businessman."

Is that how she viewed him?

The six-year-old seemed confused by the explanation. "Oh. I thought it must be a dress or pair of shoes."

"Why?"

"Because I heard Mrs. Franklin say it was a shame that yours was all soiled."

Eli stiffened, reflexively putting a hand at Sadie's back in support. He wanted to take away some of the sting she must be feeling, but wasn't sure how to do it. Then again, perhaps if she felt the full brunt of this *now* it would serve to shorten the time it took her to come to her senses.

Luckily Viola seemed to lose interest in the conversation, and skipped back to rejoin Audrey and Penny without pressing for further explanation.

"Are you all right?" Eli pitched his voice so that only she could hear him.

"Yes." But she didn't sound quite as confident as she had before.

He took advantage of the situation to press his case again. "Are you convinced now?"

"That there will be wagging tongues? Yes. I had hoped for better but I suppose it was inevitable."

He made an impatient gesture. Why did she insist on not seeing what was so obvious to everyone else? "You know that wasn't what I meant. And I would appreciate it if you wouldn't make light of the situation. We need to announce our engagement as soon as possible."

He could tell by her expression he'd gotten her back up again.

"And I would appreciate it if you would respect my wishes and stop pestering me with your talk of marriage." She raised her chin. "This talk will blow over soon, you'll see. And once I'm back at Hawk's Creek, that will be the end of it."

Was she just being stubborn, or was the idea of marrying him so abhorrent to her? "Perhaps as far as you are concerned, though I somehow doubt that. But what about the rest of us? What about me and Penny and even Viola, who all make our home here?"

He saw the argument forming on her lips and held up a hand to forestall her. "Very well," he said. "I will hold my peace for now. But we *will* talk of this again." With a short bow, he left her and headed to his room.

He paused in the doorway as he realized Penny had followed him, with something obviously on her mind. Had she heard any of the gossip?

"Did you need something?" He mentally held his breath, preparing himself for an uncomfortable discussion.

"Is your foot feeling better today?"

He relaxed. She was only worried about his injury. "Some. Don't you worry. I'll be as good as new before you know it."

She sat in a nearby chair and started swinging her legs. "Why were you and Sadie out there in the woods?"

A trickier question. "We were trying to replace the honey Miss Lassiter spilled the other night. There's a special place out there Mrs. Collins gets it from."

Penny's nose wrinkled. "Sadie didn't spill that honey, Eli. I did."

Eli stilled, staring down at his sister. "You did? But I saw Miss Lassiter…" He hadn't actually seen her spill it, just trying to clean up the mess.

He sat down hard on the bed. He'd made the wrong assumption and the maddeningly stubborn woman hadn't bothered to correct him.

Seems he wronged her yet again.

Sadie sighed in frustration as she climbed the stairs to her room. The man just didn't know when to let it go.

She'd found herself watching as he hobbled down

the hallway. It was amazing how, even with his limp, he could make a dignified exit.

But as she entered her room, Sadie felt her determination waver just a bit. She'd faced condescension and criticism before, but never this questioning of her very character. Perhaps she should talk about cutting her visit short. If push came to shove, she'd find a way to make Cora Beth accept her offer to hire help to take her place. The thought of not seeing Penny again, though, saddened her to no end.

She refused to think about how the thought of not seeing Penny's brother again made her feel.

Chapter Nine

"Sadie, I feel responsible." Cora Beth, stood at the counter while Sadie washed the lunch dishes, looking genuinely contrite. "If you hadn't come here to help—"

Sadie raised a wet hand before Cora Beth could say more. "This is *not* your fault. Coming to Knotty Pine was entirely my idea, not yours. And taking that detour to collect the honey Friday was *also* my idea. My very ill-conceived idea as it turns out." How in the world could she have anticipated that what seemed nothing more than a quick side trip to help a friend would land her in this mess?

"Have you reconsidered Mr. Reynolds's offer?"

Actually, she'd thought of very little else since he'd so matter-of-factly proposed Saturday morning. Not that she'd changed her mind. "Like I told you before, I can't—"

Before Sadie could finish the sentence, the door flew open and a familiar figure came striding in.

"Griff!" She quickly dried her hands on her apron. "What are you doing here?"

Her brother crossed the room in ground-eating strides

and grasped her by her shoulders. He looked deep into her eyes, his expression tense, worried. "I heard what happened. Are you all right, Sadie girl?"

Sadie shot Cora Beth an accusing glance then turned back to her brother. "I'm fine, really. There was no need for anyone to worry you with this silly kerfuffle. And certainly no need for you to come hightailin' it out here to check on me." Why did her brothers continue to treat her like a helpless schoolgirl? Even their pet name for her, Sadie girl, made her feel relegated to the status of a child.

Cora Beth stepped toward the doorway. "I'd best go see what the twins are up to."

Griff barely acknowledged her exit as he continued to study Sadie. "You don't look fine to me."

He was too perceptive by half. She pretended indignation. "Griffith Michael Lassiter, I might be your little sister but that doesn't give you call to insult me like that."

But he wasn't to be sidetracked. "You know what I mean. I can tell this whole thing's not sitting right with you."

"Of course it's not. Getting caught out in that storm was more than a little inconvenient and unexpected. And yes, I might be a little worse for wear, but I truly am fine. In fact, now that it's over, I'm looking back on the whole thing as a great adventure."

Griff relaxed enough to smile at that. "Sadie girl, I do believe you could see a barn on fire and spin it into a yarn of high adventure."

"Nothing wrong with looking for the positive in things."

Griff turned serious again. "Is this Eli Reynolds fellow around?"

Sadie didn't like the way he said Eli's name, as if he planned to dislike him on sight. "Not right now." She tried again to deflect his focus. "Anyway, who's keeping an eye on the ranch while you're here playing overprotective big brother? Aren't you in the middle of spring branding?"

Griff shrugged. "Red can handle things for now." He stepped back and crossed his arms over his chest. "So where is he? I'd like to have a word or two with him."

Uh-oh, that had an ominous sound to it. "Don't you go doing anything rash. Mr. Reynolds feels bad enough for what happened as it is, even though it was more my fault than his. He even offered to marry me." As soon as the words were out of her mouth, Sadie wished them back. But it was too late.

Griff got very, very still, like a predator just before it pounced. "He did, did he? And just why did he do that, Sadie girl?"

Sadie mentally groaned. Sometimes her brother's temper was too short by half. "Griff—*nothing happened.* He made the offer because he's a gentleman with misguided notions of what his duty is."

He studied her, his eyes lidded. "And did you accept?"

"No! Of course not."

At her protest, Griff's eyebrows went way up.

Had she been just a mite too emphatic?

"Are you sure nothing happened?" her brother asked.

"Positive." This time she managed to keep her tone conversational. "What I meant was, I refuse to marry *anyone* simply because circumstances beyond our control might give rise to a bit of gossip. Besides, he doesn't really want to marry me." Yet another admission she wished she could call back. What was wrong with her today?

Naturally Griff caught her slip—she could tell by the way his eyes narrowed. "Let me ask you again, where is Eli Reynolds?"

She didn't like the measured steel in his tone. "Before I tell you, you need to promise me you won't do anything rash."

Griff spread his hands in a semblance of innocence. "I just want to talk to him."

She sighed, knowing if she didn't tell him he'd find out some other way. "He's probably over at that house he's having renovated. I'll take you there."

"No thank you—just tell me the way. I think this conversation is one that should be kept just between him and me."

Sadie rolled her eyes. Whatever Griff and Eli had to say to each other, she sincerely hoped they could get past the posturing. It wouldn't do to have her husband and her brother at each other's throats.

Eli studied the new banister on the main stairway, but to be honest, his mind was not on the task at hand. The reaction of the townspeople to what had happened was just as he'd expected. Seems he'd left one scandal behind in New York just to land him and Penny in the middle of another one. If he didn't get the stubborn Miss Lassiter to see reason soon he might as well pull up stakes again and find another town to settle in.

A sound drew his gaze to the entryway and he saw a man with an intense, none-too-friendly expression studying him from the front doorway. Was he one of the workmen?

"Eli Reynolds?"

Something in the man's tone alerted Eli that he did not consider himself an employee. "Yes?" A moment later he took in the familiar features and realized who this must be. The man's next words confirmed his suspicion.

"I'm Griff Lassiter—Sadie's brother." The man's demeanor remained assessing, suspicious.

"Mr. Lassiter, I'm glad you're here." At least from a something-that-needs-to-be-done standpoint. "Let's step into the parlor. The furniture is already set up there and we might as well make ourselves comfortable. I believe you and I have quite a few things to discuss."

With a stiff nod, Sadie's brother let him lead the way.

As soon as they'd taken their seats, Eli tried to take control of the conversation. "First, I want to assure you that absolutely nothing of an improper nature occurred while your sister and I were stranded in the woods. It was an awkward situation but your sister maintained her composure and I treated her with every respect."

"So Sadie says." He didn't sound entirely convinced.

Eli pressed on. "That being said, however, I know my duty and am prepared to do it."

"Sadie says she doesn't want to marry you. In fact she was quite emphatic about it."

Eli mentally winced at the implication behind those very blunt words. "Your sister has not yet fully realized the gravity of the situation. Surely you, as her brother, understand that we have no choice."

"As her brother," Griff repeated with a flinty steadiness, "what I *understand* is that my sister has both a tender heart and a hard head. If she says she doesn't want to marry you, then there's no way that you or anyone else is going to force her." The man's eyes could have bored through granite. "And to even try, you're gonna have to come through me."

Eli understood the strong protective instincts that drove him to defend his sister, emotions he'd gotten all too familiar with in the days leading up to his and Penny's departure from New York.

He had to make Sadie's brother see that he had her best interests at heart. "Mr. Lassiter, I assure you my intentions toward your sister are entirely honorable. Surely you understand that, through no one's fault, her reputation has been tarnished. I am merely trying to put the best face that I can on the situation and lend her the protection of my name."

That only deepened the man's frown. "The protection of the Lassiter name has always been more than enough to carry her and I don't see that changing. I intend to take my sister back to Hawk's Creek with me in the morning."

It appeared stubbornness ran in the Lassiter family. "I understand how you feel, she's your sister and you'd do anything to protect her." Oh yes, he knew the feeling well. "But I believe spiriting her away so precipitously would be a grave mistake." He refused to consider that that was exactly what he'd done with Penny. His reasoning, however, had been based not on an emotional knee-jerk reaction but on a carefully controlled assessment.

He leaned forward, trying again to find common ground with Sadie's brother—his future brother-in-law if things worked out as planned. "At least stay here long enough to give your sister sufficient time to think this through. Once she realizes the extent of the situation I think she'll begin to see reason."

"Give you enough time to coerce her into marrying you, you mean."

Did the man *know* his sister? "You're giving me way too much credit if you think I can convince your sister to do something she doesn't want to." Eli had spoken without thinking, but he noted the slight twitch to his visitor's lips and felt hope flicker back to life. "Besides," he used his most persuasive tone, "you'll be right here to make certain everything is handled as it should be."

Griff's expression hardened again. "You can sure as this morning's sunrise count on that."

Did that mean he planned to stay after all? Eli held his peace. And his breath.

"If Sadie has no objections," Griff said slowly, "I suppose I can stick around until Friday." Then he gave Eli a hard look. "But the moment she says she's had enough, we're on the first train headed north."

"Your brother came to see me today."

Sadie mentally winced. Eli's tone was conversational but she could read the undercurrents. They were standing on the front porch of the boardinghouse, watching the first stars of the evening make an appearance. The others had diplomatically stayed inside, though it had taken a stern look from her to stop Griff from joining them.

She inhaled the scent of roses from the nearby bushes. That scent always reminded her of her mother. "I apologize if Griff was overbearing. He can be very single-minded sometimes."

"A family trait perhaps?"

Sadie smiled, glad that he could find some humor in the situation.

Then he waved aside her concerns. "But there's no need to apologize. He was worried about you, and rightly so. I don't think he's ready to believe that he can't protect you from this. Naturally he's determined to stand by you, whatever decision you make."

She found herself pinned by his stare and decided to let him do most of the talking.

"I think his brotherly devotion is blinding him to the gravity of the situation," Eli said evenly. "If word of this incident were to follow you to your hometown, and it almost certainly will, even your prominent family name won't shield you from the wagging tongues. More importantly, it will put your chances of eventually finding a more desirable match in serious jeopardy."

She almost protested the idea of there being a 'more desirable match', but caught herself just in time. "Are you trying to frighten me into marrying you?" she asked instead.

He didn't rise to the bait. "Just trying to help you face facts. Perhaps I was less than sensitive back there at the cabin when I made my case for the need for us to marry."

What an understatement! But that wasn't the sticking point. "Admit it," she said, going on the offensive, "you don't want this marriage any more than I do."

He didn't try to deny it. "That's beside the point. But if it makes you feel any better, it's been my intention since I arrived in Knotty Pine to seek out a proper wife, one with whom I can build my new life."

That *did* surprise her. Of course, she doubted he considered her 'proper wife' material. "Part of furnishing your household?" She wished the harsh words back as soon as she uttered them.

Something flickered in his expression, but he covered it quickly. "Let's say, rather, that it's an effort to *complete* my household. Penny is at an impressionable age where she needs a maternal influence."

"Then hire a nanny. A marriage should be based on mutual caring and respect."

She saw the muscles in his jaw tighten. "I'm sorry if what I'm offering doesn't meet your notions of what a marriage should be, but it has of necessity become my measuring stick."

It must make for such a joyless life to be so analytical about *all* aspects of one's existence. "So, are you saying you see me as someone who could provide that maternal influence to your sister?"

He shifted slightly before he answered. Which was, she supposed, in itself an answer. For a moment the only sound was that of the insects welcoming the darkness.

"You *could* be," he finally said. "Naturally we would need to come to an understanding of the sort of routine and discipline to be maintained in our household."

His main focus was *discipline?* Surely she'd misunderstood. "Those things are important, of course. But surely you're also looking out for what will make her feel loved, encouraged, supported?"

He tugged on the cuff of his shirt. "Sound discipline and a steadfast routine are required to produce true harmony in a home. Harmony, in turn, leads to contentment. Those other, more sentimental notions, can be deceptive, even harmful, if not tempered with a rational approach. Naturally I wish Penny to be happy, but not at the expense of providing a proper upbringing and considering her ultimate well-being."

"Ultimate well-being comes from God alone."

"Of course. But we must do our part, as well. And I'm determined to do everything in my power—including finding her a mother figure to provide the proper example."

Actually, it sounded like he wasn't looking for a

motherly influence for his sister, he was looking for a warden. Which meant he needed to look elsewhere—she most definitely would not fit the bill. But poor Penny.

She straightened. "Mr. Reynolds, while I appreciate that you're attempting to be gallant, I will assure you again that I'll survive this brouhaha without resorting to a hasty, unwanted marriage. Especially given that you and I have such different notions of what we want in a spouse."

He brushed at a moth flitting nearby, his frustration evident in his expression. Then he seemed to come to a decision. "I think you're under the impression that I'm doing this entirely for your benefit, and I'll confess that I allowed you to believe that. But that's not entirely true."

She eyed him suspiciously. Was this another ploy to get her to agree to his proposal?

"It isn't just *your* reputation at stake. I was there too, remember?"

What was he getting at? "But surely, I mean, you're a man."

"Yes. But do you think any woman of character will want to marry me if the perception is that you and I were…indiscreet? And that I refused to do right by you afterwards? Not to mention how this might affect Penny."

Surely none of this would affect that sweet, innocent little girl? "You're being overly dramatic again." But she felt her determination waver. What if there was some truth to what he was saying? She'd never forgive herself if Penny felt the sting from any nasty gossip.

He leaned a hip against the porch rail. "Oh, perhaps someday I might shake the stigma, but not anytime soon. And I need someone to help me care for Penny now."

Sadie started to repeat her earlier refusal, but something in his expression caught her attention. Beneath his logic and confidence, she saw another emotion flicker in his expression, something that looked very much like *need*.

It had to be her imagination. Still, it stopped her for a moment. "For someone who doesn't care much for melodrama, you seem to be quite adept at it."

His lips twisted in a wry grin. "This does seem very much like our own version of the Adventures of Annabel Adams, doesn't it?"

Had Penny planted that idea or had he come up with it on his own?

"Still, I'm asking you to think about what I just said, to take into consideration what it will mean to how Penny and I are accepted here in Knotty Pine, before you make your final decision."

She could tell that hadn't been an easy request for him to make. Did he truly *need* her? The thought confused her, set her mind spinning in a different direction. Perhaps she *had* been too hasty in making her decision. *Heavenly Father, I've been guilty of not seeking Your guidance in this matter. Guess it's time I started to do a little more listening and a little less deciding.*

"Maybe you're right," she finally said. Then she quickly held up a hand as victory flashed in his expression. "I only mean that I agree I hadn't considered how all this might affect you and Penny and that I do need to give it more thought and do some praying about it."

"Quite reasonable," he said magnanimously. "Take a few days if you need them."

She turned toward the front door, then had another thought. "Would you mind, I mean, perhaps we could pray together for heavenly guidance."

He gave her a startled look, then nodded. "Of course."

"You can start." She bowed her head and closed her eyes.

There were a few seconds of silence and then, "Lord, please give Miss Lassiter the clarity of vision to see that marriage is the only logical solution to this unanticipated situation and then give us both the wisdom to conduct our lives with honor and dignity."

She glanced up, slightly shocked. She'd never heard anyone pray in that manner—*telling* God what the outcome should be rather than seeking His will. It seemed so, well, so presumptuous.

But it wasn't for her to judge.

She bowed her head again, and added her own prayer to his. "Heavenly Father, we give You thanks for Your wonderful gift of grace, a gift You extend to us daily. And we thank You again for watching over us during that storm and providing us with the comfort of food and shelter. Those berries were especially nice. We acknowledge that You are all-knowing, all-powerful, ever-present and all-loving. Which means You already know about the pickle Mr. Reynolds and I find ourselves in. We are of two different minds on what we should do about this and are sorely in need of Your guidance. Please provide us with the wisdom to understand Your will and the courage and good sense to follow it, no matter our reservations or desires. Amen."

She opened her eyes to find him studying her with a slightly puzzled look in his face. What was he thinking? No matter, she needed to have some time to herself. "Thank you for praying with me. Now, if you'll excuse me, I think I'll retire to my room."

He straightened. "Of course. I hope you have a good

night's rest and I look forward to hearing your decision soon."

"You'll be the first person I discuss it with." She stepped back, strangely reluctant to leave him.

As soon as she entered the boardinghouse, Griff stepped out of the parlor. "Anything we need to talk about?"

Sometimes she could do with a little less big-brothering. "Not on my account. I'm going up to my room." She ignored his concerned frown and headed for the stairs.

But she was waylaid once more before reaching her destination. Penny met her at the top of the landing, an anxious expression on her face. "Are you going to marry my brother?"

Penny obviously felt strongly about this—but which way? "I haven't decided yet." She studied the little girl, trying to read her reaction. "How would you feel about it if I did?"

The child's cheeks pinkened, but her expression lost none of its earnestness. "It would be nice to have someone else in the house with us. And I like you—you smile a lot."

Now that was a telling statement. Did her brother not "smile a lot" when they were alone? "Thank you—I like you, too. And you have a very pretty smile that brightens up the room when you choose to share it with us."

"So you'll come live with us?"

She brushed a lock of hair off the girl's forehead. "I need to pray about it before I know my answer to that. And I'd appreciate your prayers, as well." She stooped down to give Penny a hug. "But whatever I decide, you know that you and I will always be special friends, don't you?"

Penny nodded.

She gave the girl a light pat on her backside. "Now scoot. I need to go to my room and I think Audrey and Viola were looking for you."

Sadie watched Penny head down the stairs, then turned to her room. The thing about this whole situation was that there was a part of her that *wanted* to tell him yes. But even that traitorous part of her wanted it only if he was going into this willingly, happily. Not because he felt he had no other choice.

Then again, was he right about how her continued refusal would affect his and Penny's standing in the community? And if he was, was that a burden she was willing to carry, that she even had a right to carry?

Heavenly Father, I'm so confused—please let me see Your will in this. It occurs to me that I've been imploring You to help me find a place where I can feel truly useful and of value, but I never imagined it might lead to this. Is this marriage truly Your will? Or should I stand firm in my refusal?

Sadie lay awake far into the night, no more sure of what answer she would give Eli than when she'd left his company.

Eli lay with his arm behind his head, staring up at the ceiling in the moonlit bedchamber.

He tried to tell himself that she would give him the answer he sought, but he wasn't quite so confident. His admission that he needed her had chipped away at her stubborn stand, but had it been enough to convince her? He devoutly hoped so, because the idea that he hadn't would mean his and Penny's position in this town was in serious jeopardy.

The strangely personal prayer she'd uttered this evening still echoed through his mind. Naturally he believed in the civilizing influence of religion. He said grace at every meal, attended church on Sundays, gave a portion of his income to the church. He took pains to make certain his sister was raised to understand moral and spiritual concepts.

But he'd never heard anyone speak so intimately and familiarly to God as Miss Lassiter had out there on the porch. It was as if the deity was not only real to her but was a close friend. As if when she asked for guidance she was confidant she would receive it. As if she had *faith,* not logic.

After the first few words he'd opened his eyes and watched her, studying her face, trying to understand what drove her. Her eyes had remained closed for a few moments after the "Amen," then she'd opened them and met his gaze with a soft smile. A smile that had made him momentarily forget all the reasons why she hadn't been his first choice for a wife.

But his head had cleared quickly. And now he was back to making certain he had things well in hand. Assuming she did agree to marry him, because the alternative was not worth considering, he needed to adjust his plans accordingly. He was confident that, give the opportunity, he could make this work.

If she could learn to control some of her exuberance and spontaneity, to think before she acted and to conduct herself with more decorum, then they would get along quite well indeed.

But that was a whole lot of "ifs."

As Eli rose from the breakfast table the next morning, Miss Lassiter cleared her throat and met his gaze.

"Before you head for the bank," she said, "I'd like to have a word with you."

Thank goodness. She'd been a little late joining them in the dining room and he hadn't been able to read anything in her expression. In fact, he'd begun to think he'd have to be the one to initiate the conversation.

She cut a quick glance toward her brother. "In private."

Eli ignored the frown on Griff's face and kept his focus on Sadie. "Of course. If Mrs. Collins would allow us the use of the family parlor?"

At Cora Beth's nod he swept out his arm, indicating Miss Lassiter should precede him. This was it, he could tell from the determined set of her back that she'd reached a decision. What would he do if her answer was still no? For that matter, what would he do if her answer was yes?

They entered the parlor without another word. Eli pulled the door to, making sure it did not close entirely.

Miss Lassiter eyed the gap, but made no comment. "Before I give you my answer," she began, "there are a couple of things we need to discuss."

He leaned back, trying not to show signs of the relief flooding through him. Surely if she was going to say no she would have come right out with it. Given the circumstances, if what she wanted was assurances, he was prepared to give them to her. "So let's discuss."

"How do you feel about dogs?"

Not the turn he expected the discussion to take. But he would follow her lead. "I have no objections to the animals in general."

"I have a dog. His name is Skeeter and I've raised him from a pup. Were I to move, I would expect to take him with me." She gave him a challenging look. "You should understand, he's used to having the run of the house."

Was that all? While he wasn't particularly enamored with the idea of giving a dog the run of his new home, and he found pampered lapdogs irritating, it was a small concession to make to get her to the altar. Besides, he could set some boundaries once they were married. "Of course. In fact, I'm sure Penny would enjoy having a pet around."

She nodded, as if his acquiescence had been a forgone conclusion.

He felt a flicker of irritation at her presumptuousness, but let it go. "So, are you prepared to give me your answer now?" Time to get on with it.

"There's one other matter we need to discuss first."

He certainly hoped this next issue was as innocuous as the first. "I'm listening."

She took a deep breath, as if fortifying herself. "I'm Temperance Trulove."

Chapter Ten

Eli felt his jaw tighten as the tolerant smile on his face froze. Of *course* she was the author of that bit of nonsense. He should have realized it before. Not only was the timing right but it was exactly the sort of thing he would expect of her.

It was several heartbeats before he could trust himself to break the crackling silence. "I see. I suppose it was harmless enough as a way to pass the time. But as my wife you will have other responsibilities to keep you busy so of course you'll give that up. I mean, there will hardly be time—"

She held up a hand. "Make no mistake, I fully intend to continue. Not only did I make a commitment to Mr. Chalmers at the *Gazette,* but I find I really enjoy writing the stories. Mr. Chalmers already has the next two installments and I had planned five more to finish off Annabel's adventures."

"Miss Lassiter, I simply cannot allow a wife of mine to devote time to such a frivolous undertaking."

She stood. "Then you have your answer, sir. We have nothing more to discuss."

GET 2 BOOKS

IF YOU ENJOY A HISTORICAL ROMANCE STORY that reflects solid, traditional values, then you'll like *Love Inspired® Historical* novels. These are engaging tales filled with romance, adventure and faith set in various historical periods from biblical times to World War II.

We'd like to send you two *Love Inspired Historical* novels absolutely free. Accepting them puts you under no obligation to purchase any more books.

HOW TO GET YOUR
2 FREE BOOKS AND 2 FREE GIFTS

1. Return the reply card today, and we'll send you two *Love Inspired Historical* novels, absolutely free! We'll even pay the postage!

2. Accepting free books places you under no obligation to buy anything, ever. The two books have combined cover prices of $11.00 in the U.S. and $13.00 in Canada, but they're yours to keep, free!

3. We hope that after receiving your free books you'll want to remain a subscriber, but the choice is yours—to continue or cancel, any time at all!

EXTRA BONUS

You'll also get two free mystery gifts! (worth about $10)

FREE!

Return this card today to get
2 FREE BOOKS and 2 FREE GIFTS!

Love Inspired
HISTORICAL
INSPIRATIONAL HISTORICAL ROMANCE

YES! Please send me 2 FREE *Love Inspired*®
Historical novels, and 2 free mystery gifts as
well. I understand I am under no obligation
to purchase anything, as explained on the
back of this insert.

*About how many NEW paperback fiction books have
you purchased in the past 3 months?*

❏ 0-2
E9ET

❏ 3-6
E9E5

❏ 7 or more
E9FH

102/302 IDL

FIRST NAME

LAST NAME

ADDRESS

APT.#

CITY

STATE/PROV.

ZIP/POSTAL CODE

▶ DETACH AND MAIL CARD TODAY! ▶

(LIH-2F-11)

Irritation and frustration warred with his desire to gain her agreement to his marriage proposal. "Wait."

She raised her brow and he realized there'd been more than a touch of command in his voice.

He tried to moderate his tone. "Please, sit back down." Looked like it was his turn to make a hard-to-swallow compromise.

The "please" mollified Sadie somewhat. And she belatedly remembered the decision she'd made this morning, and more importantly, why she'd made it. But that didn't mean she was going to just let him stampede over her on this.

"I assure you I'm quite determined."

"Perhaps we can strike a compromise. My main concern is that you don't present an improper example for my sister. If I go along with this, I would need to have your word that you won't let Penny know you are the author of that—" he caught himself "that story."

Her chin tilted up at his continued autocratic pronouncements and she mentally counted to ten. *Heavenly Father, You're going to have to help me find patience if we're going to make this work.* "I won't lie to her if she asks." She finally replied. "But I will agree not to offer up the information on my own."

He didn't seem particularly pleased with her response, but after a moment, he nodded. "Agreed." Then he leaned back. His pose was relaxed but she sensed an underlying tension. "Does this mean you are now prepared to accept my proposal?"

Was she really ready to do this? There'd be no going back if she said yes. But hadn't she already reached that point?

She squared her shoulders, said a quick mental prayer and then met his gaze. "Yes, I suppose it does."

A quickly suppressed flicker of relief was his only reaction. She hadn't expected any deep emotional response to her acceptance of his proposal, but still...

"Good." He tugged on the points of his vest. "Now that we're in agreement on that point, there are a few additional details to be worked out. First, there's picking a date for the wedding. Since time is of the essence, I trust holding the ceremony on Saturday will give you enough time to do whatever planning is necessary."

This Saturday? "But that's only five days away." She clasped her hands together in front of her. "I mean, won't such haste seem almost an admission of guilt?"

He didn't seem to share her concern. "Actually, I think the sooner we put this whole situation behind us the better it will be all the way around."

How romantic.

"Besides," he continued "I assume your brother can't stay here indefinitely. And having his presence at the ceremony will serve two purposes. First, I assume you want to have family present for obvious personal reasons and second, it would add an additional air of normalcy to have his visible seal of approval."

"Yes, of course." He'd definitely been giving every aspect of this a lot of thought. Did the man ever act spontaneously?

He smiled approvingly. "The house will be ready by then, too. It'll be a smoother transition for all of us if you can join Penny and me when we move in and immediately step into the role of lady of the house."

She took a mental breath and nodded. "Of course. I guess I just hadn't expected things to move quite so fast."

Goodness, by the end of the week she would be Mrs. Eli Reynolds. Was she ready for that? She tucked a strand of hair behind her ear, feeling unaccountably nervous.

More importantly, was *he* really ready for that?

Eli was oddly touched by the hint of vulnerability in Sadie's expression. "I know this is all a bit disconcerting and will take some getting used to, but I'll be right here to help you get through it." He chose his next words carefully "And I won't rush you into anything you're not ready for." Did she understand his meaning? From the slight blush on her cheeks, it appeared she did.

"Now, I've already spoken to Reverend Ludlow," Eli continued, "and he's prepared to perform the ceremony whenever I give him the word."

Her eyebrow went up. "Taking my agreement for granted, were you?"

The touch of dry humor in her expression was a good sign. "Not at all, though I was definitely hoping. And I wanted to make certain everything was in order in case you did, um, agree." He'd almost said *come to your senses.*

"Then I suppose there's no reason to delay. Saturday it is."

And just like that, it was settled. Eli took a moment to absorb that he was truly engaged to the woman seated before him. There was a touch of unreality to the whole situation.

As they stepped out of the parlor, he wasn't at all surprised to find Griff Lassiter standing nearby. The man didn't make any effort to hide the fact that he didn't trust Eli where his sister was concerned.

"You can be the first to congratulate us, Griff." Sadie's

smile was perhaps a bit too bright. "Mr. Reynolds and I are engaged to be married."

But her brother didn't look as if he were eager to hand out congratulations. He shot a suspicious glance Eli's way, then turned to his sister. "Are you sure, Sadie girl?" His voice was surprisingly tender.

"Quite." She placed a hand on her brother's arm. "Don't worry. I've prayed long and hard and I've decided this is not only what I *need* to do, but it is what I *want* to do." She gave his arm a squeeze. "Truly."

Her words surprised Eli and pleased him at the same time. Did she mean it? Or was it just a way to appease her brother?

He waited while Griff studied Sadie, as if looking for some sign of duress or unhappiness.

Then Griff turned his stare back his way. "Make sure you do everything in your power to take care of her." Then, without a backward glance, he marched up the stairs to his room.

When Sadie finally turned back to him, her smile seemed a bit forced. "How do you suggest we spread the word?"

"Don't worry, that will happen quite naturally. For now, I thought perhaps it would be a good idea for me to give you a tour of the new house."

"Right now?"

He'd expected a little more enthusiasm. "If it's not too inconvenient. After all, it will soon be your home as well and you've never set foot inside. This will give you an opportunity to look things over and see if there's anything you want to change."

"You would let me make changes?"

The speculative way she asked the question gave him pause. Was she already planning something? But now was not the time to second-guess himself. "Within reason, of course. I want you to be comfortable and feel at home there."

"Don't you think you ought to let Penny know about our decision before we make any announcements?"

He should have been the one to think of that. He knew Penny liked Miss Lassiter, but how would she feel about having her as part of their household? "We'll tell her together. In fact, let's invite her to tour the house with us. She hasn't seen the latest changes."

"Doesn't she have school this morning?"

"We'll call a special holiday—it's not every day her brother gets engaged." And it would probably be best to have her with them while they were touring the house. He planned to bend over backwards to follow the very letter of propriety between now and the wedding.

He was pleased to see Penny's broad smile when they delivered news of their upcoming nuptials. Sadie, with the impulsiveness he was becoming resigned to, stooped down and scooped the girl up in a tight hug. Whatever her feelings about him, Sadie seemed to have no reservations about his sister.

He studied the picture they made with their bright smiles and two heads bent together. There was a feeling of rightness there, as if they were already on the road to becoming a proper family.

When they separated, he cleared his throat. "I'm going to show Miss Lassiter our new house this morning. Would you care to join us?"

Penny's eyes grew large. "But what about school?"

"I think it will be okay if you miss just one day. What do you say?"

Penny nodded quickly. "Let me just tell the others

to go ahead without me." And she raced off down the hall.

"Since she's telling the kids," Sadie said, "perhaps we should tell Cora Beth and Uncle Grover."

Cora Beth was predictably delighted and promised to help Sadie with all the planning and preparation that went into a wedding. Uncle Grover offered congratulations and announced his intent to make them a "special gift." Since the man was an entomologist, Eli had some concerns, but decided to not add that to his current list of worries.

Later, as the three of them made their way down the street, Eli set a leisurely pace. They hadn't gone far from the boardinghouse when he spied a familiar figure. Mrs. Van Halsen—perfect.

He tipped his hat. "Mrs. Van Halsen, beautiful day isn't it?"

She paused but her smile was merely tepid. "Why, yes it is. I hope your injury is not paining you overmuch."

"It's healing quite nicely, thank you. Besides, it would take more than a twisted ankle to bother me today."

That seemed to pique her interest. "Oh?"

"Yes. In fact, I want you to be among the first to know—Miss Lassiter has done me the honor of agreeing to be my wife."

The woman's demeanor thawed immediately. "How marvelous. Have you set a date yet?"

"We want to start our married life together in our new home. So we'll speak our vows this coming Saturday. Everyone in town is invited, of course."

"Does that mean you'll be married here instead of your hometown, Miss Lassiter?"

An unanticipated question. Eli started to step into the breach, but Sadie spoke up first.

"Cora Beth still needs my help, so yes, we decided to be married here." Her voice was conversational, her expression polite. "That's why my brother will be here through Sunday, so he can walk me down the aisle."

"It's a shame you can't wait for Josie and your other brother to return from their trip."

"Yes, it is." Sadie placed a hand on Penny's shoulder, directing the woman's gaze that direction. "But Eli, I mean Mr. Reynolds, and I thought settling into our new family roles as soon as possible would be best for everyone. I know a caring mother such as yourself will understand why."

Mrs. Van Halsen looked at Penny, then back at Sadie and nodded meaningfully. "Of course, you're right as rain on that point. A mother's role is very important. I see now that it was a very wise decision on your part."

She gave a smile that took them all in. "My felicitations on your happy news and you can count on me to be there to see you wed." With another nod, she continued on her way.

Eli watched as the woman entered the mercantile and hurried over to the cluster of women gathered near the counter. The news of their upcoming nuptials would be all over town within the hour.

He turned back to Sadie. "Well done."

She gave him a smile and a shrug. "All I did was tell the truth." Then she glanced toward the mercantile. "The news will spread naturally, did you say?"

He smiled, feeling just a tad smug. "These things have a way of taking care of themselves."

After two more such encounters, they finally reached their destination. Eli opened the gate to the front walk and waved Penny and Sadie on ahead of him. He was quite proud of the work that had been done, almost as if he'd done it with his own two hands. He had, after all, directed every step of the way.

He was pleased to see the approving smile on her face as she climbed up the wide front steps to the wraparound porch that fronted the soft yellow facade. This was probably a far cry from the ranch house she was brought up in.

He opened the tall double doors that served as the entrance and waved Sadie and Penny inside.

The new wallpaper had been hung just two days ago and added an elegant touch to the entryway.

Sadie touched the paper, tracing the design. "This is lovely."

Pleased by her response, Eli turned to his sister. "Why don't we show Miss Lassiter the dining room first?"

"You know, back at Hawk's Creek we didn't stand on ceremony much, especially in how we addressed each other. Since we're engaged now, I'd take it kindly if you'd please call me Sadie."

Her words took him by surprise. But her request was logical. "If you wish."

"And may I call you Eli?"

He should have offered sooner. "Yes, of course."

"What about me?" Penny asked.

"Why, you must call me Sadie, as well. After all, we're going to be sisters." She smiled. "I've always wanted a sister—it'll be nice to finally have my wish come true."

Eli saw a shadow flit across Penny's expression. And wondered if Miss Las—Sadie, caught it, as well.

Hoping to distract Penny, he quickly led them through a door to their left. "This is the dining room. All of the furnishings come from our previous home in New York."

She looked around without a word. Was she over-whelmed by it all? Not that he would blame her if she was. He hadn't seen any furnishings of this quality since he'd arrived.

Once they'd looked their fill, he led them across the hall to the parlor.

"The doors on this room and the dining room are extra wide and made to fold away. When they're opened it makes for a large area, perfect for entertaining large groups. In fact, if you're agreeable, I thought it would be a good idea to combine the wedding reception with an open house here after the ceremony."

That should make her happy. He hadn't met a woman yet who didn't like to throw a party.

Host a large party? She could do that. She'd played hostess at the ranch a number of times. But she'd always had Inez to help with the details. Sadie squared her shoulders. She'd just have to get used to getting along without Inez's help from now on. Scary thought.

Then she realized he was waiting for her answer. "It sounds like a fine idea. It'll put us on a good footing with our new neighbors."

He nodded his approval. "Exactly."

"A party." Penny gazed up at her brother. "Can I come, too?"

Sadie didn't wait for Eli's response. "Of course you can, princess. After all, this is your house and you should help show it off, too."

After they'd admired the parlor sufficiently, Eli led them down the hall to another room. But Sadie's mind was only partly on the little tour he was giving them. The thought of her upcoming nuptials kept turning over and over in her mind. She thought she'd made peace with the idea. But now that she'd given her word, she found herself second-guessing the decision. And goodness, what had he meant when he said he'd "give her some time?"

Heavenly Father, please help me find peace with this new role I'm going to be taking on.

He strode down the hall and opened another door. "This was originally a bedchamber, but I had it turned into a library."

Sadie pulled her thoughts back to the present and gave her future husband—that thought still rattled her—her attention. She stepped inside and gaped. Three of the four walls were completely lined with floor to ceiling bookshelves. And the shelves were stocked with hundreds of books, all neatly arranged and organized. "My goodness. I thought we had a large library at Hawk's Creek, but I've never seen so many books in one place in my whole life."

She moved close enough to read some of the titles. There were texts on subjects from botany to history, from medicine to law. There were bound atlases, biographies and collected sermons. Books of poetry and music. She saw titles by Shakespeare and Dickens and Hawthorne. And so many authors that she didn't recognize. "This is a treasure trove. Have you read all of these yourself?"

He shrugged. "Most of them, but not all. Some of these were acquired by my grandfather or by my father."

What about the females in the family—didn't they like books?

"You can feel free to read any of these any time you wish," he continued. "After all, they will be yours as well as mine once we're married."

So the man had no problem with literature as a rule. It was just her penning stories that he disapproved of.

The next room he led them to was his study. Another dark somber room full of heavy, solid furniture. "It suits you."

"Thank you." Then he gave her another glance, as if suspicious of her meaning. "And how do you like what you've seen so far?"

"Everything seems very solid and formal."

He seemed pleased by her response, as if formal was exactly the effect he'd wanted to achieve.

"Did you pick out all these things yourself?"

He moved toward the massive desk that dominated the room. "Most of these pieces were taken from either my former town house or my father's country estate. Some of them are relatively new and some have a rich history with my family. This desk, for instance," he said as he ran his hand lightly across the intricately carved rosewood piece, "was imported by my great-grandfather from England. The dining room table was commissioned by my father as a gift to my mother on the first anniversary of their wedding. That tapestry that hangs in the library was begun by my maternal grandmother and finished by my mother shortly before she died."

That did put the furnishings in a different light. She still believed, though, that the home would benefit from the addition of some whimsical touches to lighten the atmosphere. But she kept that opinion to herself.

Eli spread his hands. "Of course, if there are any personal pieces of your own that you wish to add, we'll most certainly find a place for them."

She mentally reviewed several of the items from Hawk's Creek she was most attached to and just as quickly rejected them. "Most of the furnishings at the ranch *belong* at the ranch." She paused a moment, thinking about what he'd just said, about the furnishings representing bits of his family history and tradition. Those things *were* important. "Then again, there *are* one or two pieces I might consider asking Griff to send back when he returns home." She mentally winced, wondering if he'd caught her slip. Hard *not* to think of Hawk's Creek as home.

"As I said earlier, since this will be your *new* home I want you to feel free to add whatever touches you like— to put your stamp on our home, as well."

So he *had* heard her slip. At least he didn't seem particularly put out by it. And his referring to this as "our home" warmed her heart all over again.

Before he could quiz her, she moved down the hall to the next room. This one was slightly smaller and the walls lighter in color.

He stepped up behind her. "This sitting room can be reserved for your personal use."

She nodded as she looked around. "I'd like to furnish it myself, if you don't mind."

"Not at all. Feel free to equip it as you like."

Ten minutes later they had reached the back part of the house. "The kitchen is through here," Eli said. "I believe you're already aware that I plan to hire a cook and housekeeper, so you don't have to worry yourself with having to spend much time in here."

Was that a comment on her cooking skills? "Back at Hawk's Creek the kitchen was one of the brightest spots in the house."

"But this isn't Hawk's Creek." He seemed to realize how abrupt that had sounded and moderated his tone. "What I mean is, there will be other, more appropriate, places here for us to gather as a family."

"Of course."

"Naturally, as the soon-to-be lady of the house I'll

leave it to you to hire the woman who best meets your own requirements for a cook and housekeeper. I've already interviewed the three ladies Mrs. Collins recommended, but if you want to broaden the search, that's your prerogative. However, given that we'll be moving in on Saturday, I suggest you hire someone as soon as possible. It would probably also be a good idea to hire a couple of other women to help with the preparations for the wedding reception."

Goodness, so many responsibilities, and she wasn't even married to him yet. What would life be like after the wedding? Her cheeks warmed and her mind quickly shied away from that thought. "I trust Cora Beth so there's no need to broaden the search. I'll have a decision by tomorrow."

That won her a look of approval.

He waved a hand. "In the meantime, if there's anything not to your liking in here, let me know and I'll take care of it."

The kitchen was roomier than Cora Beth's and nearly as large as the one at the ranch. The stove looked brand-spanking-new and the worktable situated in the center of the room had a rack hanging above it that held a number of implements Sadie was completely unfamiliar with. She walked to one of the cabinets and opened it, noting it was well stocked.

"All of the dishes, utensils, pots and such were shipped from the kitchen in Almega. If there is something else you need, though, just let me know."

He'd been thorough, she'd give him that. Not that she was likely to know if there was anything lacking. Other than the obvious, she had no idea what an experienced cook would expect to have on hand.

She felt a tug on her skirts and looked down to

see Penny staring up at her expectantly. "Can we cook together in here sometimes like we do at the boardinghouse?"

Before she could answer, Eli stepped forward. "I'm sure Sadie will be happy to teach you all that a lady of the house should know. But you wouldn't want to get in the way of our new cook, would you?"

Penny slowly shook her head.

Sadie gave the girl's shoulder a light squeeze. "But don't you worry. You and I are going to find lots of other things to do together." She snapped a finger. "Oh, and did I mention that my dog Skeeter is going to come live with us as well?"

Penny's expression brightened immediately. "Really?"

"Uh-huh. You're going to love Skeeter." She tweaked one of the girls braids. "And I know he's going to take to you like a new sprout takes to sunshine."

Penny giggled.

Still smiling, Sadie glanced up at Eli and was caught off guard by the expression on his face. It was almost… wistful. But it was there and gone so quickly she decided she had been mistaken.

"If we're done in here," he said as he turned back toward the hallway, "why don't I show you around upstairs?"

She glanced at his walking stick. "But—"

He waved off her concern. "I won't be running any races in the next day or two, but I'm definitely up to climbing a set of stairs."

Sadie almost smiled at that—she couldn't imagine the dignified Eli Reynolds running a race under *any* circumstances.

As they climbed the stairs, Penny skipped ahead to

the room at the far end of the landing. "This one is mine," she called out. "Eli let me pick it myself." She opened the door and then waited for the grown-ups to join her.

Sadie cut him an approving smile for giving his sister that much control, then joined Penny and looked around. "I must say, you made a very fine choice."

Penny grabbed Sadie's hand and tugged her to the window. "You can see both the big oak tree and the street in front of the house from here."

"That *is* a nice feature. We'll have to frame this window with some really special curtains. Do you have a favorite color?"

Penny nodded. "Yellow."

"Then yellow it is," Sadie said. "Would you like to go with me to the mercantile tomorrow to pick out the fabric?"

Penny nodded enthusiastically, obviously pleased to be included in the decision making. Then she cocked her head to one side. "So which room is going to be yours?"

The child's innocently voiced question caught Sadie by surprise and raised questions she herself had avoided dwelling on. Eli had mentioned giving her time to adjust, but what exactly did he mean? And how much time?

Surely as husband and wife they would share a room. Or would they?

At what point did Mr. Reynolds expect them to live together as man and wife? And more importantly, what did *she* want?

Sadie studiously avoided looking directly at her soon-to-be husband as the heat rose in her cheeks.

To her relief, Eli's gaze remained on his sister. Almost as if he was avoiding looking at her, as well. "Why don't we let Miss Lassiter look at all of the rooms before she makes her pick?"

So, he *didn't* intend for them to share a room. Surprisingly, her relief was tinged with just the slightest touch of disappointment.

Penny took her hand again. "Come on, I'll show them to you."

"Besides Penny's room, there are four other bedrooms," Eli said as they moved into the hall. "The master suite, which is there across the landing, is the roomiest. You are, of course, welcome to claim that one—I can be quite comfortable in one of the others. If that's not to your liking, however, there is this one next to Penny's and two at the head of the stairs. They are basically the same with a few differences in view and wallpaper."

Sadie dutifully looked into each of the rooms, though she had to force herself to concentrate on what was in front of her when she could feel Eli's presence so close behind her.

The master bedchamber, as he'd said, was the roomiest of the bunch. It was furnished with the heavy pieces that he seemed to favor, but that she found much too oppressive.

She finally settled on one of the two rooms at the head of the stairs. It faced east, the same as her room at the ranch, and was papered with a cheery floral and striped pattern in pastel shades of green and rose. "This will do nicely."

"Are you certain you wouldn't rather have the larger master suite?"

Did he think she was just being polite? "No, this is definitely the one I want."

"All right then. Shall I have someone bring over your things from the boardinghouse?"

Since she'd only planned for her trip to Knotty Pine to last a few weeks, the only things she'd brought with her from Hawk's Creek were clothes and a few personal items. She supposed she'd have to get Griff to pack up and ship the rest of her belongings once he returned home.

Home—she had to remember that *this* place was home now. She hadn't realized when she left Hawk's Creek ten days ago that she wouldn't be returning to it, except as a visitor, ever again.

Sadie felt a stinging behind her eyes. Then she lifted her chin. No! She'd already made her decision, had felt this was the path God wanted her to follow, and she would *not* allow herself to grow maudlin over it. This would work out, all she needed was a little bit of courage. And faith.

She moved to the window to see what kind of view she would have and her spirits immediately rose. "You have a stable."

"A small one, yes. It will house up to three horses and a buggy. I suppose you have a mount at Hawk's Creek."

"Yes, Calliope. She's a sweet little mare I raised from a foal."

"Then by all means you should send for her."

Surely, once she had Skeeter and Calliope here with her, this would begin to feel much more like home.

Eli followed Penny and Sadie down the stairs, calling himself all kinds of a fool for not discussing sleeping arrangements beforehand. He and his soon-to-be bride needed to have a discussion, indelicate as it might be, before their wedding day.

As they strolled back to the boardinghouse, the two

adults let Penny filled the silence with her excited chatter, mostly questions for Sadie about how they would decorate her room.

Eli listened to the easy way Penny chatted with Sadie, saw the frequent smiles on her lips and lightness in her tone, and wondered how Sadie managed to draw her out. Why hadn't he already known his sister's favorite color or why she had picked that particular room for her own? Why hadn't he even thought to ask?

When they finally reached the front porch of the boardinghouse, Eli turned to his sister. "Why don't you go on inside and see how Mrs. Collins is feeling this morning? I need to have a few words with Mis—with Sadie in private."

"Okay Eli."

He turned to Sadie. "Would you stroll with me?"

"Of course."

He led them away from the busier part of town, taking a few minutes to gather his thoughts. He wasn't certain how she would react to the subject matter he needed to broach. "It occurs to me that we should discuss our expectations for, well, for how we will conduct the more personal aspect of our marriage." Yes, that was a sensible way to approach the topic.

He raked a hand through his hair, keeping his gaze focused straight ahead. "I mean, naturally, as husband and wife, there is a certain, um, intimacy that is normally expected."

Why didn't she say anything? Surely she understood—

He suddenly remembered she'd said her mother had passed away when she was nine—Penny's age—and that she'd been raised by her father and brothers. It was possible that there'd been no one to take on the duty of preparing her for her wedding night. The thought of taking on that duty himself made a cold sweat break out on his forehead. Perhaps he was mistaken.

"Miss Lassiter, that is, Sadie, how much, I mean, what do you know of—" he cut a glance her way.

Her expression had a gently puzzled look. "How much do I what?"

He cleared his throat and shifted his gaze forward again. She was more of an innocent than he'd expected. But if this had to be done, then best to get it over with quickly. "How much do you know about what goes on between a man and a woman once they are married?"

She bent slightly to pick a bit of lint from her skirt. "Since I've never been married myself I naturally have no firsthand knowledge."

Firsthand knowledge—good grief he should hope not! "That is how it should be. I was speaking of a more intellectual knowledge, perhaps relayed to you by a married woman of your acquaintance."

She shook her head sadly. "There are very few married women on the ranch and none that I've had that sort of conversation with."

Eli felt his collar tighten. Perhaps this was a conversation best left to Mrs. Collins. "I see. Then perhaps you can inquire of Mrs. Collins just what—"

Her laugh cut him off. "Oh Eli, I'm sorry. I know I shouldn't tease you but I couldn't help myself. I grew up on a ranch, remember? I have a pretty good idea of what you mean by *intimacies*."

His relief was tempered by a touch of annoyance. This was not a subject to make light of. At least she'd had the grace to blush on that last part. "Very well. Then, to get back to my earlier point, I'm aware that you and I are not well acquainted and that it's only natural for you to want a period of time to adjust to the idea of our being married."

"Very considerate of you."

There was a certain dryness to her tone that made him uneasy. "Of course, the current arrangement won't last forever. Eventually, that is to say, well…" Aware that he'd moved into indelicate territory, Eli wrestled himself back under control. "I want to have children of my own one day," he said matter-of-factly.

"I see." She finally smiled. "Then it's fortunate you and I are in agreement on that point."

Eli breathed a mental sigh of relief. She was not going to be coy or unduly missish over this. He found himself hoping she would not take too long to "adjust."

Sadie climbed the stairs to her room, wanting a few moments to herself before checking to see if Cora Beth needed her for anything. Fortunately Griff was nowhere to be seen. She didn't think she could deal with him right now.

She wasn't certain how to react to that unorthodox conversation they'd just shared. It had been fun, though, watching the always-in-control Mr. Reynolds squirm for a change.

Was he truly being considerate of her feelings, or just putting off what he saw as a duty to be dispatched at some point? So how did they decide the time was right? And who made that decision? Was she supposed to give him some signal? Her face grew red-hot at the thought.

Dear Lord, please see me through this.

A knock at the door provided a welcome interruption to her jumbled thoughts. "Come in."

Cora Beth opened the door and hesitated on the threshold.

Sadie popped up from her perch on the edge of her bed. "Oh, I'm so sorry. I should be downstairs helping with the cooking. I—"

Cora Beth waved her back down. "You've had a very eventful day—the chores can wait a bit." She crossed the room as she spoke and pulled the chair away from the vanity table. Turning it to face Sadie, she sat and folded her hands in her lap. "I know you had reservations about accepting Mr. Reynolds's proposal. Are you at peace with your decision now?"

Was she? "I'd be lying if I said I haven't had second thoughts. But I've been praying about it and I've come to believe this is the course I'm meant to take." She tucked an unruly strand back behind her ear. "Heaven help us both."

Cora Beth's lips twitched. "You are to be commended on your honesty at least." Then she turned serious again. "I've been praying over this, as well. Praying that God will grant you both the discernment to go forward with open minds and open hearts."

Sadie nodded. "Thank you." Then she added, "as for open hearts, I don't think the man has a romantic bone in his body."

"I think in time you'll come to think differently." Cora Beth took on a wise-woman aura. "Most men guard their more tender feelings from the world—some more so than others. But I've seen the way Mr. Reynolds looks at you."

That piqued Sadie's interest. What did she mean—the way he looked at her? Was there something—

But Cora Beth didn't give her an opening to ask. "Do you have any questions? About married life, I mean."

Had Eli asked Cora Beth to talk to her? Or did everyone think she was so uninformed? Then she straightened. "As a matter of fact, I do." She leaned forward. "How do I make sure I'm a good wife?"

"Well, there are certain, um, behaviors, between a man and a woman, that may seem a bit awkward at first glance, but that are really quite—"

Sadie stopped her before she could go any further. "That's not what I meant. I know all about *that*." At Cora Beth's shocked expression, she quickly added. "I mean, I've lived on a ranch my whole life. I've seen cows and horses and other animals mate so I understand the basics." Though she preferred not to think about doing *that* with Eli.

Cora Beth smiled. "Oh my goodness. No wonder you have that rather-not-know expression on your face. It's not quite the same between a man and a woman. Especially when they care for each other."

Sadie was caught off guard by her words. "It's not?"

Cora Beth shook her head, then shifted as if searching for the right words. "Farm animals act instinctually and pretty much indiscriminately. For people, it's different. While it may take a bit of getting used to, it's a beautiful, loving act, meant to draw two people who care for each other even closer together and prepare them to create and nourish the family God meant for them to have."

The image Cora Beth's words conjured up sparked Sadie's imagination. It sounded so…so wonderful. Would she and Eli ever…

She shook off that thought. Better not to get sidetracked thinking like *that*. "What I meant was, how do *I* make a good wife in other aspects of our life. I mean, we both know I'm no good at cooking and sewing and all those domestic tasks that normally fall to a wife. How do I learn?"

Cora Beth nodded. "I'll let you in on a little secret my momma taught me. A wife's true role in the home is to be its heart. Love and selflessness and a focus on pleasing God make for a happy home, and it'll be your job to make sure your home has that. While many women display those qualities through the way they perform household chores, that isn't the only way, or even necessarily the best way to add heart to a home."

Did Cora Beth truly believe that? Or was she just trying make her feel better. "Still, it would be a good idea for me to learn some of the basics."

"If you like. But remember, a cook or housekeeper can take care of the basic chores. The true role of a wife is to be all those things I said before and to give her husband a haven where he can feel comfortable just being himself."

She reached forward and took both of Sadie's hands. "You, my dear, are a special person and you have so much heart. Just be yourself. You can bring joy and warmth and love to that house, all the important things that make a house a home."

Sadie wished she could be as sure of that as Cora Beth seemed to be. But, with God's help, she'd sure give it her all.

Strolling through town on her own the next afternoon was an interesting experience for Sadie. Several folks stopped to offer congratulations on her upcoming nuptials. Most had sounded genuinely happy for her, some merely intrigued.

After interviewing the three women who were in the running for the job of cook, she happily settled on Nettie

Dauber. The widow, who was old enough to be Sadie's mother, was plainspoken, seemed very capable and was willing to take direction or take control—whichever was required.

Feeling good about the first decision she'd made for her new life, Sadie couldn't wait until she could tell Eli about it.

When she stepped inside the boardinghouse, Sadie saw Griff waiting for her, a big grin on his face. And he wasn't alone.

"Inez!" She flew across the distance separating them. "You came."

Inez returned her hug. "Of course I came. You don't think I'd let you get married without me here to witness it, do you, Sadie girl?"

"But Red and the others—"

"Can eat Grady's cooking for a week." Inez gave her a cheeky grin. "It'll make them appreciate me all the more when I get back."

Sadie laughed. "As if they don't already appreciate you."

"Oh, our baby girl's going to be a bride." Inez put her calloused hands on Sadie's face. "Ry is going to be so sorry he couldn't be here."

Sadie bit her lip. "There are reasons we can't—"

"I know." Inez smiled softly and gave her cheeks a couple of quick pats before dropping her hands. "Now, introduce me to this young man of yours."

"Eli is still at work. You can meet him when the bank closes."

Inez nodded. "Griff told me he's a banker. Always figured you for a rancher's wife, but you never were one to take the expected path."

What did she mean by that?

Inez stepped back. "Now, tell me what kind of reception you're wanting and how many folks will be there."

Sadie shook her head. "Oh no you don't. You're my guest. I want you at the church, witnessing my wedding, not working in the kitchen."

"Wild horses couldn't keep me away from that church when the time comes. But that doesn't mean I can't get things organized for your celebration, too. You just leave everything to me, Sadie girl."

Sadie hooked her arm through Inez's. "Well come along into the kitchen. I promised Cora Beth she could help with the planning, as well. It looks like you ladies are going to get me organized in spite of myself."

Griff shook his head. "Sounds like this is no place for a man right now. Think I'll take a ride out to Ry's place and see how things are going over there."

Griff's words reminded Sadie of her own fateful trip down that road just a few short days ago. It also brought to mind a bit of unfinished business. "If you don't mind, I'd like you to do a favor for me while you're there."

If things worked out the way she hoped, her wedding present to Eli would be truly memorable. Perhaps it would, in some small way, make up for his having had to settle for something less than that proper wife he'd hoped to find.

Chapter Eleven

Sadie set her pen down and gently blew on the paper. She'd thought, what with all the commotion happening in her life, she might have had trouble continuing her chronicle of Annabel Adams's adventures. Surprisingly, that hadn't been the case. In fact, for the last hour the words had practically flowed out of her and she'd barely looked up from her scribbling. It had been a relief to escape her world for the comparatively safe confines of Annabel's. When she finally stopped, she'd left poor Annabel in yet another tight situation and would need to think on how to get her out of it before she continued.

She was glad Eli had finally backed down on wanting her to give it up, though she was surprised he hadn't put up more of a fight. Had he seen how important it was to her? Or had he merely been trying to finally get her to the altar?

Whatever the case, she wasn't sure she could have given it up. What had started out as just a lark to pass the time while she was here in Knotty Pine had fast become a creative outlet that she couldn't imagine living without again. The story was the first thing that was wholly hers. And people actually liked it. Not merely tolerated it or viewed it as a nice little pastime for her to amuse herself with, but genuinely liked it and eagerly looked forward to seeing more. The speculation around who was behind the stories was tinged with an admiration she found guiltily exhilarating.

Sadie stood and drew her elbows back, trying to get the kinks out, then crossed to the window. It still stung a bit that Eli looked down on her work the way he did.

Not that she required his approval.

The man was still a puzzle to her—so formal and analytical in his approach to life in general. Yet there was that hint of suppressed emotion in him, as if one ever got past his defenses, one would find a deeply passionate individual.

After Inez met Eli and Penny yesterday evening, she'd given it as her opinion that Sadie had made a fine match. Sadie hadn't realized until then how concerned she'd been that Inez, the woman who'd been like a mother to her, would have reservations.

Sadie glanced at the small watch pinned to her bodice. "Oh my goodness!" Dinner preparations should have been started thirty minutes ago. She turned and rushed to the door. Hopefully she could make up some time and not be late getting the meal on the table.

When she stepped into the kitchen, however, she found Cora Beth and Inez there ahead of her. "I'm so sorry. I lost track of time."

Inez waved her away. "No worries. We have it all well in hand."

"But I'm supposed to be—"

"It's okay," Cora Beth motioned for her to take a chair. "You should be thinking about your wedding, not doing my chores."

"That's right." Inez tapped the spoon against the pot

and then set it down. "I was just telling Cora Beth here that I'm willing to stay on a few days after the wedding and help her around here since you'll have your own place to tend to. Don't see any reason why I can't start now."

Sadie closed her eyes for a moment. *Father, I know they mean well. So why do I feel like such a failure right now?*

Cora Beth motioned for Sadie to take a seat at the table beside her. "So tell me, have you thought about what dress you'll be wearing for your wedding?"

Not until just now. She feigned indifference. "It won't be a hard choice to make. Since I wasn't planning on a wedding when I left home, I only have two dresses with me that would be suitable."

"Oh my goodness, where's my head?" Inez set the cook spoon down. "I brought your mother's wedding gown with me. Thought you might want to wear it on your special day."

Sadie was taken aback. "Oh Inez, that was so thought-ful of you. But there's no way that dress would fit me." *And the elegant style definitely doesn't suit me.*

Her mother had been a graceful, delicately-built wom-an—several inches taller and much trimmer than Sadie. And that dress—ah that beautiful, frothy dress. Covered with yards and yards of lace and enough beadwork to make it sparkle when it moved, the dress had filled her with awe when she was a little girl. And she'd dreamed of one day wearing it herself.

Right up until the day she'd realized that she was not the striking, elegant person her mother was, and on her the dress would look laughably inappropriate.

But Inez was not to be denied. "You're just a mite shorter than your mother but we can take care of that with a new hem. And if we need to let out a seam or two, well, that's easy enough to do, as well."

Oh there would definitely be need. Sadie's mind was working furiously trying to come up with some convincing reason to give Inez for not wearing that dress.

"Don't you worry about a thing," Inez said. "It'll be my wedding present to you."

Sadie saw the pleased, expectant expression on the woman's face and knew she was defeated. She stepped up and gave her a big hug. "Thank you so much. It's a lovely gift."

As they were pushing away from the table that evening, Griff took Sadie aside. "I'd like to have a word with you."

"About what?"

"It has to do with finances."

"Then Eli should be included."

"I don't think—"

"Nonsense. He's going to be my husband and I don't intend for us to have any secrets from each other." Before he could protest further, Sadie took matters into her own hands. She crossed the room and touched Eli's sleeve. "Griff has something he wishes to speak to us about."

"Oh." Eli glanced across the room toward her brother. A brow went up as he no doubt made note of the glower, but he nodded. "Of course. I'm at your disposal."

Once they were seated in the parlor, Griff got straight to business. To his credit he made an effort to make Eli a part of the conversation. "This concerns Sadie's interest in Hawk's Creek. I'm prepared to make her the same offer I made Ry when he got married and put down roots here." He turned back to Sadie. "I can buy your portion of the ranch, or you can continue as a long-distance partner and I'll send you payments every quarter for whatever your share of the profits might be."

Sadie, who was as aware of the financial state of the ranch as Griff was, knew it would be stretching matters pretty thin for him to buy her out. He'd more than likely have to take out a loan and she didn't want to put him in that position. Besides, she wasn't ready to give up her share of Hawk's Creek just yet.

But it wasn't just her opinion that mattered. She glanced Eli's way. Finance was his business, after all. Did he have a preference? "What do you think?"

He met her gaze with a steady one of his own. "Your brother is right. This is your decision. And whatever you decide to do, I'll support you."

He was being gentlemanly again, not a bad quality in a husband. "But I'd like to hear your thoughts on the matter."

"Very well." Eli leaned forward. "Thinking about this objectively, if you were a bank customer asking for advice, I'd want to know much more about the operation, perhaps even have a look at it myself."

But I'm not a bank customer, she wanted to say, I'm your soon-to-be-wife.

Griff, however, seemed to see nothing wrong with Eli's statement. "I can tell Jackson, the manager over at the bank I do business with, to answer any questions you might have on the finances. And you're welcome to have a look at the place any time you've a mind to."

"That's a wonderful idea," Sadie said.

"What?" Eli looked puzzled.

"Going to Hawk's Creek for a visit after we're married."

"I don't know. I won't be able to go right away. There are some things at the bank—"

Griff stood. "No problem. This is a big decision and I really didn't expect an answer today. Hawk's Creek isn't going anywhere and my offer stands indefinitely. Discuss it together, plan a trip out there if you like. Pray about it. And in the meantime Sadie retains partial ownership, same as before."

Griff was wrong—nothing was the same as before. She might remain partial owner of Hawk's Creek, but it would no longer be her home. How strange to think about living in town permanently, about living among folks she barely knew.

If nothing else, experiencing this unsettling, set-adrift-in-unknown-waters feeling for herself made her even more sympathetic toward Penny. Whether Eli knew it or not, she was going to be a very good big sister for Penny.

Eli watched Griff leave the room. It was edifying to know that his independent-minded fiancée not only welcomed but actually sought his opinion, on this matter at least. Was it because she was finally beginning to recognize the value in his analytical approach to decision making? Or because it was how he made his profession? Or rather, was it because, now that they were engaged, she was ready to show him just a bit of deference? He could live with any of those answers.

But whatever the case, he was determined not to disappoint her. "Your brother seems a fair man."

"As fair and honest as they come. He doesn't know any other way to be."

What it would be like to have her speak of him with such admiration and certainty? He shook off that nonsensical thought. "I appreciate your asking for my input in this."

"We're going to be married. It's only right we share in making these decisions. And that we pray over them together."

This tendency she had to want to pray over every decision left him uncomfortable. Isn't that what God gave man a brain for—to reason things out and make decisions? But maybe it was just her way of organizing her thoughts.

He spread his hands. "Of course. But getting back to the current question, just to make sure I understand the situation, when faced with the same choice, your brother Ry sold his interest in the ranch when he married Mrs. Collins's sister, is that correct."

"Yes, but you can't really go by that. Ry is the owner of his own ranch now. And he took a piece of Hawk's Creek with him, in the form of his prize stallion and a string of mares."

There was something she wasn't saying but he was having trouble figuring out just what was going on in that unpredictable mind of hers. "So, if we sold your interest to Griff, is there some element of Hawk's Creek you'd want to take with you?"

She chewed her lip for a moment. "I hadn't really thought of it that way before, but no, I don't think so."

Still he could sense something was bothering her. Then he remembered how sentimental she was.

On impulse, he leaned forward and placed a hand over hers. Doing his best to ignore the sudden and very uncharacteristic urge to lift that hand to his lips, he stared straight into her eyes. "Sadie, I realize this is your home we're talking about. You must have strong feelings about which way you want this to go. Tell me."

Her hand, so small and fragile-seeming under his own, continued to stir protective instincts in him.

Her gaze dropped to his hand and she stared, as if mesmerized. Finally she looked up again, but there was an endearing hint of distraction now. She nodded. "Hawk's Creek. Yes." Her focus sharpened. "Of course I do. Hawk's Creek is the only home I've ever known. The thought of selling off my piece of it, even if it's to Griff, seems as unthinkable as selling off a piece of my arm." She took a deep breath. "I'm not saying what Ry did was wrong, but it was different for him. He'd already found other things to tug him away, other places to call home."

Would Sadie find those other things, other places that she could comfortably set down new roots? Would what he could offer her be enough?

But she was right. He supposed, for an emotional woman such as her, such attachments were important. If she wanted to hold on to a piece of her childhood home, who was he to say nay? "If it means so much to you, then there's no need for me to perform any sort of analysis. Of course you should maintain your interest in Hawk's Creek."

The smile she gave him made his small gesture worthwhile. Then she straightened. "I hope this doesn't mean you don't want to visit Hawk's Creek now. I'd really enjoy showing you around the place."

"Of course. But as I told your brother, not right away. I've only just taken over the reins at the bank and I wouldn't feel right being gone for an extended period right now."

Her smile dimmed for only a heartbeat and then she rallied. "I understand. After all, school won't let out for a few more weeks and we'd want to take Penny with us."

She knew good and well that wasn't his reason. Was

she lying just trying to save face? That uncharitable thought was quickly followed by a sharp jab of guilt. After all, even if it had been for her own good, he'd all but forced this wedding on her. And he wasn't allowing any time for a honeymoon trip. Perhaps, once they were settled in and school was out, he'd suggest she and Penny take a trip to Hawk's Creek without him. That should cheer her up. After all, given their relationship, she wasn't likely to really care that much if he was along or not.

And, strangely, that thought bothered him much more than he'd expected it to.

The days leading up to the wedding passed more quickly than Sadie would have thought possible. It seemed every time she turned around she was either being asked to make a decision or being asked to approve a decision someone else had already made.

The highlight, for her, was looking over the trio of horses Griff brought over from Ry's ranch. She had no trouble at all picking out the one she wanted, a lively brown mare with strong lines and a sassy spark in her eyes.

At least she was keeping too busy to worry over what her new life would be like. Except when she lay awake at night, staring up at the ceiling. Was Eli feeling the same sense of unreality, of rushing headlong into something before either of them was ready?

She awoke Saturday morning to an absolutely perfect day for a wedding. Gone were the storms of the previous week. Instead, the sky was bright and sunny with a few fluffy clouds scattered across the blue expanse, a slight breeze wafted in to keep the heat from being overbearing, flowers bloomed everywhere—it was everything a bride could ask for.

By one o'clock, Sadie stood at the back of the church, wearing her mother's wedding gown, feeling like a little girl playing dress up. At least she'd managed to convince Inez to simplify the dress a bit, explaining that the church in Knotty Pine was not a magnificent cathedral and the people who would be in attendance were not Philadelphia's social elite. Still, she felt out of place, like a magpie pretending to be a hawk.

She had thought that by now it would all have felt right. But this lacey confection was not right for her, this ceremony was not being held at her home church as she'd always imagined it would be, and most calamitous of all, the groom waiting for her at the altar did not love her.

Heavenly Father, I know that not every path You lead us down is a comfortable one, and I know Your hand is on us always. But right now I can't see the rightness of this, so I need Your blessed assurance more than ever.

She took a deep breath and willed herself to have only positive thoughts. *I'm going to make Eli the best wife I possibly can. I'm going to make certain Penny has a house filled with as much joy and love as I can manage. And, dear Lord, I'm going to make sure You are a part of this family, too. As Cora Beth said, I'm going to strive to be the heart of our home. These two people need me, whether they know it or not.*

Her stomach settled and her smile relaxed. It was time.

Sadie turned to her brother, who stood waiting for her to give the signal that she was ready.

Griff tugged at his shirt collar. He looked mighty fine in his Sunday suit, but the concern on his face was entirely unsuitable for a wedding. "Are you sure this is what you want?" he asked. "It's still not too late to back out."

She knew without a doubt that if she asked him to, Griff would escort her out of the church and purchase a ticket on the next train headed north. He'd always looked out for her, had always been there when she needed him. With Ry spending so much time in Philadelphia, it had been just her and Griff for the most part after her father died.

And for the first time it struck her that this marriage signaled a change for him, too. He would be alone now. The last Lassiter left standing at Hawk's Creek. Would he miss her company? She put a hand on his arm and looked deep into his eyes. Seeing the concern and love there, she felt a deep, bittersweet ache. "Eli and Penny *need* me, Griff." Those words went a long way toward settling her own nerves.

He stared at her a moment longer, as if trying to peer into her heart, and finally nodded, as if satisfied with what he saw there. "I want you to know you always have a place at Hawk's Creek. You can come back any time, for however long you need to, no questions asked."

She reached up and smoothed his collar. "I know, and that's a lovely, comforting thought. But this *will* work out. I'm sure of it."

She moved her hand back to his arm. "Now, walk me down that aisle and make all the female hearts go pitter-patter at the sight of you."

With a grin, Griff tapped her nose and then placed a hand over hers where it rested on his arm, straightened and faced forward. Sadie did likewise.

As they took the long walk down the aisle, Sadie studied Eli's face. Was he feeling any qualms or doubts, was he disappointed that he'd wound up with her instead of the "perfect wife" he'd hoped for?

But she saw no sign of regret or resignation on his face. In fact, if she didn't know better, she'd almost believe it was satisfaction and encouragement. He'd quit using the walking stick on Thursday, though she noticed he still favored his left leg ever so slightly when he walked.

Just before Griff placed her hand in Eli's, her brother bent down and kissed her forehead. Then he stepped back and joined Uncle Grover, Inez and the children in the front pew.

A moment later she was standing before the preacher, her soon-to-be husband at her side.

Cora Beth stood at her left and Sheriff Hammond stood beside Eli. But the only person her senses could take in was Eli. Standing tall and straight, his broad shoulders set off by his dark suit, the comforting feel of her hand in his, the subtle clean scent of bay rum and leather and masculine spices that seemed to be uniquely his—this man was to be her husband, hers to learn to love and cherish the rest of her days. The thought almost overwhelmed her.

When it came time for them to speak their vows, Eli held both of her hands in his, his gaze holding hers just as securely. She felt strength and promise and approval in there.

And her heart seemed to swell until it filled her chest. For the first time she felt genuine hope that perhaps they could be happy together—not merely accepting or okay, but genuinely happy.

When he placed the ring on her finger, Sadie stared at the sparkling bauble. It was a lovely thing—a diamond and two sapphires mounted on a gold band.

"You may now kiss the bride."

Reverend Ludlow's words caught Sadie off guard. Her gaze flew to Eli's, trying to gauge his reaction. This could get very awkward.

She saw a heartbeat of hesitation flash in his expression. Then he seemed to collect himself and with a reassuring smile he leaned down, apparently intent on following the preacher's suggestion.

Sadie had a split second to anticipate, and then their lips touched. Her eyes closed and she opened herself up to the sensation. There was an unexpected gentleness and warmth there, and a touch of something else, something that took her by surprise and left her slightly breathless. But before she could quite figure out what that something was, or get her fill of it, he pulled away.

Her eyes remained closed for a few seconds longer and she could still feel the tingle of his lips on hers. Then she opened her eyes and was pleased to see the same bemused surprise on his face, as well. Then he smiled and there was a touch of satisfaction and a totally masculine cockiness to it.

A moment later he seemed to pull himself together and turned to face the congregation with his usual businesslike demeanor. But as he escorted her down the aisle, she was pleased to note how securely he kept her arm tucked in his.

It was done. Eli felt a sense of elation. Sadie was his wife now and there was no going back. Not that he wanted to go back.

When she'd stepped into the church on her brother's arm, he'd been astounded. Her wedding dress had transformed her from a hoyden to a lady. She'd sought out his gaze and latched onto it as if wanting to find shelter from a storm. And he'd found himself more than ready to offer her that protection.

And that kiss they'd sealed their vows with. She'd responded with such sweetness, such trust, it had taken him completely by surprise. His hand involuntarily tightened its hold on her arm at just the thought.

When they stepped outside, Danny stood on the church lawn, holding the lead of a sleek brown mare, and grinning at the two of them like a generous uncle bearing gifts. Eli paused, staring at the lovely animal as she tossed her head, obviously aware she was on display.

"Her name is Cocoa," Sadie said. "Do you like her?"

"She seems a fine animal. Is she yours?"

"No, she's yours." Sadie colored slightly, but her face wore a wide grin. "It's my wedding gift to you."

Eli didn't know what to say. He was well aware that she'd entered into this marriage reluctantly, that he'd backed her into a corner. And still she'd taken the time to find a gift that would be both thoughtful and meaningful to him. He was oddly touched.

Sadie's smile faltered and he realized he'd been silent way too long. "If she's not what you had in mind, we can select another—"

He rushed to reassure her. "No. That is, I like her very much. It's just that I wasn't expecting—" He stopped, taking a moment to collect his thoughts. "Thank you."

He didn't have anything to give her. How could he have forgotten a bride gift?

"I know it's not as fine as what you gave me."

What was she talking about? Then he noticed her gazing down at the ring on her left hand, the one that had belonged to his mother. He covered her hand with his. "It's the perfect gift. In fact, I couldn't have asked for anything finer."

He turned back to Danny. "Can you take her to my stable. And see that she has enough to eat."

Then he patted Sadie's hand. "Shall we find Penny, then lead the way to our new home and prepare to greet our guests, *Mrs. Reynolds?*"

He saw the pink creep into her cheeks and the sparkle in her eyes and suddenly felt several inches taller.

A few minutes later Eli stood inside the foyer of his new home, between his wife and sister, greeting wedding guests and accepting their well wishes. He decided that standing between the two ladies in his life was a very comfortable place to be.

The conversation flowed over him like a stream over stones.

"The ceremony was just beautiful."

"Mr. Reynolds, you've done a wonderful job restoring this old place. It looks even better than it did when it was brand new."

"Sadie, my dear, we're so tickled to welcome you as a permanent resident of Knotty Pine."

And so on.

Sadie was radiant. He would have liked to have her more genteelly reserved, but somehow her informality worked. Today was a special day, after all. Time enough for subtle grooming later.

And people seemed to take to her quite well, smiling tolerantly at her fulsome laughter and occasional faux pas. Penny, too, seemed to be enjoying herself.

When the last of the guests had been formally received, he allowed Penny to go in search of Audrey and Viola while he and Sadie separated to mingle with their guests.

The women Sadie had hired to prepare the food had done a good job. Even though it seemed every citizen of Knotty Pine was here, there was plenty of food to go around, and he was pleased to see that his home was up to the task of accommodating everyone. The guests seemed equally impressed with the reception and with the viewing of the now completed house.

At some point Sadie slipped upstairs to change out of the elegant wedding gown and into another, no doubt more comfortable dress.

As he mingled, Eli found his gaze returning time and again to Sadie. She was animated and the smile never seemed to leave her face. Her laugh was not the gentle, ladylike titter he was accustomed to hearing from females. Rather, it was delightfully infectious. Once, when her gaze met his, she sent a soft, intimate smile his way that warmed him through and through.

Sadie watched as Griff approached her. With the exception of family and near-family from the boardinghouse, the last of the guests had departed for their own homes, and evening was approaching.

Her brother stopped in front of her and leaned back on the balls of his feet. "Well, Sadie girl, it's done. You're a married lady now with a fine new home and a fine new family. I'm very proud of you." Then he took her hand and said softly "But then, I always have been."

His words both surprised and touched her. "Oh, Griff." She launched herself into her brother's arms, doing her best not to cry. "You're the best big brother a girl could ask for.

He laughed. "Why don't you say that sometime when Ry's around? He could stand to be taken down a peg or two."

She stepped back with a laugh. "You know I love Ry, too." Then she gave him an arch look. "Besides, I rather enjoy letting you two fight for my affections."

He laughed and tapped her nose. "Tease." Then he sobered. "Just don't ever forget where you came from."

"How could I? I'll always be one of the Hawk's Creek Lassiters, no matter where I am."

He nodded and shoved his hands in his pockets. "Guess I'll be saying my good-byes now. I plan to head back to Hawk's Creek on tomorrow's train."

Sadie gave him another bear hug, then abruptly released him. "Just a minute—I almost forgot." She raced up the stairs and returned, clutching a piece of paper. "Here. Inez knows about the clothing and such, but this is a list of the other things I'd like to have packed up and sent here. Would you mind handling it for me?"

Griff glanced at the list and his eyebrow went up. "Are you sure?" He looked around, as if gauging where she would be placing her things.

"Oh yes." She gave him her most demure smile. "Eli told me I could add some of my own things to this place if I wanted to and I plan to take him up on it."

Griff's answering grin had a devilish edge to it. "If there weren't so many chores waiting for me back at the ranch I'd be tempted to deliver these things personally."

"I'm sure I have no idea what you're talking about," she said airily. Then she laughed. "And, once he gets used to my lighter additions to his st—*solid* furnishings, I'm sure he'll appreciate them." She'd caught herself just in time. It wouldn't do to describe Eli's efforts as stuffy to Griff.

Griff looked skeptical. "If you say so." Then he gave

her an awkward, big-brother hug. "I hope that husband of yours knows what a lucky man he is." His voice was suspiciously gruff.

He stepped back and jammed his hands back in his pockets. "Now, I'd better go take my leave of your husband."

Inez came up next, her eyes misty as she took both of Sadie's hands. "You made such a beautiful bride, Sadie girl. Your daddy and dear momma would have been so proud."

"Thank you. And thanks for everything you did to make this reception, this day, so wonderful."

Inez waved off her thanks, then gave her hands another squeeze. "I'm just pleased to see that you have yourself a lovely home and a lovely new family. I never would have pictured you as a city girl but I think you're going to do just fine here."

She most sincerely hoped so. "I agree. But I'm glad you think so, too."

Inez stepped back. "Oh and I like Nettie Dauber. I think she's going to do a fine job for you as cook and housekeeper."

"With that kind of endorsement, I know I have nothing to worry about." She glanced up and saw her brother watching them. "I think Griff is ready to escort you back to the boardinghouse. But I'll see you again before you head back to Hawk's Creek on Wednesday."

Inez nodded. "She insists she'll be back to full strength by then. I think she's rushing it a bit, just like that man of yours did with his cane."

That man of yours. Sadie glanced toward her new husband and found him watching her, as well. Their guests would all be gone soon, Penny would be tucked into bed, and they would be alone. What then?

* * *

Sadie watched as Eli closed the door behind Griff and Inez. Cora Beth had taken her children home earlier, most of the cleaning up had been done, and what was left could wait until morning.

"Well, Mrs. Reynolds, I think the party went well."

Did he use her married name because he liked the sound of it as much as she did or was he just trying to get accustomed to having a wife? She decided to focus on the first reason. "Thanks to Mrs. Dauber and Inez."

"Yes, well, I'm certain you had a lot of input into the planning."

She found his attempt to praise her both endearing and encouraging. Another hint that he was willing to make the effort to ensure this arrangement would work out, after all. She felt a definite bounce to her step as she moved toward Penny, who was curled up on one end of the sofa. "Come along, princess, time to get you to bed." She stroked the child's hair. "Would you like me to tuck you in and hear your prayers?"

Penny nodded and placed her hand in Sadie's as she stood. Sadie felt her heart do a flip-flop, oddly touched by the trusting gesture. It didn't matter what Eli had to say about routine and discipline, she was going to make sure this little girl had lots of reasons to smile.

As she climbed the stairs, she could feel Eli's gaze tracking her progress.

And that set her heart flip-flopping in an altogether different manner.

Eli watched until Penny and Sadie reached the top of the stairs, then turned sharply and stepped out on the front porch. His first night in his new house. With his new wife.

Where was the sense of accomplishment, of pleasure at the culmination of all his plans? Why did he feel this restless energy instead?

But there was a sense of anticipation, of better yet to come, as well. Eli leaned against the porch rail and stared out at the night sky.

Seeing her with Penny just now had driven home the fact that, no matter how he'd arrived at it, this had been a good choice for his sister. Not perfect, perhaps, but good nonetheless.

He could sense the potential in Sadie even stronger now, could see where this match could really work with just the right bit of guidance from him. Yes, with his gentle coaching, she could become a lady fine enough to grace the halls of society ballrooms.

The three of them would become valued members of this town, Penny would grow up protected and happy, and ready to face the world with assurance and confidence.

He was startled out of his thoughts by the sound of the door opening. He turned to see Sadie standing there, silhouetted like a cameo in a broach.

"Penny's asleep," she said, joining him at the porch rail.

"She's had a long day."

"We all have." She hooked an arm around one of the support posts and sighed. "But it was lovely."

Eli leaned his elbow on the railing again, but surreptitiously studied her. "I'm glad you think so. A bride should have fine memories of her wedding day." Why had she joined him out here? Was there something she wanted?

She smiled as if he'd just said something exceedingly clever. "Memories are wonderful things, aren't they? Especially when you can share them with others." She lifted her face to the stars. "I think the three of us are going to make some wonderful memories in this house."

That didn't seem to require an answer.

She finally looked at him and there was a curious mix of vulnerability and determination in her expression. "I know I'm not the wife you wanted, Eli, but I promise to try to make you a good one." She gave him a crooked smile. "No promises as to how successful I'll be at it though." With that she lifted up on her toes, kissed his cheek and scurried back inside the house.

Eli stood there a bit longer, staring at the door and stroking his cheek where her lips had been. He could still feel the petal-soft warmth of that kiss, could detect the faintest hint of the floral scent she'd worn.

His thoughts shifted of their own accord to the kiss they'd shared earlier, at the wedding ceremony. The sweetness of her response, the bemused softness of her expression afterwards had tightened his chest, had made him want to live up to the trust he saw in her eyes.

This kiss, though, had been different. While a bit more chaste, it had been sweet and spontaneous, and more significantly, she had initiated it. It was as if she'd given him a very special, aching, filled-with-promise kind of gift.

He wasn't certain exactly what to make of it. But, all in all, it seemed a very promising beginning to their married life.

Chapter Twelve

Eli escorted his sister and new wife into church the next morning. This time they were greeted with warm smiles and felicitations. Eli settled into the pew feeling as if all was finally right with the world again.

After the service, Penny raced off to join Audrey and Viola, Sadie stopped to chat with a group of women which included Inez and Mrs. Collins, and Sheriff Hammond drew him into a small circle of men who were discussing the latest news on national politics. It was edifying to discover the men listened attentively to his opinions. His hard work to make himself a valuable member of the community was beginning to bear fruit.

He found his gaze drawn to his new wife. Her expression was bright and animated. Yes, she still had a bit of a childlike look about her, but instead of putting him off, he was beginning to see it as an asset.

Last night, when he'd stepped into his room, alone, he'd found himself wondering how long she would need to come to terms with their being married, to be ready to join him in the marriage bed.

Had it been a mistake to hold off? She professed to understand that aspect of marital relations, but how did she feel about it? Living up to his word might be more of a challenge than he'd expected.

A question from Horace Danvers forced his focus back to the conversation at hand. But not for long. When he finally excused himself, there were several knowing glances that passed between the men, but he ignored them. After all, from an appearances standpoint, he was newly married and it was normal to want to spend time with his bride.

Sadie entered the library, looking for something she could read to Penny. Once they'd eaten lunch, Eli had gone to his study, leaving her and Penny to amuse themselves as they saw fit.

She searched the titles and quickly discovered there was not much material designed to capture and hold a child's interest. Thank goodness that was one of the things she'd put on the list for Griff to send her—copies of her own childhood favorites. Many of them were sadly dog-eared, but the words were still as entertaining and spellbinding as ever.

Perhaps they could do something else. She looked around—the house felt so formal, so stiff, as if it were a sour schoolmarm who forbade anything resembling horseplay in her classroom. She missed the casual, comfortable atmosphere of the house at Hawk's Creek, the feeling that it was okay to laugh, to get a bit rowdy, to really spread out. Maybe, once her things arrived, it would feel a bit more like home around here.

In the meantime, she decided to take advantage of the large piano in the parlor and she convinced Penny to play a number of duets with her. Apparently, Penny felt repressed by her surroundings as well, but once Sadie was able to get the girl to relax and not take things so seriously, they had a grand time improvising with both tempo and melody.

Later, she glanced out the window and spied the stable. Spinning back around she smiled at Penny. "I think I'll go down and check on Cocoa. Want to come?"

"All right."

"Good. And since I plan for us to get good and dirty, we probably ought to change into our oldest clothes." She crouched slightly, as if at a starting line. "I'll race you to see who can get changed and make it back down here first."

With a giggle, Penny made a mad dash for the stairs.

Sadie changed into one of her older dresses, then waited until she heard Penny's footsteps race past her door before stepping out of her room.

Penny stood at the bottom of the stairs grinning smugly as she watched Sadie descend.

Sadie had never before felt this good about losing a race. It would be fun finding new ways to make this little girl smile.

Distracted by the sound of clattering footsteps and feminine laughter, Eli stepped out of his office. And came face to face with two breathless females. Their laughter stopped abruptly and they faced him with identically sheepish expressions.

"Oh, sorry if we disturbed you." Sadie's expression was that of a kid on a lark. "Penny and I are headed out to check on Cocoa. Want to join us?"

He waved a hand toward his desk. "I've got some paperwork that needs my attention."

"Penny tells me she's never learned to ride a horse. Do you mind if I teach her?"

He looked at his sister. "Do you *want* to learn?" His stepmother had always frowned on the practice, deeming it unfeminine.

"Oh yes. Sadie says it's quite fun and zilerating."

He smiled at her mispronunciation. "She does, does she?"

Penny nodded.

Sadie gave him a reassuring smile. "Don't worry. I've been riding since I was five years old and I'm much more graceful on a horse than on foot. She'll be safe with me."

"Please, Eli?"

He was no proof against the two of them. "Very well. But take it slow."

Penny skipped forward and gave him a hug around his waist. "Thanks."

He stroked her hair, then rested his hand lightly against her back. When he looked up, he found Sadie studying the two of them with a soft smile. He'd give a pretty penny to know what she was thinking.

Then his sister stepped back and took hold of Sadie's hand. "I'm ready. Let's go."

He frowned. "You're not going to teach her right now, are you?"

Sadie shook her head. "Today, we're going to work on how to groom a horse. We'll move on to riding lessons in another day or two."

Good. That would give him time to find Penny a suitable mount. Eli watched the two of them move toward the rear entrance and for a moment was tempted to join them.

After breakfast the next morning Eli headed to the bank and Sadie walked Penny as far as Danvers's

Mercantile, where she met up with a group of children on their way to the schoolhouse.

Sadie headed back home, wondering what she was going to do with herself all day. Feeling at something of a loss, she drifted into the kitchen where Mrs. Dauber was already at work chopping vegetables. The woman glanced up at Sadie. "Will Mr. Reynolds be home for lunch?"

Would he? Sadie perked up. Of course he would. He'd always returned to the boardinghouse, after all. "Yes, he'll be here."

"Then I'll make certain I fix enough for two."

After a bit more discussion about the menu, the conversation dragged and Sadie wandered out to the stable. She saddled up Cocoa and rode her at a sedate pace round and round the tiny paddock. She would have to talk to Eli about providing proper exercise for the mare. A nice long ride across the countryside sounded very appealing right now.

She cleaned up, then headed to the library where she found an interesting-looking book and curled up on the window seat to read. Fifteen minutes later she found herself too restless to continue.

So what now? If she'd been at the ranch she'd have gone for a ride in the south pasture or checked on Dusty's new foal or maybe even seen if Clem needed help mending tack.

Had Griff had time to get her things together yet? If she was lucky, maybe they would arrive in the next few days. Cocoa was a fine animal but she missed Calliope. Perhaps, when Calliope arrived, she and Eli could go riding together.

And there were all those furnishings and ornamental pieces, too. Normally she didn't pay much attention to how a house was decorated, but in this case she couldn't wait to add a few touches of Hawk's Creek to this place.

Sadie decided to walk down to the boardinghouse and visit with Cora Beth and Inez. Perhaps Cora Beth could clue her in as to what the womenfolk did around these parts.

By the time Eli returned for lunch, she was full of news about what she'd learned.

"Cora Beth invited me to join the Ladies's Auxiliary. They help with keeping the church clean and tidy, and they fix food baskets and do chores for folks who are ailing and need a bit of help." He should be happy as a tic on a hound that she was finding ways to get involved with the community. It's one of the things he'd wanted in his "perfect wife" after all.

"Sounds like a worthy cause."

She ignored the hint of condescension in his tone. "Of course, I'm not good at cooking or sewing, but I can clean as well as the next person and there's all kinds of chores I can do like milking cows and caring for livestock. And, since I'm not as busy as most of the other ladies around here, I can deliver things, as well."

He frowned at that. "I'm not certain it's appropriate for you to go traipsing around the countryside on your own."

Not appropriate? "I did it all the time at Hawk's Creek. Rode all over the six hundred acres of the ranch and the half dozen or more miles it took to visit some of our neighbors."

"This is not Hawk's Creek."

"And I'm not your little sister. I'm a grown woman."

They glared at each other for several long seconds

before Sadie backed down. He was only worried about her. "I'm sorry. It's just that I'm not used to having to check with someone before I do something."

Some of his stiffness eased. "I apologize, as well. It's just that now you are in my care, and you are part of my family. I'm responsible for keeping you safe."

Sadie felt a stab of disappointment. Appearances and duty again. He'd been worried about how it would look, not about her well-being. "If I need to make deliveries that are very far from town, I'll find someone to go with me." "Very far" being a relative term. "Griff will be sending over Calliope, my horse, when he sends Skeeter. I trust you have no objections to me riding alone."

He gave her a long look. "As long as you're not going far."

By mid-morning on Tuesday Sadie was getting cabin fever. She'd already written a long letter for Inez to deliver to Griff, and The Ladies's Auxiliary didn't meet until tomorrow, so she was at loose ends. To top it off, Eli had said not to expect him for lunch—he was scheduled to look at a farmhouse a local was wanting to borrow money on.

What was she supposed to do with herself all day? She was pretty far ahead on Annabel Adams's story, but perhaps she would do some more writing just the same. She actually had an idea for a new story that had fired her interest and now might be the time to experiment with it a bit.

Before she could get started though, a knock at the door brought a welcome distraction. Calling out to Mrs. Dauber that she would get it, Sadie headed for the door, hoping whoever it was had come for a long visit.

Then she heard a familiar bark and raced forward,

throwing open the door. As soon as she did, she was nearly knocked over by fifty pounds of barking dog. "Skeeter!" She knelt so that her ecstatic pet could have access to lick her face, which he did with great enthusiasm. "Oh, I missed you too, boy." She laughed and finally held him back.

Then she looked up to belatedly greet the man who'd accompanied her pet. "Hello, Red."

The weathered ranch foreman tipped his hat. "Hi Miss Sadie. Or should I say Mrs. Reynolds?"

"Sadie will do just fine. Thanks so much for bringing Skeeter to me."

Red grinned. "He was moping so much it was an act of charity."

"Well, come on in and rest yourself a spell."

Red pulled off his hat and entered the foyer. "Thanks, but there's a whole lot more to deliver. Griff sent everything you had on that list of yours. They're over at the train station, waiting on transport."

"Everything?"

Red Grinned. "Calliope is already stabled at the livery."

Sadie felt a flutter of excitement in her chest. It had been so long since she'd had herself a good gallop—she hadn't realized until just now how much she missed it.

"Did she make the trip okay?"

"Like a trouper. Almost like she knew you were at the end of the line. She's been fretting for you ever since you left. She'll be mighty glad to see you." He tilted his hat back. "I suppose you're just as eager to see her. So get your hat and let's go."

It was tempting, but she knew Red had had a long day.

"Time enough for that in a bit. Come on into the kitchen and get yourself something to eat first."

She ruffled Skeeter's fur one more time for good measure, then led the way down the hall.

Mrs. Dauber took one look at Skeeter and crossed her arms over her chest. "Animals don't have no place in my kitchen—especially not one as big and rambunctious at that one." The woman seemed adamant, but with some cajoling on Sadie's part she reluctantly allowed it "just this once." Sadie did notice, however, that within ten minutes the cook was slipping Skeeter little tidbits of food.

After Red had a chance to eat and refresh himself, Sadie, with Skeeter at her heels, allowed him to escort her to the livery. Knowing Calliope was waiting, it was all Sadie could do to maintain a sedate pace. Along the way, she recruited a couple of strapping youths, Harry and Wilbur Browder, to help Red with the loading and unloading.

Once they'd arranged for a wagon and horse to transport Sadie's possessions, Red and the boys headed for the train depot while Sadie spent time with Calliope. Borrowing a set of brushes, Sadie spent the next thirty minutes happily grooming her horse and chatting away about all that had happened, just as if the animal could understand her every word. She paused occasionally to say something to Cocoa who was in the next stall.

Red sent Wilbur to fetch her once the wagon was loaded, and Sadie reluctantly left. But as she headed home she was surprised by the tingle of anticipation. Who'd have thought she would get so all fired up about decorating a house?

By the time she reached the house, the men were already unloading the first of the items. There were several trunks that no doubt contained her clothing and personal items. But it was the crates she was more interested in.

She couldn't wait to get everything unloaded. Sadie had the Browder brothers carry her trunks up to her room, absently directing them to stack them as best they could. But she had the rest of the items placed in the foyer where she could inspect them herself. As soon as the last of the crates were brought in she had them opened up. With the men's help she unpacked every item and laid them out where she could see them all. Then she started grouping them based on which room she thought each should go in.

For her sitting room she set aside the brocade wingback chair and small writing desk that had graced her own mother's sitting room—she thought of it that way even now—as well as a small table that had stood in a corner near the main stairwell.

For the front parlor she quickly grouped the rug, the painting, the lamp and the chess set.

The two pottery bowls and the hawk came next—where would they look best? She finally settled on placing the bowls on the sideboard in the dining room and the hawk on the table in the entry.

The books, of course, would go in the library.

That only left the pair of porcelain figurines. She finally decided to put those in her sitting room, as well.

Skeeter trotted at her heels wherever she went, as if determined to never let her out of his sight again.

When the work was finally done, Sadie stepped back and admired her efforts. The eclectic, colorful pieces she'd selected had gone a long way toward brightening up the formerly somber parlor. She bent down and rubbed

Skeeter's head. "What do you think, boy? Do you think Eli will appreciate the change?"

Then she snapped her fingers. "That's right, you don't know Eli. It's okay. He takes a bit of warming up to but I promise you it's worth the effort. And you're really going to like Penny. She's sweeter than buttermilk pie and cute as a bunny in clover."

"You always talk to that mutt as if he can understand you."

Sadie smiled at Red over her shoulder. "That's because he can."

She heard the front door open and Skeeter's ears went up. They stepped out into the hall in time to see Penny shut the door behind her.

The little girl halted in her tracks, her eyes widening as her gaze latched on to Skeeter.

"Is that your dog?" she asked without glancing up.

"Yep, this is Skeeter. Come on over and get acquainted."

Penny set her books down on the entry table, only sparing a quick, surprised look at the hawk, then approached the dog cautiously.

"Hold out your hand and let him sniff it."

Penny bravely did as she was bid, and stood with a stoic expression while Skeeter licked her hand.

"I can see he likes you."

"He does?"

"Absolutely. Go ahead, pet him if you like."

She watched as Penny gingerly smoothed a hand across the dog's head and nape. When Skeeter gave an encouraging woof and started wagging his tail, at first she looked startled, then grinned.

"He *does* like me."

"I told you."

Penny knelt down and giggled as Skeeter attempted to wash her face with his tongue.

Sadie couldn't help but smile at the picture they made. Skeeter liked children as much as she did. She only hoped Eli took to her pet as well as Penny had.

Penny finally looked up from the dog and pointed to the entry table. "Did that bird come from your ranch, too?"

"Uh-huh. Do you like it?"

Penny stared at the hawk. "It's different. What's it made from?"

"It's made from the horn of a bull. Would you like to hear the story that goes with it?"

"There's a story?"

Sadie smiled. "Of course. Most everything has at least one story to go with it. We just don't always know what that story is."

"Then yes, I want to hear the story that goes with your bull horn bird."

Sadie grinned at her descriptive. "Ok. And afterwards I'll show you all the rest of the pieces that came from my old home."

"Do you know their stories, too?

"Of course. That's why they're each special to me. And I promise to tell you each and every one."

Eli strode into the house and halted on the threshold. Penny sat on the floor like a scullery maid, playing with an oversized, rough-looking dog of questionable breeding. He'd already gotten word of the shipment that had arrived from Hawk's Creek. Was *this* Sadie's pet? With a name like Skeeter he'd been expecting a lap dog whose biggest drawback would be an annoying yip. This animal was large, well-muscled and must weigh at least fifty pounds. Its short-haired coat was gray with black spots, and its tongue seemed as long as Eli's hand and wrist. He couldn't tell what breed it was—seemed to be a touch of collie, a touch of greyhound and a touch of who-knows-what-else in the animal.

Where was Sadie and why wasn't she supervising? Was it really safe for his sister to be behaving so familiarly with the beast? "Penny, what are you doing down on the floor with that animal?"

Penny, however, seemed oblivious to any danger the animal might pose. "Look Eli, Skeeter's here. Isn't he great?"

Great was *not* the word he'd use. "I had expected something...smaller."

Sadie stepped out of the parlor. "Skeeter isn't a 'something'—he's a dog."

From the bristle in her tone he could tell he'd gotten her back up. "My apologies. It's just, I thought your pet was a lapdog. This looks more like a guard animal."

Her frown deepened. "I never said anything about him being a lapdog—he comes from working stock."

A strange man appeared from the vicinity of the kitchen just then. "Miss Sadie, I— Oh, sorry, didn't realize you had company."

"Red, this is my husband, Eli Reynolds."

Before the man could do more than nod, she turned and completed the introductions. "Eli, this is Red Hannigan from Hawk's Creek. He was kind enough to bring Skeeter and most of my belongings here for me."

Eli extended a hand. "Mr. Hannigan, Sadie and I thank you for your trouble."

The man pumped Eli's hand with what seemed unnecessary force. Mr. Hannigan seemed to be sizing him up. "It's just Red. And no need for thanks—it wasn't any trouble. Fact of the matter is, I had to arm wrestle three other hands for the chance to come down here and check out the fella who managed to capture Miss Sadie's fancy."

Did the man think this was a love match? Eli wasn't certain what he thought of that.

"Red's going to be staying the night at the boarding-house and escorting Inez back to Hawk's Creek in the morning."

"Mrs. Collins runs a clean, comfortable place."

"So I've heard." Red turned back to Sadie. "If you don't need me to help you arrange any more of your things I think I'll be heading on over to the boarding-house now."

What "things" had he been helping her arrange?

"You're free to do as you please, Red, you know that. I appreciate all your help today. Let Inez know I'll come by to see you both off at the train station tomorrow."

He nodded. "Will do." Then he tipped his hat Eli's way. "Nice meeting you, Mr. Reynolds. You take care of our Miss Sadie now."

As Eli watched Red head out the front door, his gaze was caught by a carving on the entry table. What was that? A closer look showed it to be the head of a bird— hawk maybe—carved out of what seemed to be an animal horn and mounted on a block of polished wood. He moved closer to get a better look, not believing what he was seeing.

"It's a hawk," Sadie said. "It sat in my father's study for as long as I can remember. Do you like it?"

So this had sentimental value to her. He just wished she had found a less prominent place to display it. "I've never seen another quite like it," he said diplomatically.

Her bright smile told him she hadn't picked up any

undercurrents in his statement. "Yes, it's very special."
She waved him forward. "Come on in the parlor and I'll
show you some of the other pieces I had sent over."

"Other pieces?" Eli braced himself. Surely it wasn't
more of the same.

Penny stood, dusting her skirts. "Oh, just wait until
you see all of the other things she's brought, Eli. They're
absolutely splendid."

His sister's words did little to reassure him. Nor did
the fact that Sadie's "pet" seemed even larger now that
it was standing.

Sadie was happily chatting as she led the way into the
parlor. "I made a list for Griff so he'd know just what
items to send. And they look even better than I imagined
they would."

"You should have waited until I got home so I could've
helped you unload and set out your things." And perhaps
influenced *where* they were set.

"Red helped. He's a very handy fellow. Besides, I
wanted it to be a surprise."

He was surprised all right. With some trepidation
Eli moved to the parlor. And stopped on the threshold
to stare at the transformation she'd wrought.

A bearskin rug now lay in brutish state in front of the
fireplace. A colorful but amateurish picture of a ranch
house hung on the bit of wall that separated the two tall
windows on the far side of the room. A hobnail cranberry
glass lantern presided over the small table next to the
sofa, replacing the more traditional, elegant lamp that
had been there this morning. And a rustically carved
chess set occupied the table near the piano.

"What do you think?"

Eli tried to pull his thoughts together. Did *all* of these

items have sentimental value? "You've certainly put your stamp on this room."

"That was the plan," she said happily. "Isn't it wonderful the way your things and my things go so well together even though they're so very different?"

She thought these items went well with his furnishings? He hadn't realized her taste was so underdeveloped. "Is this everything?" Please say it is.

"Oh, no. I wanted to spread things around a bit. I put some things in the dining room and in the library and in my sitting room. Come on, I'll show you the rest."

Eli studied the two bowls that now anchored each end of the sideboard. They were crafted of glazed pottery, painted in a bold shade of blue and decorated with flowers—one had two roses and the other had five lilies.

The bright colors were a jarring note in the otherwise elegantly-appointed room.

"I thought these would brighten up the room a bit. My mother had a whole collection of these—sixteen in all. The daisies and lilies were always my favorite though." He supposed he should be grateful she hadn't had the entire collection brought in.

Next she led the way to the library where his gaze was immediately drawn to two porcelain figurines situated on the low table that fronted the fireplace. At least these were finely crafted pieces, but they were badly cracked and chipped.

Sadie, however, fingered them as if they were priceless treasures. "I used to play with these when I was a little girl."

Another sentimental attachment. He supposed he should be thankful she hadn't *all* her playthings with her.

He expected to find a whole trove of her "treasures"

when they moved to her sitting room, but he was surprised to find it still woefully under furnished—a tasteful wingback chair, a delicately constructed writing desk and chair and a table that had seen better days but were obviously of good quality. These furnishings were a bit delicate for his taste but were of a quality and workmanship much more refined than the pieces she'd placed in the more public areas of the house. Why couldn't she have swapped the placements?

"Why so sparse?"

She shrugged. "I don't really need a lot right now." She ran her fingers lovingly along the top of the chair back. "These pieces came from my mother's study and I didn't want to strip it bare."

Too bad her taste didn't mirror her mother's.

"I figure I'll do what she did," Sadie continued. "Find pieces over time that I like and make it more of a personal haven."

He mentally winced at the thought of just what her personal taste in furnishings would do to this room if the other items she'd brought into the house were a reflection.

As they returned to the parlor, Sadie spun around to face him. "So, what do you think of my additions?"

Hearing the note of worry in her voice, Eli did his best to answer diplomatically. "The pieces certainly are colorful."

Her eyes lit up. "Exactly! They brighten up the rooms and give them character."

Changed their character more like. From elegant and sophisticated, to a mishmash of unmatched styles and garish colors.

All through the evening meal, the gaudy blue bowls taunted him, set his teeth on edge. Afterwards, as they sat in the parlor, he was acutely conscious of the bearskin rug. How could they possibly entertain guests with that atrocity sitting there? But how could he broach the matter to Sadie without hurting her feelings?

Chapter Thirteen

The next morning Eli came downstairs prepared to deal with her tasteless additions. Perhaps some of the less egregious items could stay, but items like the bearskin rug and carved hawk would need to find new homes. He'd pondered the situation as he lay in bed last night and finally decided the best course of action was to try to be subtle but firm.

Once breakfast was served, he cleared his throat. "About those things you had delivered from Hawk's Creek."

Sadie glanced up. "Yes?"

"I was just thinking, I mean since the pieces are all so special to you, and since your sitting room seems so bare, maybe you'd like to move them there, where you can surround yourself with familiar objects."

"Oh, but I like having them scattered around where we can all enjoy them. And I don't mind sharing."

She wasn't making this easy on him. "That's quite generous of you, but perhaps the colors are a bit *too* bright…"

Her smile slowly faded. She stared at him for a long

moment, then her chin came up. "You don't care for them." The words were flat, emotionless.

He tried to smooth things over. "I didn't say that. I only meant they don't match—"

She brushed his words aside as if he hadn't spoken. "So you didn't really want me to put my stamp on the entire house, just my isolated, private portion of it that neither you nor our guests will have to be bothered with."

"You're twisting my words."

"Am I?"

He set his fork down in exasperation. "Yes, you are. I was just thinking that it might be better if perhaps we shop for some new pieces together, pieces that we can both enjoy and maybe build new memories around." Sentimental memories seemed to be important to her.

But she wasn't appeased. "I see. Does that mean we will be replacing your desk or your grandfather clock."

He frowned. "Those are family heirlooms."

"And mine are mere bric-a-brac. Don't worry, I'll have everything moved to my sitting room and bedroom as soon as possible." She set her napkin on the table.

"Feel free to hire whatever help you need."

"Of course. Because money is the answer to everything." She stood. "Now if you'll excuse me, I need to speak to Mrs. Dauber about today's meals."

Eli stared at her back as she turned and marched stiffly out of the room. That didn't go quite as he'd hoped.

"That wasn't very nice, Eli."

He'd forgotten his sister was even present. "Come now, Penny, she might be a bit put out right now, but she'll be fine once she thinks on it. Perhaps I was a bit too straightforward, but I'll help her pick out new things that both she and I like."

Penny's gaze still condemned him. "But it won't be the same."

He certainly hoped not.

"These are her *story pieces*." Penny said that as if it explained everything.

"Story pieces?"

Penny nodded. "That's what she calls them. I asked her why she chose these things out of all the things in her house, and she said it's because there's a story she can tell about each of them." Penny crossed her arms. "Sadie likes stories."

A bit too much perhaps. "Stories are fine for children, but grown-ups must learn to set make-believe behind them and deal with the real world."

"Why?"

"Because when you're an adult you have adult responsibilities, you have people depending on you and you can't just pretend things are something that they're not. You'd never get anything done if all you cared about was fun and make-believe."

"But Sadie has fun and she gets things done." Penny tilted up her chin. A gesture she'd no doubt picked up from Sadie. "When I grow up, I want to be like Sadie." She stood up from the table. "May I be excused, please?"

"Yes. Collect your books and head out for school."

Penny paused next to her brother and placed a hand on the arm of his chair. "Eli," she looked at him with a surprisingly adult disappointment, "I know her things are different from yours, but I like them, and you would, too, if you heard her stories. I think you should ask her to tell them to you."

"We'll see."

Eli rose from the table and straightened his cuff. He refused to feel guilty. It was important that Sadie learn good taste so that Penny would also grow up with an appreciation for the finer things. Some things he could overlook, but bearskin rugs and carvings made from bull horns—no. He knew he was in the right here.

So why did he suddenly feel so wrong?

Sadie managed to keep her emotions under control through most of the morning. She walked Penny to the mercantile as usual. The little girl's sympathy and obvious outrage at her brother's actions forced Sadie to defend Eli—not an easy task with her emotions still roiling around. But by the time they parted, they both agreed that Eli had a right to his own opinion, and his was no more right or wrong than theirs.

Then she met Red and Inez at the train station to see them off. Inez took one good look at her and knew something was wrong. Sadie waved off her concerns with a laughing comment about adjusting to life in the city.

When she was finally alone, she headed straight for the stable. She fed Cocoa a bit of extra grain and promised to exercise her later. The she saddled Calliope and mounted up. She rode sedately until she was well out of town. But as soon as the last of the buildings were behind her she let the horse have her head.

For several minutes she just let everything else go except the exhilaration of galloping across the long stretch of flat, open road. The feel of the sun on her skin, the wind on her face, the smell of dust and grass and wildflowers, the sound of crows and jays and pounding hooves—if she closed her eyes she could almost imagine herself back at Hawk's Creek. When she passed a buggy headed into town she finally slowed her horse to a walk.

And allowed her emotions to come flooding to the front. Anger, frustration, disappointment, hurt—all the wasplike, hurtful emotions that prick and sting. She should have known better than to think Eli would appreciate her additions to their home. The man was too set in his ways, too focused on appearances.

His disregard for her feelings *was* hurtful, but she could deal with that. What bothered her more was the thought that this might be an indication of how he felt about her personally. Was he ashamed of her? Did he see her as an embarrassment, as someone to keep out of sight as much as possible? After all, he'd only pressed his suit with her because he'd felt honor bound.

He'd admitted he'd been seeking a wife, a *proper* wife, before their "little incident" forced his hand. Perhaps he'd already set his sights, his affections, on someone else here in Knotty Pine. Oh—what if he was nursing tender affections for another woman? Jealousy added its own sting.

She tried to forcibly put that from her mind. Whatever the case, she and Eli were married now. So it was up to the two of them to make the marriage work. For Penny's sake, if not their own.

As Cora Beth had said, as Eli's wife, it was up to her to bring the heart to their home. Perhaps, in time, he would come to value her viewpoint. For now, it was enough that he seemed to at least be trying to be kind.

She tugged on the reins, turning Calliope back toward town. "Come on, girl. I have some things to take care of back at home."

* * *

By the time Eli returned home for lunch, all traces of Sadie's additions to the household furnishings had been removed from at least casual view. And Sadie herself seemed calm and relaxed. There was no mention of this morning's conversation, no mention of where her things had gone.

He waffled for a minute about whether to ask what she'd done with the missing pieces, but finally decided to not ruffle the feathers.

She chatted with him about seeing Red and Inez off at the train station, about her morning ride and about the upcoming Ladies's Auxiliary meeting. "Cora Beth tells me the ladies alternate which home they meet in," she told Eli. "They're meeting at Mrs. Danvers home this afternoon and at the boardinghouse next week. I thought I would volunteer to have it here the following week."

"That sounds like a fine idea."

The conversation lagged for a few minutes, then she broached a new topic. "Do you ever do much riding?"

"When I have someplace to go. And more often than not it's by carriage."

"But don't you ever ride horseback just for the pure enjoyment of it?"

"Pure enjoyment?" Where was she going with this?

"Yes. You know—the exhilaration you get from galloping across the countryside, letting the wind whip at you and the sun warm you, knowing you can control the powerful animal beneath you with just a touch."

Was she worried he didn't appreciate her wedding gift to him? "Cocoa is a beautiful mare. I think she'll make a good carriage horse but you're right, it might be enjoyable to ride horseback occasionally. Perhaps, once we have a suitable mount for Penny, we can ride as a family."

Sadie nodded, smiling as if he'd given her a gift. "That would be nice. In the meantime, I'll alternate my daily rides between Cocoa and Calliope so they both get exercised."

Was *that* the point she'd been trying to make. "I can hire someone to exercise them if you like."

"No, please don't. Riding is something I've always done and always loved. It would be foolish to hire someone else to do it."

Not her point then. "As you wish."

Her smile was his reward. Yes, she seemed as cheerful and carefree as always with no lingering resentments. It appeared he'd been right when he told Penny she would get over her hurt feelings quickly. She seemed to have a fleeting attention span—moving from one emotion to another as easily as she moved from one topic to another.

He'd been right to speak his mind earlier. His worry about hurting her feelings had been entirely unfounded.

When Eli stepped through the front door that afternoon, he was greeted by the sound of Penny's laughter. He followed the sound to Sadie's sitting room and stood in the doorway staring at the transformation she'd made. Here were all of the items that had come from Hawk's Creek.

"Oh Eli, isn't this the most amazing room?" Penny exclaimed.

Sadie glanced his way with a smile. "I took your suggestion and brought all my things from Hawk's Creek in here. You were right, they make this room into something special."

The hodgepodge of items was startling when brought together. The colors clashed, the styles were all over the place. The elegant little table with the knick on it held the hobnail lamp and stood right beside the bearskin rug. The cracked porcelain figurines overlooked the chess set and hawk's head carving. The blue bowls sat in garish splendor on the mantle, flanking either side of her watercolor. And so on around the room.

Yet somehow it all looked like it belonged together. As did Sadie, Penny and Skeeter.

Where did that leave him? "There was no need for you to bring it all in here. If you want to leave a few things, like the lamp and the figurines—"

"No, no, you were right, these pieces belong together." She stood. "Penny, I believe you have some homework to do. And Eli, if you'd like to relax in your study, I'll check with Mrs. Dauber and see when we can expect her to serve supper."

Within seconds he was left standing alone. Even her dog had followed Penny out. He moved slowly toward his study trying to figure out why he felt this sudden restlessness.

This was what he'd been hoping for. A wife who would run his household and take her place in the community beside him. Someone who would not just take care of his sister but who would come to love her, who would give her the attention and discipline she needed, while at the same time keep her happy and entertained.

And Sadie was well on her way to providing all of that.

Even though she'd gone off in a bit of a huff this morning—and no matter how his conscience tweaked he would not allow himself to feel any guilt for that—she had come to her senses and was behaving quite decorously this evening.

So why wasn't he feeling more pleased with the way things were shaping up?

Chapter Fourteen

"And how was the Ladies's Auxiliary meeting?" Eli was hoping to draw Sadie out a bit as they sat around the dining table.

"Mrs. Danvers put me on the broom brigade," she said proudly.

"The broom brigade?"

"Yes. We're divided into three groups—the sewing brigade which mends the altar cloths and curtains and anything else around the church that needs that kind of attention. Then there's the polishing brigade which, of course, polishes the pews and other woodwork. And us, the broom brigade which takes care of the floors." She waved her fork in a tight circle. "Mrs. Van Halsen was a member of that group but she's moved over to the sewing brigade so they needed a new person."

"And that's where they put you—sweeping floors."

Sadie nodded. "It's work that needs doing and I don't mind. But that's just the once-a-week work. We do other things, as well. There's some folks here in town who need someone to check in on them occasionally and I volunteered to help out with that, too. After all, I'm not as busy as some of the other ladies."

Eli nodded, pleased to hear she was finding her place here. Charitable undertakings were an important part of community life.

The subject of Sadie's things was not broached again. Eli watched her closely for signs of unhappiness or discontent over the couple of days, but saw none. Her disposition remained sunny and open.

He wasn't sure whether to be pleased or concerned.

He *did* notice that she and Penny spent a great deal of time in her sitting room rather than the parlor. And for some reason that made him feel left out. Not that he wasn't welcome there. He just didn't feel quite comfortable there.

It was almost as if her things were frowning at him. That highly fanciful notion was so unlike him that he found himself feeling even more out of sorts.

Friday, Charlie Jamison stopped by the bank to make a deposit. He stuck his head in Eli's office. "Just wanted to let you know how much we appreciate that missus of yours."

Eli leaned back in his chair. "Is that so?"

"Yep. My pa has been real down since he hurt his hip last month. He's not one to take to just sitting around. But Miss Sadie, she didn't just drop off a meal. She cheered him up real good yesterday with her checker playing and reading to him. Tickled him to no end when that little slip of a thing beat him two games out of three."

"You don't say."

"I do. Hadn't seen pa this lively since his accident."

After Charlie left, Eli set his pen down. So, Sadie was doing more than delivering food baskets, was she? Why hadn't she said anything? He couldn't remember—had he asked her about her day yesterday?

An hour later, Bart Dugan stepped in his office. "I suppose you already know this, but that's one fine woman you married, Mr. Reynolds. She brought a bowl of soup to my Martha this afternoon and stayed to take care of our young'ens. First chance I've had to come to town and get supplies since Martha got sick."

Later, when he headed home, Mrs. Nelson stopped him. "Please tell Sadie how much we appreciate her visit to Granny Lawrence this morning. Having someone to listen to her reminiscences and read to her just cheered her up so much. She's missed getting around on her own since her sight got so bad."

His wife had certainly been busy.

"So how did your day go today?" Eli asked as he passed the platter of bread at supper that evening.

"Oh, nothing much." Sadie took a slab of bread and passed the platter to Penny. "I took a ride on Calliope, enjoyed the fresh air, visited with a few folks."

Eli took his own seat at the table. "Anyone I'd know?"

"I met Mrs. Nelson today. Do you know her?"

"I don't believe I've had the pleasure."

"A wonderful character, full of salt and vinegar. She's nearly blind but that doesn't stop her from speaking her mind. We had a great conversation about how she used to play the fiddle when she was a girl."

Eli listened to her chatter on about Mrs. Nelson and then Mrs. Dugan and her kids. Not once did she mention or even imply that she'd paid a charity call on any of her new friends. Instead she made it sound as if she'd had interesting encounters with intriguing people who were their neighbors.

And her stories were full of humor and wit, but always

kind. The only person to come off in a bad light was herself. He could see why Penny enjoyed listening to her so much.

And he was beginning to understand just how complex a person she was. But he couldn't decide if that was a good or bad thing to have in a wife.

Saturday morning, Sadie and Penny were out at the stable, grooming the horses. Sadie was working with Calliope and Penny was imitating her every move as she worked with Cocoa.

Sadie had just batted a horsefly away, when she looked up and spied Eli headed toward them. "Oh, hello. Finished with that stuffy old paperwork?"

"Thought I'd take a break and see what you two are up to."

"Just working with the horses." She glanced toward Penny. "That sister of yours is really taking to it. I think we'll be able to move on to riding lessons soon."

Penny's face lit up. "Really?" She turned to her brother. "Oh Eli, can I? I promise to be really careful and do everything Sadie tells me."

"Not today," he said, "but soon."

Sadie mentally winced as she saw Penny's expression droop. She should have waited to talk to Eli before speaking up. When would she learn to think before she acted?"

"I have an idea for something almost as good, though."

Penny stared at him dubiously.

"Why don't we go for a ride?"

The little girl's eyes grew large. "All of us?"

"Of course all of us. You can ride up on my horse with me."

Sadie stared at him. Her sweet-but-stuffy husband was offering to go horseback riding with them? Then she gave her head a mental shake. Whatever had gotten in to him, best take him up on the offer before he found an excuse to change his mind. "You heard your brother—let's get changed and saddle up."

"Can we race to the house?"

Sadie took a quick glance Eli's way and decided not to press her luck. "I have a better idea. Let's show your brother what perfect ladies we can be when we set our minds to it, what do you say?"

Thirty minutes later they were setting off at an easy walk to the edge of town. Though they rode side by side, Sadie let Eli set their course. She watched Penny and Eli riding together, saw the happy look in Penny's eyes and wanted to sigh in contentment. This was just what that little girl needed. More time and attention from her brother. Did Eli realize how much his sister loved him, how desperately she craved his approval?

They were on their way back to the house when Penny brought up the subject of Hawk's Creek.

"While we were grooming Cocoa and Calliope today, Sadie told me all about Hawk's Creek," she told Eli.

"Did she now?"

Sadie laughed. "Not *all* about it princess, that would take much longer than one afternoon."

Her eyes widened. "There's more?"

"There certainly is. I saved some of the best parts for another day. And I'll bet Viola could tell you some stories about it, too. She's been up to visit a half dozen times."

"Can *we* go visit?"

Sadie cast a quick look Eli's way before answering. "Of course we can. But we'll have to sit down and figure out a good time. Your brother is very busy with his job right now."

"Couldn't we go without him?" Penny looked up at her brother. "You wouldn't mind, Eli, would you? I mean, you don't care about tadpoles and fishing holes and cows and tree swings, do you?"

Was that a wince that crossed Eli's face? It was there and gone so quickly Sadie couldn't be sure.

"Actually, I might be able to get away for a little while," he said slowly. "If we left on a Friday morning and came back on Monday I'd just be away from the bank for two days."

Sadie couldn't believe she'd heard right. First this horseback ride and now an offer to travel to Hawk's Creek. Was he finally trying to meet her halfway?

Penny had no trouble believing him. She was practically bouncing in the saddle. "Do you mean tomorrow?"

He laughed. "No. But Wednesday is the last day of school for the summer so maybe we can plan for next week." He looked over at Sadie. "What do you say? Is that time enough to plan a trip?"

"Absolutely. I'll send a telegram to Griff on Monday to let him know to expect us."

She turned to Penny. "In the meantime, young lady, we need to work on your riding lessons. You'll want to be able to ride a horse on your own when we get there."

Sadie felt the bubble of happiness in her chest expand until she was certain it was visible on her face. Could it be that Eli was making a true effort to do something to please her? If so, he'd found a great way to do just that.

Did he know that she cherished the effort every bit as much as the end result?

* * *

Sadie leaned forward to get a look at the passing landscape. She and Eli sat in the backseat of the buggy with Penny between them, while Skeeter got the place of honor up front with Manny. For the past several minutes the road they were traveling had been cutting through a corner of the rolling green hills of Hawk's Creek ranch. It had been nearly a month since she'd left the place but right now it seemed as if she'd been gone forever.

Once they made it over the next rise, the house itself would come into view. Sadie leaned forward a bit more, as if that would help her see it faster.

Sure enough, as soon as they topped the hill, the arched ironwork gateway sign guarding the drive came into view and there was the house itself, with the barn and other outbuildings behind it.

"There it is!" She couldn't keep the note of pride from her voice. There was nowhere else like Hawk's Creek, and no matter how many times she left or how far she traveled, returning here always felt like returning home.

"Look Eli," Penny said. "It's kind of like Amberleigh."

Sadie turned back to her. "What's Amberleigh?"

"It's where we lived before we came to live with Eli."

"We?"

Penny's expression sobered. "Susan and me."

Confused, Sadie started to ask who Susan was. Then she caught sight of Eli who gave a slight shake of his head and mouthed the word *Later* before taking the conversation on a tangent.

"Amberleigh was built along a much different style,"

he said. "But it did have a lot of open ground like this place and a large stable area."

Penny seemed to have rallied a bit. "I wish we'd brought Cocoa and Calliope with us so we could go horseback riding again while we're here."

Sadie laughed. "Don't worry, princess. There are plenty of horses here—I'm sure we'll find some we can borrow."

As soon as the buggy rolled under the arched Hawk's Creek sign, Skeeter bounded off the wagon seat and raced on ahead. By the time the buggy came to a stop in front of the house, Griff was waiting to greet them.

He stepped over to Sadie's side and grabbed her by the waist to swing her down. "Glad to see you remembered your way back to the place."

Manny set the brake and handed a slip of paper to Griff. "Curtis asked me to deliver this telegram that came for you."

Griff opened the paper and his face split into a smile.

"Ry and Josie are back in the States. They want me to meet them in Tyler when the train comes through on Wednesday for a short visit because they don't plan to delay getting back to Viola and their place a moment longer than they have to."

Sadie smiled as Eli handed her down. "Viola will be so happy to hear that. I know she's been missing them something awful."

Griff waved them toward the house. "Y'all come on inside. I know you'll want to freshen up after that long trip."

Manny followed them into the house with their bags. "Where do you want me to put these?"

"I put you and Eli in Mother and Dad's old room, and Penny in your room, Sadie."

Sadie stilled. She hadn't thought far enough ahead to realize this would be an issue. Of course Griff would expect them to share a room. She cut a quick glance Eli's way.

Griff, sensing something was wrong, frowned slightly. "If that's a problem, we can shuffle things around a bit. Just let me know what arrangements you'd prefer."

Eli saw the panicked look in Sadie's eye. Was she worried what her brother would think if she asked for separate rooms? Or what he would think if she didn't? He decided to take the burden of replying off her shoulders. "I'm sure the arrangements you've made will work just fine."

He was rewarded with a quick look of gratitude from Sadie, closely followed by a telltale pinkening of her cheeks as she looked away.

"Yes, of course," she said. "Sorry, I hadn't thought far enough ahead to wonder about the sleeping arrangements." She turned to Eli and Penny. "I'll show you the way and we can all get freshened up before we say hi to Inez."

Griff laughed. "She's been cooking all morning. Think I saw some of her special pot roast and smothered potatoes on the stove."

"Ummm—my mouth is watering already." Sadie placed her hand at Penny's back. "Come along, you two, our rooms are this way."

Eli waited in the room Sadie had pointed out to him while she got Penny settled in. It was spacious, with a large bed, a large armoire, a chest, a dressing table and several chairs scattered about. A folding screen discreetly guarded one corner of the room and a hat stand and bootjack sat in another.

He'd just picked up the picture of a lovely woman that sat on a bedside table when Sadie walked in.

"That's my mother." She crossed the room and touched the frame. "Dad never quite got over her loss."

"You look a bit like her."

She shook her head, then dropped her hands. "I'm sorry about the room assignments. It never occurred to me—"

"No need to apologize. I should have thought ahead, as well. But it's just for a few nights." He could tell she was still agitated. "I'm sorry if this makes you uncomfortable. I promise to be a gentleman. But we can make an excuse for you to sleep with Penny, if you prefer."

"No. I'll be fine."

Her answer pleased him. Not only had he not been looking forward to facing Griff's inquisitive looks if they asked to sleep apart, but he didn't like to think that she feared him, or worse, was repulsed by the idea of them sharing a room.

In fact, this might be just the thing to ease her into the idea of sharing a room with him permanently.

Several minutes later, as they headed down the stairs with Penny between them, Eli took the opportunity to look around. He'd been too focused on what she might be feeling earlier to focus on anything else. And surprisingly there were more than a few touches of elegance amongst the expected rustic trappings. The first thing he noticed was the intricate stained glass window, a match for anything he'd seen in the grand estates of Almega, that let colorful patches of sunlight into the landing.

A fine crystal chandelier graced the front entryway.

Of course, just below it was a plain braided rug covering a large area of the polished oak floors.

Still, the juxtaposition of the elegant and the rustic seemed to create a comfortable, inviting environment.

When they reached the bottom of the stairs, Sadie waved a hand to her right. "We better step into the kitchen and tell Inez hello or I'll never hear the end of it."

The kitchen was a large open room with lots of windows and counter space. Not only did they find Inez there, but Griff as well, munching on a piece of pecan pie.

Inez immediately set down her rolling pin, wiped her hands on her apron and bustled over to greet them. After welcoming Eli with a smile and Sadie with a hug, she turned her full attention to Penny. "My goodness, don't you just look sweeter than molasses in sugar."

Penny grinned. "You talk just like Sadie."

"Well I should think so," Inez answered. "I practically raised the gal."

After Inez had plied them with cookies, Sadie led them away, proclaiming it was her turn to play tour guide.

As she led them from room to room, Eli again noted the little touches of refinement and sophistication mixed in with the more functional items.

When they reached the sitting room, he was struck by the subtle elegance of the furnishings.

"This was my mother's special place," Sadie said. "I can see her in just about every piece in here." Sadie moved to a colorful globe that was stuck over in a corner of the room. "Her father gave her this as a wedding present when she left Philadelphia. He told her he wanted to make sure she knew how to find her way back home if she ever tired of married life out in this 'uncivilized territory.'" Sadie gave the globe a dismissive spin. "I never saw her look at the thing, even when she told me that story."

"But she brought some of her former home with her, didn't she?" Eli asked. "I mean I see touches that could only have come from New England or abroad."

Sadie laughed. "Oh yes. Mother always liked to surround herself with pretty things. But she wasn't obsessive about it. She always said she held to the notion that beauty was in the eye of the beholder. She was just as pleased with a drawing one of us kids did for her as she was with an expensive painting." She pointed to a crude drawing of a horse that had been framed and prominently displayed on a sofa table. "See here? Ry drew this and gave it to her one year for her birthday. Even when he got older and was embarrassed by it and wanted her to hide it away, she refused. Said it was her favorite piece."

So, she got her sentimental streak from her mother.

"My father's taste was quite different," she continued. "But he always tried to get her pretty things to make her smile."

"Like the blue bowls," Penny said.

Sadie gave her a quick smile. "That's right."

"Can we see the rest of them?" Penny asked.

She took Penny's hand. "Of course. Come on, they're in the parlor."

Eli was left to follow behind them.

Sadie crossed the room and pointed to a glass-fronted curio cabinet that reached nearly to the ceiling. "Here they are."

Eli found himself staring at a dozen or so bowls, the exact same shade of blue as the ones Sadie had had delivered to Knotty Pine. Why these bowls? Why not the beautiful crystal bowl or china vase he could see displayed elsewhere in the room.

"One rose, two petunias, four calla lilies…" Penny called out the design on each of the bowls.

Was there some significance he was missing here?

Griff joined them just then. "Ah, showing off the infamous anniversary bowls, I see."

"Anniversary bowls?" Eli repeated.

"Don't tell me Sadie never told you the story?"

Eli glanced Sadie's way. "No."

Griff laughed. "I'll let Sadie tell it to you when she's ready. She does a much better job of it than I do."

Penny tugged on Sadie's skirt. "Can I play on your swing now?"

"Of course you can, princess." Sadie glanced up at her brother. "And I'll just bet your Uncle Griff would be glad to give you the same big old pushes he used to give me."

Griff shot her a puzzled look before he turned to Penny. "Come on, buttercup, let's let these two sit here all lazy-like while we see if that old swing still works."

Taking hold of Griff's outstretched hand, she let him lead her from the room, Skeeter at their heels.

As soon as they were gone, Sadie turned and Eli braced himself for the question he knew was coming.

"Who is Susan?"

Chapter Fifteen

Sadie saw the slight tensing of his jaw, saw the shadow of grief and something else darken his eyes.

"Susan was our sister," he answered

Was? Her heart immediately went out to both him and Penny. "Oh Eli, I'm so sorry. What happened to her?"

"My father married Adelle, my stepmother, when I was seventeen. Adelle was a widow and already had one daughter at the time—Susan. Penny came along a few years later."

So he'd had a stepsister and a half-sister. Yet she could tell he'd loved them both.

He raked a hand through his hair. "Father passed away six years ago. I had already moved out by then—I inherited a house in town from my maternal grandparents that suited my needs much better than my father's country estate. While my stepmother relied on me to take care of her financial affairs after she was again widowed, she and my sisters spent most of their time at Amberleigh, and I stayed close to my business interests in the city. Then Adelle passed on several months ago and I suddenly found myself the guardian of two girls, my own sisters, whom I hardly knew at all."

She could imagine how that must have thrown his orderly world upside down.

"Susan was fifteen at the time," he said, "and Penny had just turned nine. I hired a well-recommended nanny and moved them all into my house, turning the third floor entirely over to them."

His jaw tightened. "Adelle had mentioned to me once that Susan had been found walking in her sleep on a few occasions, so I asked the nanny to be particularly watchful. And I checked on her in the evenings before I turned in, as well. There was no sign that she'd resumed her sleepwalking."

He was silent for so long that Sadie wondered if he had decided not to finish. Then he inhaled deeply. "I came home from a late meeting one evening about ten weeks ago and found Susan's body on the flagstone terrace, just below her third story window."

Sadie's hand flew to her throat. "Oh, how awful! But, Eli, please don't tell me you blame yourself. I'm sure you took every reasonable precaution."

She saw his hands fist at his sides. "She was my responsibility. And I let her down." His voice was tight, almost raw. "I don't intend to make the same mistake with Penny."

"Of course you won't." This explained so much about him, about his drive to find a suitable wife, about his inordinate concern over her and Penny's welfare.

"Penny had nightmares for weeks afterwards," he added. "But once we moved here, and she was able to put some distance between herself and all the reminders, she seemed ready to move on."

"Poor little sweetheart. To lose so many loved ones at such a young age—it's amazing she's come through it all with such a sunny disposition. She's lucky to have a brother like you."

"That's a matter of perspective."

"I won't let you talk about yourself like that."

That earned her a startled glance, then he gave a crooked smile. "Loyal and forthright as always."

Sadie placed her hand on his arm. "I promise you I will help you protect and cherish Penny," she said fiercely. "And ask the Good Lord to help us to know how best to guide her." She gave his arm a light squeeze. "Thank you for sharing that with me. I know it wasn't easy. But now you have someone to share that burden with."

He looked slightly uncomfortable. Was it her praise or her offer to share his burden that bothered him?

"Speaking of Penny," he said, obviously ready to change the subject, "perhaps we should see how she's doing."

"Don't worry, she's in good hands with Griff. But come on, I'm ready to get outside, too."

As they stepped outside, Sadie offered up a silent prayer. *I know why You put me in this position now, Lord. They're both hurting and grieving, and I'll do everything I can, everything You show me to do, to help them heal.*

When Griff caught sight of them, he stopped pushing and the swing gradually slowed to a stop.

"Hey you two," Sadie called out, "we're headed out to the stable to take a look at the horses. Want to come along or are you having too much fun?"

"Can we go for a ride?" Penny asked.

"Not today. We've been traveling all day and I'm ready to just relax for now. But tomorrow I can show y'all around the place all good and proper."

"The fishing hole and the lightning tree and the new barn."

Sadie laughed. "All of it."

Griff shook his head. "Sounds like someone has been spinning stories again."

"Sadie tells the best stories ever." Penny's tone dared anyone to dispute her statement.

"That she does, buttercup. Been doing it almost since the day she started talking. Hadn't been able to shush her since."

"Is that so, Mr. Too-Big-for-his-Britches Lassiter?"

Griff raised his hands in surrender. "Hey, I was just stating facts. I never said it was a bad thing."

He turned to Penny. "Someday you need to get my little sister to tell you the story about how Ry and I tricked her into sitting smack dab in the middle of a mud hole."

Penny immediately turned to Sadie and clamored for the story.

"Come along," Sadie said with a martyred sigh, "I'll tell you about my dastardly brothers while we walk to the stable."

That evening, Sadie didn't intend to linger long over the nightly ritual of hearing Penny's prayers and then tucking her in. Eli had diplomatically let her know that he would wait a bit to follow her upstairs. She just wasn't certain how long "a bit" was. But Penny was full of talk about the new experiences and it was several minutes before her yawns finally overcame her chatter.

Sadie made quick work of changing into her bed-clothes, but she was still at her mother's dressing table, pulling a brush through her hair, when a soft knock signaled Eli's presence. Fighting the urge to scamper across the room and dive under the shelter of the bedcovers, Sadie took a deep breath. "Come in."

Eli opened the door and stopped in his tracks. Rather than lying under the covers, his wife sat there, robed in a dark green dressing gown, brushing her hair. And what hair! For all that they had been married two weeks now, this was the first time he'd seen it down.

She looked softer this way, more feminine. Not like a child—no, not at all. Like a woman, a gentle, beautiful woman. His wife.

But he'd promised her he wouldn't make this uncomfortable for her. "I'm sorry. If you need more time I can—"

"No, don't be silly. I'll be done in a minute."

He sat in a chair by the window and began pulling off his boots. But he couldn't take his eyes from her. He was mesmerized by the rhythmic motion of her hairbrush as it slid through her hair, by the way the auburn tresses shimmered in the glow of the lamplight, by the fluid motion of her free hand as it separated the locks and held them away from her head for the brush to caress.

What would it be like to take the brush from her hand and perform that service himself? To bury his face in the silky tresses? To— With a mental oath he forced himself to look away.

When he heard her set the brush down, he looked back up, just in time to see her rise. Her hair was braided now and his fingers itched to set it free again. Then he noticed the color in her cheeks. Was she merely embarrassed at the thought that they would share a room tonight or was she worried that he would break his word? That thought splashed cold water on his runaway imagination.

She waved a hand toward the large folding screen that

guarded one corner of the room. "There's clean cloths on the stand and fresh water in the ewer." Her hand fluttered in an uncharacteristically nervous gesture. "If you should need anything else—"

"I'll be fine.

She nodded and turned down the bedcovers. He deliberately turned his back before she could shrug out of her robe.

When he stepped from behind the screen he found her under the covers but still wide awake. His nightshirt should be enough to keep from embarrassing her, but still, crossing the room under her silent scrutiny was almost his undoing. He might be a gentleman, but he was also a man. And the woman in that bed was his wife.

But how could he know if she was ready? If only she would give him the least little sign—

Then he remembered that this was her parents' bed. And her brother was sleeping right down the hall. This was perhaps not the best time to try to woo his wife.

He turned down the one lamp in the room she'd left lit, then slid into bed, careful not to do anything to alarm her. As he let his eyes grow accustomed to the dark, he could hear her breathing, could tell she was trying to regulate it and was failing. And the sudden overwhelming urge to protect her, to put her fears at rest, swept over him and overtook his other, less altruistic urges.

"Good night, Sadie," he said softly. Then he rolled over, turning his back not so much on her as on his own desires.

Sadie stared at Eli's back. She'd thought for sure tonight he would make her fully his wife. She'd saw the look in his eye when he first walked in and spotted her at the dressing table. She'd watched surreptitiously in the mirror as he'd stared at her brushing her hair. There'd been something there, something that called to her in a visceral way.

She'd been tingling with anticipation, wondering what it would be like, remembering what Cora Beth had said *"...it's a beautiful, loving act, meant to draw two people who care for each other even closer together and prepare them to create and nourish the family God meant for them to have."* Those words had painted such a deeply touching image, had planted the seed of want inside her, that Sadie found herself yearning to experience it, to become truly one with her husband.

Why didn't he seem to want that as well?

Chapter Sixteen

By the time Eli reached the dining room for breakfast the next morning, Sadie and Penny were already seated and attacking their plates. He hadn't slept well last night, lying awake long after Sadie's breathing evened into the steady rhythm of sleep, and when he had finally dozed off he'd woken twice when his sleeping wife rolled over against him. He wasn't certain he could take another night of such sweet torture.

His mood hadn't improved any when he woke to discover Sadie already up and gone from their room. Apparently *she* hadn't had any trouble sleeping. He should have been pleased to know she trusted him so fully, but somehow that hadn't been his primary emotion.

Sadie looked up and saw him just then. "Good morning, sleepyhead."

Penny gave him a worried look. "I told Sadie you must be ill because you *never* sleep this late but she said you were probably just tired because you always work so hard."

The door opened and Inez stepped through with a plate piled high with eggs, biscuits and steak. "Hope you woke up hungry."

"I'm fine," Eli addressed Penny's fears first as he took his place across from Sadie. Then he smiled up at Inez. "Thank you, it smells delicious."

"Griff is already out checking on the herd." Sadie slathered jelly on her biscuit. "Said for us to entertain ourselves today and he'll see us this afternoon." She plopped the two halves of her biscuit together. "I thought this morning might be a good time for us to ride out over the place and let me show you some of my favorite spots."

"Can I ride my own horse?" Penny asked.

Eli was pleased to see Sadie looked to him to answer Penny's question. "You've been coming along really well, but riding across an open field is a bit trickier than riding in a paddock or on a hard-packed road."

Penny's face fell.

"But," he continued, "if Sadie can find us an easy-tempered horse and we take it nice and slow, I might see my way toward allowing it."

His sister's expression immediately brightened, as did Sadie's.

"Oh, please say you have an easy-tempered horse, Sadie."

"I know just the one. Buttermilk is as gentle as they come."

"Can we go now?"

Sadie laughed one of those infectious laughs he was learning to appreciate. "Let's give your brother a chance to eat his breakfast first, what do you say?"

"And here's the pond I told you about."

Eli studied Sadie's happy smile. It was obvious how much she loved this place. Did she resent that he'd been the cause of her having to leave it?

"It's so big." Penny turned to him. "This is where Sadie's father taught her how to fish, and where her brother Ry taught her how to swim and where her brother Griff taught her how to skip stones."

It seemed Sadie had shared a lot of her history with his sister that she hadn't with him. But then again, he'd never shown any interest in hearing about it. "Sounds like a special spot."

"Sadie has lots of stories about this place." Penny sat up taller. "Like the time she pushed her brother in because he was teasing her about getting mud in her hair. And—"

Sadie laughed. "I'm sure your brother isn't interested in those stories right now." She prepared to dismount. "Why don't we let the horses drink and graze a bit while we get down and try some of that lunch Inez packed for us?"

Eli quickly dismounted as well and went to help Penny down. It was amazing how quickly she'd taken to riding horseback. He suspected part of it was because she wanted to emulate Sadie.

"This place is ever so much bigger than Amberleigh."

"That it is."

Sadie had taken them over acres and acres of open land earlier. At one point they'd topped a rise and were able to see a large herd of cattle contentedly grazing some distance away. "That's the main herd. Griff is over a bit east of here, culling out some of the young bulls."

She'd taken them to a large structure she called the north barn, which she proudly declared Griff had designed himself and gone into detail about just why his design was so superior to others. In fact, everywhere they went she had personal anecdotes to relate. She told

how the charred tree they'd passed about thirty minutes
ago had been struck by lightning just one day after she'd
picnicked in that very spot. And how the creek they were
crossing had flooded one spring and washed out a long
string of fences. And so many more tales, all of them
told with her signature humor and vividness.

"Well looky here." Sadie had already spread the
picnic blanket and was on her knees digging through
the sack of food Inez had provided. "We're in for a real
treat. Inez packed us up some of her best-you-ever-tasted
fried chicken and biscuits. Looks like there's some of her
pecan cookies, too." She glanced up at them. "Anybody
hungry besides me?"

"I am." Penny plopped down on the blanket beside
Sadie.

Thirty minutes later Penny was off gathering flowers
to braid into a crown and Sadie sat with her arms propped
behind her, staring dreamily at nothing in particular.

Eli settled down beside her. "I can see how much you
love this place."

She gave him a curious look, then smiled. "Of course
I do. It's where I grew up. Don't you feel the same about
Amberleigh?"

He shrugged. "I suppose, but perhaps not as intensely."
He doubted he felt *anything* as intensely as Sadie. "Just
like I liked my house in the city and I like my—our—
new home in Knotty Pine. They are merely places and
are what you make of them."

She slowly nodded. "In a way I suppose that is true.
Because when it comes down to it, it's the memories
you have about something that make it feel special. So
much of a person's childhood is filled with wonder and
discovery and the feeling that we are safe and so can be

as adventurous as we like. And where you grow up is all tied up in those feelings."

Is that what her childhood had been like? He reached over and pulled a leaf from her hair.

Before he could coax her into saying more, Penny was back.

Sadie sat up straighter. "What a lovely crown you're wearing. You look just like a woodland princess."

Her praise made Penny laugh and preen a bit. "Can you teach me to skip a stone across the pond?"

To his surprise, she didn't jump right up. "Why don't you ask your brother if he will?" she said instead.

Penny turned to Eli uncertainly. "Do you know how to skip stones?"

Unaccountably pleased to be asked, Eli stood. "I most certainly do. I'll have you know I once had a stone skip five times before it sunk."

Penny's eyes widened. "You did?"

"Come along young lady, and I'll see if I still have it in me."

Eli sat in the backseat of the buggy next to Sadie while Penny sat up front with Griff. They were headed to Sunday morning service, at a church that was apparently some distance away from the ranch. While Penny chattered on to her captive listener, Eli tried not to let himself fall asleep in the morning sunshine.

Last night he'd waited over an hour after Sadie went up to bed before joining her. Her soft breathing when he entered the room had let him know she was sleeping and he'd gone to great pains to make certain he didn't wake her up. Unfortunately, while she slept, he hadn't gotten much sleep at all. Good thing there was just one more night of this. Perhaps, once they returned to Knotty Pine where he wasn't so conscious of being in her parents' room and of her older brother sleeping—or not—right down the hall, he could talk to her about—

"We're here!"

Eli peered across the way at the whitewashed country church which, he'd learned, was built on a small corner of Lassiter property. There were an amazing number of wagons and horses tethered nearby and the churchyard seemed to be filled with simply-dressed folks mingling and visiting with each other. He imagined in rural communities such as this the Sunday service was the one time of the week when neighbors saw each other.

As soon as she dismounted, Sadie was surrounded by the folks there, all welcoming her back and wanting to congratulate her on her wedding. The women oohed and aahed over her ring and made a fuss over her new status. The single men all proclaimed themselves to have had their hopes dashed and their hearts broken, and the others just generally welcomed her home.

In short order Eli and Penny were pulled into the crowd, as well. Penny, who shyly clung to Sadie's skirts, was fussed over. Eli received a number of slaps on the back and congratulatory comments for his good fortune in marrying Sadie.

Watching her amongst her friends and neighbors, Eli was struck again by how much she'd given up to become his wife. Here, among these people, she was obviously well loved. Her family was both prominent and respected. In Knotty Pine she'd had to start over, to try to build relationships with people she barely knew. Building a new life there had been his choice, but not hers. No wonder she'd held out so long.

If he were to return to Almega tomorrow would there be anyone to make a fuss over him this way? He sincerely doubted it.

As they entered the church Sadie paused to greet an elderly, bespectacled gentleman. "Reverend Martin, it's so good to see you again."

The man took both her hands in his own. "And you too, Sadie my dear. I hear felicitations are in order."

"Thank you. Let me introduce you to my new family." She placed a hand on Penny's shoulder. "This is Penny, my pretty new sister."

"Hi there little lady, welcome to Everlasting Love Church."

"Thank you very much, sir."

"And this is my husband, Eli Reynolds."

Eli took the minister's hand and found his grip surprisingly strong.

"It's an honor to meet the man who claimed our Sadie's heart."

Eli mentally winced at the reverend's turn of phrase. Claiming Sadie's heart was not something he could boast of having achieved. "A pleasure to meet you as well, Reverend."

He cast Eli a severe look over the top of his spectacles. "Young man, I hope you know what a treasure has been given into your keeping."

Sadie rescued him from having to answer. "Goodness gracious, Reverend Martin, enough of that. You're going to embarrass me." She linked her arm through Eli's and took Penny's hand. "Now, we are going to find our pew. I look forward to hearing another of your rousing sermons."

Eli could hear the man of the cloth chuckling behind them as they walked up the aisle.

* * *

By Monday evening they were back home in Knotty Pine. And to Sadie's surprise, it did indeed feel like coming home. Amazing how quickly a place could grow on a person. She suspected, though, in spite of what she'd said to Eli, that it had more to do with the people in a place than the place itself.

She had enjoyed her trip back to Hawk's Creek though. Showing Eli and Penny around had been fun, but more than that, it had been a chance to say a proper good-bye to her childhood home, the chance she hadn't had before her wedding.

That chapter of her life was closed now, and she was looking forward to seeing what this new chapter held for her.

Eli knocked on the door of the sitting room and stepped inside to find Sadie at her writing desk. "Am I interrupting?"

"Not at all. I'm ready for a little break."

"Where's Penny?"

"We just came in from making sure Buttermilk was settled in nicely."

Griff had given the horse to Penny, saying it was a welcome-to-the-Lassiter-family gift and that she'd spoiled the horse for other riders anyway. Penny had been thrilled to finally have her very own mount. However Eli wasn't quite sure how he felt about it yet. But he couldn't bring himself to say no.

"She's in the kitchen with Mrs. Dauber now," Sadie continued. "Trying to talk her into making a cherry cobbler for supper I believe."

Good. It would give him a chance to speak to Sadie alone. He crossed the room until he was standing nose to toe with the head of the bearskin rug. He still couldn't figure out what she saw in the thing, but he was ready to find out. If he'd learned anything the past few days it was that Sadie usually had a reason for the things she did. And most of the time, it was a very good reason. "Penny tells me these pieces you had shipped here from Hawk's Creek are what you call story pieces."

She gave him a startled look. "They are."

"I imagine the story that goes with this rug is a good one."

"It is."

For a normally chatty person she was being frustratingly terse at the moment. "Mind sharing it with me?"

She stood and crossed the room to stand beside him. "Well, the rug itself is from the pelt of a bear killed by my grandfather. He shot the critter when it was trying to make dinner out of one of his prize cows. But that's not the reason it's special to me." She stooped down and softly stroked the fur. "When I was little, this rug lay on the floor of my father's study. One of my earliest memories is of my mother laying on the floor beside me on this very rug, next to the fireplace, reading from a book."

She straightened. "It was just her and me and I can still remember the sound of her voice though I don't remember the words. And I can picture the dress she was wearing that day just as clear as if it were here in front of me. It was lavender with little yellow flowers and had a narrow ribbon of lace all around the bodice. And I remember feeling that I had the most wonderful mother in the world."

She smiled self-consciously. "Of course, I'm sure every child feels that way about her mother. It's just that the memory is so clear and perfect, and every time I see that rug, I get a little bit of that feeling back."

Definitely a strong sentimental attachment, especially if it could evoke such emotions. Did all her pieces have strong emotions tied to them? "And this picture?" he asked, waving to the framed watercolor above the mantel. "I can see now that it's a depiction of Hawk's Creek. Did you know the artist?"

She nodded. "My mother painted it. She wasn't very happy with the way it turned out but Pa insisted on hanging it in his study. Said he'd rather have something she'd created than anything he could find in a museum. Mother pouted a bit that he wouldn't let her burn it like she wanted, but just to tease him. She then said she'd let him keep it only if he made something for her." She pointed to the chess set. "That's why he carved that chess set, as a gift to her." She sighed. "They were so in love."

It seems that the romantic streak in her went deeper than he'd imagined. And that she came by it honestly.

"How about that table over there?" He figured it was a safe guess that the cracked and badly-repaired leg was going to be part of its "story."

She eyed him suspiciously. "Now you're just being nice."

He grinned. "And is that such a novel idea?"

She tossed her head. "At times like this it is. But if you really want to hear the story…"

He followed as she drifted closer to the table.

"Do you see that broken place on one of the legs?" she asked.

He felt a smug satisfaction that he'd guessed correctly.

"It happened one rainy day when I was six years old," she continued. "The weather was near as bad as that storm you and I got caught out in, and Ry, Griff and I were playing tag in the house—something we weren't supposed to be doing. We ended up knocking over that table and busting the leg. The three of us found some nails and tried to fix it ourselves—or at least my brothers did while they set me to be the lookout. Of course Pa noticed it right off and we had to come clean. We were given extra chores for a week."

"And that's a *good* memory?"

Her smile turned wistful. "The three of us were having a good time up until the accident. My brothers were even treating me as if I wouldn't break if I got rowdy right along with them." She traced the edge of the table with a finger. "It's the last clear memory I have of the three of us being so carefree before Mother passed. Then afterwards, Ry went off to visit Grandfather in Philadelphia and the three musketeers were never quite the same."

Eli touched her arm in sympathy. "I'm sorry."

She refocused on him. "Thanks. But it's okay to sometimes remember the sad things in our past as well as the happy. Gives us perspective."

Always reaching for the silver lining. "You know, if you wanted to move one or two of these pieces into other parts of the house, like the parlor or library, that would be all right with me."

"Thank you, but I think I like them all together this way." She gave him a sassy look. "But that doesn't mean I won't pick up new things from time to time to brighten those other rooms." Her smile softened. "I'm ready to make some new memories."

Eli bolted straight up in bed, awakened by the sound of terror-filled cries. Penny! Her nightmares must have returned.

Within seconds he was tearing down the hall headed for his sister's room. He'd nearly passed Sadie's door when he realized the cries were coming from her, not Penny. He threw open her door to find her buried under her bedcovers, flailing in an attempt to find her way out, crying about not being able to breathe. He rushed to her side, trying to talk to her, to reassure her that he would help her, but he couldn't seem to get through her hysteria and the more she flailed the more tangled she became. It was several eternal seconds later before he finally freed her and she fell against his chest, sobbing. He held her close, rocking her and making soothing sounds, the way he'd done with his sister so many times before. But this did *not* feel like his sister.

"What's the matter with Sadie?" Penny's fear-shaken voice came from just inside the doorway.

Sadie still clung to him as if he were a lifeline and her whole body trembled with alarming force, but Eli tried to keep his voice calm and reassuring. "She's just had a bad dream." At least he devoutly hoped that's all it was.

"Is she going to be okay?"

Both of his girls needed him. Sadie was still trembling, but not so violently now, and her breathing had eased somewhat. He loosened his hold just enough to motion Penny forward.

She ran into the room as if afraid he'd change his mind and stood beside the bed staring at the two of them with wide, frightened eyes.

He took one of her hands. "Do you remember those bad dreams you used to have?"

She nodded.

"It was scary and very upsetting, but afterwards, when

you woke up and realized it was all a dream, you were okay, weren't you?"

She nodded. "Because you stayed with me and made me feel better."

His heart hitched at her trust in him. "And just like with you, Sadie will be okay soon, too. She just needs a few minutes to let the dream fade."

He felt Sadie take a deep shuddering breath, then she pushed back enough to meet Penny's gaze. Even in the shadowy room he could see the effort she made to pull herself together. "I'm so sorry I woke you up, princess. But I'm okay now." Her voice was husky, but she managed to smile.

"Do you want me to stay with you?" The little girl still wore a worried frown.

Sadie managed another smile at that. "That's very sweet of you, but I'm fine, truly."

Eli squeezed his sister's hand. "Don't worry, I'll stay with her until she falls back asleep. Just like I did for you. Okay?"

Penny nodded. "Okay." She turned to Sadie. "Eli helps keep the bad dreams away."

"I'm sure he does."

Once they heard Penny's door close again, Eli pulled Sadie's cheek back against his chest. He brushed the hair from her damp forehead and then rested his chin on her head. "Would you like to tell me about it?"

She shook her head. "It's nothing really. Just a bad dream."

"It didn't sound like nothing. It sounded like you were terrified of something." He couldn't imagine what it would take to make his brave spitfire react with such terror. "It might make it less overwhelming if you talk about it."

She picked at her sleeve. "I guess I got tangled under the covers somehow while I was sleeping. That must be what brought it on."

He held his peace, hoping she'd say more.

"It's just that, I can't bear to be in a crowded, dark, enclosed space."

He gave her shoulders a squeeze. "Most folks would feel the same."

She shook her head. "You don't understand. Whenever it happens, I panic and succumb to all-out, screaming, crying, uncontrollable hysteria. It's all so silly and embarrassing, but I can't seem to control it."

Again he brushed the hair from her face, trying to calm her with his touch. "Some things we just can't control."

"The first time it happened was when I was six years old. Inez asked me to fetch her something out of the root cellar. I didn't really want to go, the root cellar always made me uncomfortable, but Griff and Ry had refused to let me join them in one of their games earlier, claiming I was too little, and I wasn't about to admit that I was scared."

So she'd been defiant even at six.

"Anyway, somehow the door shut behind me and I couldn't get out. The fall crops had just come in so the root cellar was full—someone had stacked the potatoes so high they blocked the one window so it was pitch-black. I suddenly felt as if the walls were closing in on me and that I couldn't breathe—almost like being buried alive. I don't think I was down there very long but by the time someone found me I was screaming and sobbing hysterically."

She shuddered. "Ever since then, I have to force myself just to go into a pantry or small storeroom, and I always double-check that I can't get locked in." She gave a self-conscious laugh. "I told you—silly. A grown woman, panicking at being trapped under her bedcovers."

"No more silly than a grown man twisting his ankle trying to scramble away from a harmless king snake."

"That was different."

"No, it wasn't and I only wish I'd had the courage to be as honest about it at the time as you are tonight."

She gave him a trembly smile. "Thank you for trying to salve my pride. You, Eli Reynolds, are a very kind man."

He reached up and with one of his thumbs wiped a tear from her cheek. "No, I'm not," he said softly. "But you make me want to be."

Surprise and then something else warmed her eyes. Her lips curled into a soft smile and her eyes closed as she turned her face into his hand.

The gesture was so tender, so trusting, that almost before he realized what he was doing, Eli had lowered his lips to hers.

He'd wanted to do this ever since that first kiss they'd exchanged to seal their vows. She was so sweet, so soft, so giving—he wanted to protect her from nightmares and from dark places and from hurtful things. He wanted to always be the one she turned to, whatever her need.

She seemed ready to return his fervor. The tension eased from her muscles and she seemed to melt against him. Her hand reached up to stroke his cheek. And her kiss tasted of sweetness and trust and joy.

When he finally broke it off, Eli drew her head gently against his chest and stroked his hand across her head while he tried to get his own suddenly ragged breathing back under control. Her nightmare struggles had partially loosened her braid and he decided to finish the job. Using his fingers to comb through the tangles, he watched the tresses tumble free.

"Eli?"

Her soft question echoed pleasantly against his chest. "Yes?"

"Do you love me?"

His hand stilled. It seemed she still clung to those romantic notions of hers. Love was the stuff of make-believe and fairy tales, an ideal that was mostly unattainable. "You are very dear to me, Sadie," he said carefully. "I admire you a great deal. And I would protect you with my own life if need be."

"I see." She drew back, her expression reflecting disappointment and brittle dignity. She folded her hands in her lap and met his gaze head-on. "Thank you for being so kind and patient with me tonight. I'm sorry I woke you and that I upset Penny." She attempted a smile. "I think I'll be able to sleep now."

She was dismissing him? Didn't she realize that he was offering her something much more substantial than some fleeting emotion? But she sat there, composed and utterly determined.

He stood. "Then I will wish you a good night." He almost reached a hand out to brush her cheek but stopped himself just in time. With a nod, he turned and took a seat in a chair across the room.

She frowned. "That's not necessary. There won't be a repeat of my nightmare, I assure you."

He crossed his legs. "I told Penny I'd stay with you until you fell asleep. I pride myself on being a man of my word."

She stared at him for a long minute, then finally nodded. Carefully folding the covers back, she lay down on top of them and curled on her side with her back to him.

There was something almost forlorn about the way she lay there, something that made him ache to comfort her, to promise her whatever it was she needed.

But she'd asked for the one thing he wasn't able to give her.

It was a long time before he heard her breath even out into a sleeper's rhythm, saw her form relax into the numbness of sleep. Still he stayed there, watching her. Longing to hold her.

He could almost wish he shared that special relationship she seemed to have with their Maker. Maybe if he did, he could ask God to give him some insights how to win her back.

Because something told him he was not going to be able to accomplish it on his own.

Chapter Seventeen

When Sadie woke the next morning she knew even before she opened her eyes that Eli was no longer in her room. She'd felt his presence last night, strong and brooding, until she'd finally fallen asleep. And while she'd lain there, there'd been something comforting in his presence as well, a sense that no harm could get to her with him standing guard.

Why had she spoiled the mood with her question? After that achingly sweet, utterly wonderful kiss. And he'd been so kind to her, so gentle and understanding about her irrational fears. She'd felt safe and secure in his arms, as if nothing bad could reach her there. And more than that, she'd felt *cherished,* had felt as if she'd finally found where she was meant to be. Why couldn't she just be satisfied with that?

Because she deserved to be loved, that's why. The way her parents had loved each other. The way Ry and Josie obviously loved each other.

But more than even that, Eli had to learn how to express love. If not to her, than to Penny. He felt it, she was certain of it. He just hadn't learned how to show it yet.

Heavenly Father, please don't let me make a mess of this. For Eli's and Penny's sakes, let me help him find his way.

Before she could get out of bed, her door inched open and Penny stuck her head inside. "Good morning." It was more of a question than a statement.

Sadie sat up and gave Penny her brightest smile. "Good morning, princess. Sleep well? After I woke you, I mean."

Penny nodded. "How are you feeling?"

Sadie patted the bed and Penny rushed over and scrambled up bedside her. "I'm feeling just fine. I'm so sorry if I scared you last night."

"That's okay. I get bad dreams sometimes, too."

Sadie pulled the girl against her and stroked her hair. "They're not very fun, are they?"

Penny shook her head. "Did Eli hold your hand and make you feel not so scared?"

"He did."

"And stay with you until you fell asleep?"

"Uh-huh. And I didn't have any other bad dreams the rest of the night."

Penny nodded in satisfaction. "That's what he always did for me too. Sometimes he was still there when I woke up the next morning."

Not so with her. But what did she expect, after the way she'd pushed him away last night. "We're very lucky to have your brother to look out for us. He does a very good job of keeping us safe." She gave the girl one last squeeze, then straightened.

Her stomach rumbled and Penny giggled.

"You think that's funny, do you?" Sadie asked with mock-sternness. "I'll have you know bad dreams at night always make me hungry in the morning." She grimaced. "Of course good dreams leave me hungry, too."

Penny giggled again and Sadie made a shooing motion with her hand. "Now scoot. I'm hungrier than a plow horse after a long day in the field. Time for me to get up and get dressed. And after breakfast we can plan what we're going to do today while Eli is at work."

"Okay." Penny gave Sadie an impulsive hug around the neck, then scooted off the bed and crossed the room with much lighter steps than she'd had when she entered.

There was one Reynolds, at least, who didn't have trouble expressing love.

When Sadie came downstairs, Eli was already finished with his breakfast and preparing to leave.

Was something wrong? "I hadn't realized I was so late."

"You're not. I just decided to go to the bank a bit early this morning. I'm sure there are several matters requiring my attention since I've been away for a couple of days."

Was that really the case or was he running away from her? "Of course. We'll see you at lunch then."

He shook his head. "Probably not. I had Mrs. Dauber fix me something to take with me."

"I see." She forced a smile. "Then we'll see you this afternoon."

As he shrugged into his coat, she remembered how her father and mother had never parted without a quick peck-of-a-kiss good-bye. What would Eli think if she initiated the same practice?

Only one way to find out. Impulsively she stepped forward. "Eli?"

"Yes?"

She reached up to straighten his collar. "There, that's better." Then, before her courage could abandon her altogether, she placed a hand on his chest, popped up on her very tippy-toes and gave him a quick peck on the side of his chin, which was the best she could do given the difference in their heights. Then she stepped back and smiled, pretending she didn't see his startled expression. "Don't work too hard."

Eli strolled down the sidewalk, ignoring the urge to reach up and stroke the spot that she'd kissed. What was with the woman? Was she deliberately sending him mixed signals? Pushing him away last night after a kiss that he'd considered next to perfect. Then, just when he'd accepted that she wanted nothing to do with him, popping up out of the blue to kiss him good-bye. She couldn't have it both ways. And if she kept trying it would drive him mad.

No, he needed to regain control of the situation. He'd let his emotions get the better of him. But no more. He would speak to her tonight and make certain she understood.

"We went exploring today and found a great spot for a picnic." Penny said to him. "It's a secret place that's not easy to find. We just came on it all accidental-like. Sadie says that's 'cause God wanted to show it to us. Of course it wasn't like the fishing pond at Hawk's Creek but Sadie said it was time to find some new memory places. Oh and you should have seen Skeeter. He chased a rabbit and jumped in the creek and when he ran out he shook himself all over and sprayed my dress and hair. But I didn't mind because it was a hot day and it felt kind of good."

Her chatter seemed to be liberally sprinkled with the phrase "Sadie said." "Sounds like the two of you had quite a day."

"Oh and we saw a possum up in a tree and watched a hawk catch a field mouse. And we even tried to fish with a string and a bent hairpin, just like Annabel Adams."

He stiffened. "Penny, have you been reading that story after I told you not to."

"Yes." Her lip poked out in a pout. "But I don't see why you don't like it."

Eli was well aware of Sadie's presence in the room, but continued to focus on his sister. "I just think there are more uplifting stories for you to focus your mind on. Fairy tales and silly make-believe just fill your head with romantic notions that bear no resemblance to real life." Was Sadie paying attention to what he'd said?

"But it's a fine story, Eli. Annabel Adams is a sure enough heroine." She spun around, looking for support. "Tell him Sadie."

To her credit, Sadie showed no sign of being torn. "I'm sorry, Penny, but Eli is your brother. If he feels this strongly about it, then I'm sure we can find lots of other stories to read that will meet with his approval."

"But if he knew you wrote it—" Penny slapped a hand over her mouth.

Eli went very still. "What's this?"

But Penny was staring at Sadie with wide liquid eyes. "I'm sorry. I didn't mean to tell your secret."

So Sadie had told Penny about being the creator of Annabel Adams. "I thought we had an agreement."

"We did." She held up a hand as he started to say more. "Not now, Eli. Can't you see she's upset?"

She turned back to Penny. "Hush now, princess, it's all right. Eli already knew, so you see you really didn't let the cat out of the bag, after all. And a family shouldn't keep secrets from each other anyway."

Penny spun back around. "You already knew Sadie was Temperance Trulove? Then why are you so against it?"

Eli didn't like the accusatory way his sister was staring at him. "It doesn't matter who writes the stories, Penny. I don't think they are appropriate reading for little girls. Now, I think you should go up to your room while I have a little talk with Sadie."

"Please don't fuss at her, Eli. I won't read about Annabel any more, I promise."

"Penny, please—"

"It's okay, princess. Your brother won't scold, the two of us are just going to have a chat about what is best for you. Because that is what we both really want. You just go on along to your room, and take Skeeter with you."

Penny looked from one to the other of them, then with dragging feet, left the room.

As soon as she was gone, Sadie turned to him. "Eli, I assure you I kept my word. I did *not* tell Penny that I wrote the Annabel Adams story."

He wasn't buying it. "Perhaps not directly, but I can see how it would be tempting to brag a bit. After all the two of you have become quite close and she enjoys the tales. If she somehow saw a bit of your work laying around then you would be free to bask in her praise."

Red flags appeared in each of her cheeks. "How dare you? Do you think I prize my word so little that I would skirt around it in such a way? And for your information, Penny and I have many other activities we can enjoy together. I've no need to seek her praise in this way."

"Whatever the case, by accident or design, it seems you not only let your little secret get out, but the example you've set for her has taken a biddable girl and made her outright rebellious."

Sadie stood and fisted her hands on her hips. "Eli, she's not rebellious. Yes, she has a mind of her own and is learning to express it, but you don't want her to be a silent twit, do you? And she would *never* disobey you or do anything to hurt you, you must know that."

"It's your culpability we're talking about, not Penny's."

"My—" She took a deep breath. "Eli you're acting irrationally and that's not like you. Would you please tell me what it is you find so distasteful about my story?"

"They fill little girls's heads with romantic nonsense. With tails of heroes and heroines, of romantic love and happily ever afters."

"And is that so terrible?"

"You like stories? Let me tell you some. My mother was a romantic. So much so that when it became obvious my father didn't share her tender feelings she let it cripple her emotionally. She took to her bed and became a semi-invalid until the day she died. Her two sisters, Aunt Sophie and Aunt Genevieve, were the same. Aunt Sophie gave up everything to marry a man beneath her station and he ended up abandoning her and leaving her heartbroken. Aunt Genevieve never married because the man she considered her one true love died before they were wed. And Susan—"

He stopped himself before he said too much. "Well at any rate, romantic notions are nothing but trouble and I won't have you filling Penny's head with them. Better that she learn to be sensible, that she look at the world in a rational, no-nonsense manner. That's the way for her to find security and happiness."

Her expression had softened. "Deep, abiding love does

exist, Eli. Not everyone finds it, and I'm sorry for your mother and your aunts. But I saw it in my parents. I see it in Ry and Josie. It's there if you are but brave enough to reach for it."

"I'll thank you not to put such notions in Penny's head." He collected himself. "And now that your secret is out, perhaps it would be best if Temperance Trulove retired."

"I suppose I could write the next story under my real name."

"You know that's not what I meant. And what do you mean—next story?"

"I've already turned in the last installment of Annabel Adams's story. I talked to Mr. Chalmers about starting a new one once that one is out."

"Tell him you've changed your mind."

"But I haven't." She gave him a hard look. "What if I asked you to stop working at the bank because I had an aversion to bankers? Would you do it?"

"That's entirely different. Your writing is merely a hobby. I work at the bank to support our family."

"Poppycock!"

"What?"

"You heard me, Poppycock. Balderdash. Hogwash. Piffle. Horsefeathers. Pick your favorite—they all mean one thing. You don't work at that bank because you need to. You admitted yourself that you're already as rich as Midas. You work at that bank because you want to and because it gives you a sense of purpose. I'm not saying that's a bad thing—after all, they do say idle hands are the devil's workshop—but don't you stand there all righteous and tell me you have to work to support us. And I'm saying that's the same as writing is to me."

"Has nothing I said made an impression on you?"

"*Everything* you said made an impression on me, Eli. You think romantic notions are bad for a girl just because things turned out badly, in your estimation, for your mother and your aunts. And you think my writing my stories is going to fill Penny's head with romantic nonsense and that she'll end up just like they did."

"That's an edited version, but that's the gist of it, yes."

"So you see, I heard you. I just happen to disagree is all." Her expression asked for his understanding. "You can't protect a person from all of life's heartaches no matter how much you might want to. And you sure as springtime can't tell them how to feel and who to love. Childhood is a time for make-believe and daydreams and carefree play—don't take that away from your sister. Penny is a smart girl and she has you and me to guide her along the way, to teach her to turn to God when she has tough decisions to make, and to know that we will always stand behind her, no matter what. That's what's going to shape her life more than anything else. So trust her to make the right choices when the time comes. And trust yourself to know when to let go."

"I'll let go when she is safely married and under her husband's care."

"I know you care for her, Eli, but you've got to do more to show it or she may never realize just how much she means to you."

If Sadie only knew how much he'd done to protect his sister she wouldn't speak to him like that. "Of course I care for her."

"Then show her. Spend time with her. Talk to her. Better yet, listen to her. Let her know the small milestones of her life are important to you, as well. Help her build happy memories that include you."

"Fine words, but you've never had responsibility for a young child before, have you?"

The bitterness in his voice startled Sadie. Was he referring to Susan? Her death had been tragic, but what did it have to do with the matter at hand? "Why, no, I haven't, but surely—"

"Then I will ask you to defer to me in this matter." His expression softened just a bit. "Sadie, I know that you believe all you just said to be true, and for you perhaps it is. But look where your carefree tendencies landed you—compromised and forced into a marriage not of your choosing."

Sadie winced. Is that how he saw her role in this marriage?

"And you're an adult. Yes, when she is grown up she will make her own choices, find a fine young man to marry and I will have to let her go. But in the meantime it's up to me to lay the proper foundation, to protect her from herself if need be, so that she can grow up to be the fine young woman you see in her already."

"But—"

"Penny is my sister and I'm asking you to trust that I know what is best for her."

But did he really? Or was he blinded by his own experiences? "I'll think on what you've said and pray about it."

His fist came down on the arm of his chair. "Hang it all, Sadie! Not every decision requires prayerful consideration. Some are simple enough for us to make on our own."

This time his words shocked her. Did he truly feel that way?

He seemed to collect himself and he raked a hand

through his hair. "I'm sorry, I shouldn't have done that. But this is not some question of what you happen to think might give her fleeting pleasure. I'm looking at the bigger picture."

"I'm sorry, Eli, but I disagree with what you said a moment ago. We should always turn to God to help us make the right choices." She clasped her hands in front of her, as much to keep them from trembling as anything else. "I can see now how strongly you feel about this and I understand how your first thoughts must always be for Penny. But please, understand that I care about her just as much and right now I'm confused. I need time to sort this out to make sure I know what truly is best for her."

He nodded stiffly. "Looks like we are at an impasse. It's time for supper. I'll fetch Penny while you let Mrs. Dauber know we're ready."

After he left, Sadie sat back down, her heart weighing heavily in her chest.

Heavenly Father, every fiber of my being tells me he's wrong, that if he hedges Penny around too tightly he'll lose her. But is my writing the stand I need to take? Or should I let this go and find some other way to help him see the right path?

Supper that evening was a subdued affair. Eli said very little and Penny kept glancing from her to him, as if looking for some sign that things were returning to normal. Sadie did her best to keep the conversation light, talking to Penny about Buttermilk and about Ry and Josie's imminent return when Eli proved uncommunicative.

Later, when it was time to tuck Penny in, she lingered a while, trying to place the little girl more at ease.

When it was finally time to go, Sadie leaned forward and kissed Penny's forehead. "Sweet dreams, princess."

"It's all my fault that Eli's angry."

Sadie took Penny's hand. "It's not anyone's fault and Eli is not angry. We just need to work a few things out between us." She slipped Penny's hand under the covers. "Now, I don't want you to give any more thought to all this folderol. Tomorrow, you and I are going to go to the train station and meet my brother Ry and his wife when they come back from their trip to Egypt. And we're going to listen to them tell us all about the grand adventures they had. Won't that be fun?"

Penny nodded her head.

Sadie tapped her nose. "So make sure you get lots of sleep because you'll want to be wide awake to hear every bit of what they have to say."

With another nod, Penny rolled over on her side and closed her eyes. Sadie watched her for another minute, then made her exit. She stood on the landing, chewing at her lip. What now? It was too early to retire. But she knew Eli was not ready to talk to her yet.

Perhaps she'd find herself something to read. The lamps in the hallway were still lit, which meant Eli was still up. The sliver of light escaping from under his closed study door told her exactly where he was. She paused. Should she go in, try to talk to him again and see if they could work out their differences?

Her shoulders drooped as she turned toward the library. Perhaps it would be best for them to both get a good night's sleep first.

She circled the room, looking at the books, trying to find something to take her mind off the tangle she and Eli had gotten themselves into. She spied an atlas and pulled it down, carrying it to a nearby table. She figured looking up some of the locations Ry and Josie had been to would be a good way to pass the time. It would be good to see Ry again. And since they would be seeing Griff first, he and Josie would already be forewarned about her newly-married status. She was grateful she wouldn't have to deal with that at any rate.

Sadie closed the atlas and returned it to its place on the shelf. Then her eye was caught by an old leather bound volume on a stand in the far corner of the room. Curious, she strolled over and discovered it was a bible. Opening it, she found a family history recorded in the front. The entries ended with Eli's birth. Why wasn't Penny listed? Then she looked more closely at the names and realized it was Eli's maternal ancestry, so Penny would not be part of the line.

She looked at the entry for Eli again and blinked. My goodness. His birthday was coming up soon—Saturday. Perhaps she and Penny could plan a small family celebration. It would be something fun to take Penny's mind off the current tension in the house and might in fact go a long way toward easing that tension.

Feeling considerably better about things herself, Sadie closed the bible and decided she was finally ready for bed. She glanced at the clock in the hall and realized it had been over an hour since she'd tucked Penny in. And the light still shone in the study. Did Eli really have that much paperwork to do?

She climbed the stairs, still feeling buoyed by the thought of planning a birthday surprise for Eli, when a sound caught her attention. At first she thought Skeeter was whining to get out, but as soon as she opened Penny's door she realized it was Penny herself. Rushing over to the bedside she sat and gathered the girl in her arms. "What is it, princess? Did you have a bad dream?"

Muffling her sobs against Sadie's chest, Penny nodded.

"Well I'm here now. You just cry all you want to until you get it all out. Then we'll talk, okay?"

Penny took her at her word, crying with wracking sobs for a good while longer, before she finally began to calm down. The most terrible thing about it was that she tried to cry quietly, as if something terrible would happen if her crying was overheard.

When the crying finally stopped, Sadie gently pushed her far enough away to look into her eyes. "Feeling better now?" she asked as she brushed the hair off her forehead.

Penny nodded but Sadie could still see the haunted look in her eyes. "Do you want to tell me about it?"

This time Penny shook her head.

"Should I get Eli for you?"

Penny's hand tightened on her arm. "No, please."

The vehemence of her response startled Sadie. "Sweetheart, you need to talk to someone about this."

"It was just a bad dream."

"And what was this bad dream about?"

The little girl hunched her shoulders and refused to look Sadie in the eye. "You'll think I'm a bad person if I tell you."

Sadie gave her a fierce hug. "Penny, I could *never, ever* think of you as a bad person. Whatever it is, tell me and we'll figure out how to make it right together."

"I dreamed about the terrible thing I did. And nothing can ever make it right."

What in the world had happened to so wound this

child? Perhaps she should get Eli? But Penny had been so insistent…

"Just tell me. I promise you'll feel better once you do."

Penny took a deep breath, then let it out in a rush. "It's my fault Susan died."

Chapter Eighteen

"I didn't mean to, I promise. I would never hurt Susan on purpose."

"Oh baby, of course you wouldn't. Tell me what happened." Sadie was horrified that Penny had borne all this inside her and was trying desperately to make sure she said the right thing. Oh, why hadn't she gotten Eli?

"It was right after we got back from a visit to Amberleigh. Susan was so sad and she didn't look well at all. I wanted to tell Nanny to fetch the doctor but Susan said I mustn't bother her or Eli, that she was certain everything would be better by morning. It was very stuffy and she asked me to open her window, so I did, even though Eli said we were not to. She just looked so pale."

The sobbing started again and Sadie rocked her in her arms.

"She hadn't gone sleepwalking since we moved in with Eli," Penny continued between sobs, "so I thought it would be all right. Only it wasn't. She fell out of the window and it's all my fault."

Her voice broke on those last words and Sadie gently cupped her chin and forced her gaze up. "Listen to me, Penny, this is not your fault. No one could have foreseen what would happen. If she hadn't fallen out the window she might have fallen down the stairs or off the landing."

She held the girl's face between her hands. "Look at me. You are *not* to blame yourself for this. Susan fell, pure and simple. Yes, it's an awful thing to have happened, but no one is at fault."

"But—"

Sadie put a finger to the girl's lips. "No buts. I don't care how that window got opened, it was *not* your fault. Understand?" She had to convince the child, had to ease what must be an overwhelming sense of guilt.

Penny finally nodded.

"Have you told Eli about this?"

"No!" She grew agitated again. "He would hate me."

"He most certainly would not. Eli loves you, princess."

"But only because he doesn't know—"

"It doesn't matter. He loves you because you're you. And nothing you can do will change that."

She seemed reluctant to believe that. Then she gave a big yawn. Her hand snaked out and took hold of Sadie's. "Thank you for being so nice to me."

"How about we say a little prayer together? Would that be okay?"

Penny nodded.

Sadie took her hand, then bowed her head. "Heavenly Father, we ask that you bring healing to this sweet little girl's heart. Let her know that You love her and cherish her and will always be there to comfort her in her times of trouble. Bring her that promised peace that passes all understanding. And let her dreams always be filled with light and laughter. Amen."

Penny echoed her amen, then snuggled deeper under the covers.

"Do you want me to sit with you until you fall asleep?"

Penny seemed to think about that for a minute, then she shook her head. "I'm okay now. And I have Skeeter with me." She gave Sadie a conspiratorial smile. "Don't tell, Eli, but sometimes Skeeter jumps up in bed with me."

"It'll be our little secret."

Penny yawned again and Sadie patted her through the covers. "Sweet dreams, princess."

"Sweet dreams, Sadie."

Had she done enough to ease Penny's burden of guilt? Would the child be able to rest easier now? What a tremendous burden for such a little girl to be carrying. How could Eli not have known?

As she closed Penny's door she caught sight of Eli climbing up the stairs. Good, it would save her the trouble of seeking him out. She waited for him at the top of the stairs, arms crossed.

Eli was two-thirds of the way up the stairs when he saw Sadie waiting for him at the top. He paused. "Sadie. What—"

She put a finger to her lips and pointed to Penny's door.

He clamped his mouth shut. What now? He was tired and not up to another confrontation with her.

As soon as he stepped off the top stair she whispered, "We need to talk."

At this hour? She was carrying her penchant for melodrama just a little too far. "If you want to rehash—"

"No." She put her finger to her lips again. "Not here."

She marched to his bedchamber and waited for him to open the door.

She definitely had his interest piqued now.

Eli stepped past her, opened the door and waved her inside. Once he'd closed the door behind him, he waved her to a chair, which she refused.

"Do you mind telling me what this is all about?"

"It's about Penny. She had another nightmare tonight."

He came fully alert, every muscle tensing. "Is she all right? I should probably go to her."

"She's fine for now and she doesn't want to see you."

He froze as her words sunk in. Penny didn't want to see him? Had she completely lost faith in him? All because of his aversion to Sadie's stories?

Sadie's expression softened a fraction. "That came out wrong. She still loves you and craves your approval. She just—oh hang it all Eli, have you ever really talked to her about what happened to Susan and how she felt about it?"

Why wouldn't she sit down so he could as well? Her words weren't making a lot of sense to him. "Yes, I mean no, I mean, well naturally she was grieving. She was really broken up about it. She thought the world of Susan and her mother had passed on only a couple of months earlier."

He tried to pull his thoughts together. "Is that what her nightmare was about, Susan's fall? I assure you I never let her see the body." It was enough that he'd seen the mangled remains of his once-lovely stepsister. He could never have subjected Penny to that horror. But had she somehow seen it before he had the body covered?

"Eli, she thinks Susan's death was her fault."

Everything in Eli went still. "That's impossible. Penny had nothing to do with what happened."

"Of course she didn't. But it's her you need to convince, not me. Penny was the one who opened Susan's window that night. Apparently, Susan was feeling sickly and Penny thought the fresh air might help make her feel better. So now she thinks if she hadn't left the window open, Susan would never have fallen."

Bile and self-recrimination rose in his throat. How could he not have realized what Penny was feeling all this time, how could he have let his young, innocent little sister carry such an undeserved burden of guilt? "Why didn't she tell me?"

"Apparently, you'd warned them not to leave any windows open. She was afraid you wouldn't love her any more if she admitted what she'd done."

The words sliced through Eli like a knife. He felt blindly for the mattress that he knew was behind him and sat down hard. "How could she think that?"

Sadie stood in front of him and crossed her arms again. "She's nine years old, she felt guilty, and you were the only person left in her world. She didn't want to risk losing you, too."

Eli heard the thing she'd left unsaid just as clearly as if she'd shouted it. He'd never told Penny he loved her, never given her reason to believe he would stand by her. "I have to go talk to her."

"Of course. But do you know what you're going to say?"

Eli eased back down. What indeed? "I can't tell her the truth."

Sadie frowned. "Why not?"

"Because I'm not sure she's old enough to understand.

And because it might tarnish her memory of her sister. I could never do that to her."

He was surprised when she didn't ask him to explain. Glancing up he saw only concern and patience. He took a deep breath. "I suppose I owe you the rest of the story."

"Only if you want to tell me."

Surprisingly he did. "I told you I came home that evening to find Susan's body on the flagstones below her window. What I didn't tell you was that she jumped out of the window of her own accord."

There was a sharp intake of breath and then Sadie was sitting beside him, taking his hands in both of hers. "Oh Eli, how horrible. Are you certain?"

"She left a note." Sadie's hands gave his a squeeze and he squeezed back, comforted by her touch. It was such a relief to finally share the story, the horror of that discovery, with someone, someone he could trust to hold it close to her heart.

"I should have realized what was happening, should have seen there was more than grief eating at Susan. It turns out that before her mother's death she had been… intimate with one of the servants at Amberleigh. It was only after I moved them to the city with me that she realized she was with child." Had he shocked her, repulsed her?

But again there was only sympathy. "She must have been terrified."

"She was convinced that if she could just talk to the bas—fellow, he would do right by her. Of course I never knew any of this until I read her note. I took her constant begging to visit to Amberleigh to be mere homesickness."

"Eli, you were doing the best you could."

He wished he could believe that. But he knew better. "When I finally did take the girls back to the country for a short visit, the man in question apparently refused to take responsibility and was gone from the property the next morning. The first night of our return is when she jumped from her window."

"It must have been horrid for you to have to go through this alone. And then to shield Penny as you did. That's why you sold everything and moved here, isn't it?"

How had she known? "I did my best to put it forth as an accident. But some ugly rumors began to surface almost at once. I couldn't let Penny grow up in the shadow of that. I couldn't."

"Of course you couldn't." She lifted a hand to his cheek. "You were incredibly strong and generous and someday Penny will understand all that you've done for her." Her expression softened. "But for now you'll just have to make do with the understanding that *I* know and I think you are the most selfless, heroic man I've ever met."

Her words were like a balm to his soul. He captured her hand and held it against his cheek. "Ah, Sadie, what did I ever do to deserve you?"

She gave him a gentle, teasing grin. "You helped me harvest some honey."

That surprised a chuckle out of him. "That I did." He sobered almost immediately. "I can't tell Penny any of this."

"Perhaps someday, but you're right, this might be just as hard for her to deal with." She touched his arm with her free hand. "The most important thing is to let her know that you know what she did and that you don't blame her, that you still love her unconditionally. That'll go a long way to easing her fears."

"But I can't let her continue to carry the guilt around."

"Maybe there's a way. What kind of windows were in Susan's room?"

That was an odd question. "What do you mean?"

"Were they short like these in here, or were they the tall, narrow ones some houses have?"

"Tall and narrow, why?"

"And do you remember how you found them? I mean if someone was going to climb out on a ledge I would think they would want to open the window just as far as it could go."

He was beginning to see what she was leading up to. "You're right, the window was opened all the way up. Penny could never have pushed it up so far."

"There you have it. You can tell her with complete honesty that Susan opened them up further after she left the room, that it wasn't her fault at all."

Eli gave her a hug. "Thank you."

The clock downstairs chimed midnight. In the distance a dog howled and was answered by another. Closer by, he heard the soft whicker of the horses, no doubt disturbed by the dogs. But all of that was mere backdrop to the beating of his and Sadie's hearts as he held that hug for a few seconds longer than absolutely necessary.

When he pulled away he saw the flush of awareness staining her cheeks, saw the longing in her eyes and he bent down to taste another of her oh-so-sweet kisses.

Sweeter than honey, special or otherwise, warmer than sunshine, gentler than a butterfly's touch—her kisses were like nothing he'd ever experienced. The fact that they were for him alone filled him with an overpowering joy. She was his—to protect and cherish and share the rest of his life with.

When they separated, he looked down into her

bemused face and traced her lips with his finger. She was so beautiful, so absolutely kissable. "Someday, *Mrs. Reynolds,* in the very near future you will be sharing this room with me, I promise you, and we will be starting that family we discussed. But first we have a few matters to settle between us. And a little sister to help find peace."

Sadie gave her head a mental shake. His kisses were so wonderful. They made her feel like she was special, as if she were enveloped in a bubble of love and protection.

But he was right. Much as she wanted to explore this new side of their relationship, tonight they had to think about Penny.

He kept one arm around her and while she was glad of the contact, it did make it harder for her to concentrate.

"So what now?" he asked. "I want to just go marching over there and tell her all the things she needs to hear."

Sadie shook her head. "She was yawning widely when I left. I would guess she's sound asleep by now." Just the thought of it made Sadie yawn herself.

"You're right. It probably wouldn't serve any good purpose for me to wake her just to set her fears at rest. Perhaps I should wait until morning."

"Good idea." Sadie yawned again and felt her eyes drift close. With an effort she opened them wider. "But then you should talk to her first thing."

"Of course."

Was that a hint of amusement in his voice? If she wasn't so sleepy she'd call him on it.

When Sadie opened her eyes again, the black of night had turned to the hazy gray of pre-dawn. It took her another moment to realize she wasn't in her room. Turning her head, she met the amused gray-eyed stare of her husband. "Good morning."

Sadie sat up, not at all sure how to react. "Good morning." Taking quick stock she realized that both of them were still wearing the clothes they'd worn last night, though Eli had shed his coat and vest, and both had been laying crosswise on the bed, on top of the covers.

"You should have woken me up and sent me to my own room last night," she said, feeling slightly grumpy but not sure why.

"Ah, but you looked so comfortable I hadn't the heart to wake you."

"What if Penny had needed me for something?"

He waved a hand toward his door. "I left the door ajar so I could hear her if she stirred. There's been nary a sound."

She slid off the bed with as much dignity as she could muster.

He slid from the bed, as well. However his height allowed him to do it with much more grace than she'd been able to conjure up. Which was entirely unfair on a number of levels.

"Well then, thank you for your hospitality, but I think I'll return to my own room for my morning ablutions. I'll see you at breakfast."

"Of course." He made an exaggerated bow and then to her surprise followed her from the room.

"Where do you think you're going?"

"Why, to check in on Penny, of course. I'd like to talk to her before breakfast if she's awake." He grinned. "Where did you think I was going?"

Not bothering to answer his question, Sadie flounced

toward her room with a swish of her skirts. His warm chuckle followed her all the way to her door.

A moment later though, his exclamation pulled her back into the hall and rushing toward Penny's room. What was wrong? Had she had another nightmare?

She turned into Penny's room and at first didn't understand what she was seeing. Eli sat on his sister's bed, but Penny didn't seem to be there. Then she saw he was holding a piece of paper.

He looked up, holding out the paper, his expression stricken. "She's run away."

Chapter Nineteen

Sadie took the note from him and quickly scanned the lines, written in Penny's childish hand.

> *Eli, it's my fault that Susan fell out of her window. Sadie can tell you about the terrible thing I did. I didn't mean for her to get hurt, honest. I'm sorry I didn't tell you before but I was afraid you wouldn't want me around any more. Please don't be mad at me.*
>
> *I know what I did was wrong and that I need to do something to make up for it. I don't know anything big enough, so I'm going to do like Annabel Adams and try to go around helping people and doing good things. I will miss you both and hope you will miss me a little bit, too.*
>
> *PS*
>
> *I hope you're not going to be angry with me, Sadie, but Skeeter wants to come with me so I'm going to let him.*

Sadie's hands began to tremble and the letter fluttered to the floor. Penny was out there somewhere, trying to emulate Sadie's adventurous make-believe heroine. Sadie's knees buckled and she had to grab the bedpost to keep from falling. Eli had been right—she never should have written that story. She'd never be able to forgive herself if something happened to Penny before they could find her.

The only prayer she could form was *Dear God, keep her safe, keep her safe.* Over and over, the words tumbled through her mind.

Eli shot up, as if shaking off his momentarily paralysis. "She can't have gotten far. You let Sheriff Hammond know. I'll start looking."

"Of course. And she's got Skeeter with her, he'll watch over her." Then she had a sudden thought. *Please God, let me be wrong.* "Eli."

He paused in the doorway.

"Check the stable."

His expression whitened a bit more, but he gave a short nod and headed back to his room with long, impatient strides. She paused only long enough to jab a few pins in her hair, wash her face and put on more serviceable shoes. Yesterday's dress and less than tidy hair would have to do for now.

She headed out the back door and found Eli leading Cocoa out of the stable. He clinched his jaw and she saw a tic pulse at the corner of his mouth. "Buttermilk's missing." He mounted up and then looked down at her. "Tell Sheriff Hammond that I'm headed south and I'd appreciate it if he could go north."

Without waiting for her answer he set the horse in motion. Sadie dashed around the house and hit the sidewalk at a fast clip. It was still barely light out and not many folks were up and about. The few who were gave her curious looks but she didn't give them the opportunity to speak to her.

She reached the sheriff's office to find he was not yet in. What now? She had no idea where the man lived. But she knew who would know.

She set out immediately for the boardinghouse, a small part of her hoping that Penny had sought refuge there.

She burst in through the kitchen door without so much as a knock and almost sobbed with relief to find Cora Beth already busy stoking her stove.

"My goodness, Sadie, you gave me quite a start. What are you doing out this way so early?"

"Is Penny here?"

"Penny, why no—" Cora Beth seemed to finally take in Sadie's appearance and the import of her question. "Oh my goodness, is she missing? You sit yourself down here before you fall over, and tell me what happened."

"No time. Penny's run away and I need to let Sheriff Hammond know so he can help search for her. Only he wasn't at his office and I don't know where he lives. She's on horseback, Cora Beth, *horseback* and she's probably been out for hours so there's no telling how far she's gone. And it's all my fault. If anything happens to her—" Sadie felt her barely-held control start to unravel as a sob escaped.

Cora Beth took her arm and led her to the table. Then she handed her a cup of coffee. "Here now, you get this down while I go fetch Danny and send him for the sheriff. We'll find her, you'll see."

Sadie didn't know how long she sat there. She was vaguely aware of Cora Beth sitting next to her, offering food and comfort, but she didn't emerge from her mind-fogging fear until Sheriff Hammond strode into the room. "Danny tells me little Penny has gone missing."

Sadie jumped up from her seat. "Yes. She ran away."

"You're sure she's not just hiding somewhere back at your place. Kids do that sometime when they're looking for attention."

If only that were the case. "No, sir. She left a note and her horse and dog are missing."

"Anything in the note or anything she say last night give you an idea of where she might be headed?"

"She just said she wants to be like Annabel Adams." Sadie's voice broke again but she managed to get herself back under control.

"Off looking for adventure, then." He rubbed his chin. "I take it Eli's already out looking for her."

"Yes. He left about thirty minutes ago. Said to tell you he was headed south and would appreciate it if you'd head north."

"I'll round up a few good men and we'll start checking all the roads and trails. I suggest you head home and stay there."

"But I want to help look for her."

"It's best if someone is at home in case she gets tired of adventuring and decides to come back on her own." He raised a hand to stall her protests. "And I'll pass the word to anyone that your house is our command post. All searchers are to check in with you from time to time to give you updates and see if she's been found."

Sadie nodded, still not happy with being on the sidelines but prepared to do her part.

The sheriff gave her a reassuring smile. "Don't worry, we'll find her."

After asking Cora Beth to get a telegram off to Griff,

Sadie headed home. Not that she expected Penny to get that far, but somehow she felt better knowing her brother was aware of the situation. She also wanted him to call in favors from everyone he knew between here and there.

She turned in her front gate hoping against hope that Eli would have found her already or that Sheriff Hammond's prediction that she'd come home on her own would come true. But the only person she found when she arrived was Mrs. Dauber. She apprised the woman of the situation, then went up to her room to freshen up and change her clothes.

Then the excruciating wait began.

To keep herself busy, Sadie went to work setting up the command post Sheriff Hammond had requested. She had Mrs. Dauber prepare and keep at the ready plenty of coffee and food to feed any of the searchers who needed a quick break. She kept meticulous notes of every report that came in. Danny found her a detailed map Josie had made of the area and she used pins to mark the location of every road, trail, building or hidey-hole that had been checked. She took down the name of every person who had been talked to. And she kept the searchers updated as they came in and noted where each planned to go next.

Eli checked in about an hour after the search started. Sadie stepped right into his arms and he held her stiffly for a moment before his embrace momentarily softened. The stubble from his unshaven jaw scratched at her forehead, but she didn't care, she needed to give and take what comfort she could.

Neither said a word and after a few short seconds he pulled away and reached for the cup of coffee Mrs. Dauber had at the ready. His jaw was clenched so tight Sadie didn't know how he managed to gulp it down.

While he drank, he listened closely to the information she had gathered, then with barely a word, he set out again.

After he was gone, Sadie sat for a long time staring down at her map without really seeing it. She knew she shouldn't read anything into his stiffness, his silence. Naturally he was deeply worried about Penny. But she couldn't help but wonder if he blamed her for this as much as she blamed herself.

Then another pair of searchers stopped in and she was back into her role as information gatherer.

By the time she heard the train whistle shortly before noon, Sadie was beside herself. Penny still hadn't been found and she was going mad just sitting here waiting for the news to trickle in. She should be out there looking for her little princess.

When Griff and Ry came striding into her parlor Sadie felt a sob bubble from her throat and she threw herself into their arms. She quickly tamped down the urge to cry but her eyes were still moist when she pulled away. "Ry, it's so good to see you." She swiped a hand across her eyes. "I'm sorry I wasn't there to meet you but—"

"Hush, Sadie girl, I heard all about it." Her oldest brother offered her his handkerchief. "We were there when Griff got your telegram."

She looked past her brothers. "Where's Josie?"

Ry grinned. "She's at the boardinghouse getting showered with affection and questions by Viola."

Sadie put a hand to her mouth. "Oh! Ry, what was I thinking? That's where you should be, too. Viola will—"

"Time enough for that later. Right now it's another little girl who needs our help."

Griff put one of his arms around her shoulder. "Now, buck up and tell us what we can do."

With a nod, Sadie waved them over to her map.

By the time her brothers had determined where they would search, Josie was striding into the room, Viola in tow. As soon as Viola spotted Ry she ran across the room with her arms outstretched. "Daddy!"

Ry lifted her off the floor and twirled her around. "How's my special girl? I've missed you."

Sadie felt the tears prick the back of her eyelids again. What she wouldn't give to see Eli and Penny share such an embrace. *Heavenly Father, please given them that chance.*

Josie gave her a quick embrace, then stepped back. "What can I do to help?"

That was Josie, ready to dispense with the amenities and get right to the point as always.

"You can take over for me here. I'm going to help find Penny."

"Hold on a minute, Sadie girl—"

Sadie gave Griff and Ry both a hard look. "That's Penny we're looking for, and I'm as good at scenting a trail as either one of you. Y'all are going to have to hog-tie me to keep me from going out." She placed her hands on her hips. "And I promise even then you're going to have a fight on your hands."

Josie put an arm around her shoulder. "Ignore them, they're just being men. I'd do the same thing if it was Viola and there'd be no stopping me. Now, show me what you need me to do."

Griff and Ry headed out while Sadie quickly explained her system to Josie. While she was studying the map to pick out her own search area, though, she had an epiphany. Of course. Why hadn't she thought of this sooner?

"I'm going here," she said firmly. She placed her finger on the spot where she estimated the spot was that she and Penny had found yesterday, the special place that was just theirs.

Josie narrowed her eyes. "You know something." It was more statement than question.

"I think, I mean I don't know, maybe, but I may be wrong."

Josie made a shooing motion with her hands. "Then get on out of here. Go find your little girl."

Sadie was looking for the spot to turn off the main road when she heard a horse galloping up behind her. She turned in the saddle to find Eli bearing down on her and so she slowed her horse to a walk. Had Penny been found?

As soon as he got close enough for her to see his expression, she knew that wasn't the case.

Eli pulled alongside her and matched Cocoa's pace to Calliope's. "I checked in right after you left. Your sister-in-law says she thought you were on to something."

Sadie nodded. "I remembered the place where we went exploring yesterday and noticed no one had checked it out yet. It's kind of hard to find, but I thought maybe it was somewhere she'd try to go."

"Show me."

Sadie studied the tree line to their right. There were certain landmarks she had pointed out to Penny so they could find it again. "The trail cuts into those woods at an angle so you don't notice it unless you're looking for it. We only spotted it because Skeeter went chasing a rabbit that way."

Eli turned his horse from the road and moved closer to the trees.

"We're looking for a pair of pecans next to a cotton-wood with a broken branch. The trail starts not too far from there."

Eli nodded, his eyes never leaving the tree line. A moment later he pointed. "There!"

Sadie moved up ahead of him and started counting oaks—it should be the third one. Even so she almost passed right by the trail. She pulled her horse up short and turned her toward the roofed opening. "You'll have to duck under these branches here," she told Eli. "But the trail opens up pretty quick once we get by this oak. And our spot's not very far in."

Eli let her lead, but he rode close behind her, so close Calliope could just about swish the flies from Cocoa's face with her tail. The trail was twisty and narrow so there was no question of riding side-by-side. They took turns calling Penny's name, then listening for a response.

Then she heard something that made her heart leap. She held up a hand to silence Eli. Then she heard it again. "That was Skeeter. We've found her."

Sadie nudged Calliope into a faster walk, continuing to call Penny's name. Why didn't the girl answer?

The trail widened just before they reached the clearing and Eli was immediately beside her. They entered the clearing side by side and saw Penny sitting under a tree with muddy tear tracks on her face and her arms around Skeeter. Buttermilk grazed nearby.

Eli vaulted from his horse almost before the mare had stopped.

Sadie, who was suddenly trembling so hard she wasn't sure her limbs could support her, dismounted more slowly. *Heavenly Father, thank You, thank You, thank you.*

By the time she reached them, Eli was on his knees with his arms around Penny and he was rocking her back and forth.

Penny clung to him as if she would never let him go.

Sadie let them have a minute, then knelt down beside them. "Mind if I share a part of that hug?" Her voice was as shaky as her hands, but she didn't care. Eli and Penny separated just enough to let her in, and all the pent up emotions of the day finally broke free in a flood of tears.

Chapter Twenty

Eli held tight to both of them, giving silent thanks to God that they had finally found Penny. He felt he'd aged ten years today. All sorts of horrors had been clawing in his mind since he'd first found her note. And threaded through all of it was a fierce, soul-wrenching regret that he'd never told Penny how very dear she was to him. He'd prayed all morning to have a chance to rectify that, and now that he'd been given that chance he wasn't about to let it pass him by.

As soon as Sadie's tears subsided, he broke off the hug and looked Penny in the eye. "Are you all right?"

"I hurt my foot and my arm is all scratched."

"Let's have a look at you."

Sadie scrambled up, pulling a handkerchief from the pocket of her skirt. "I'll wet this and be back quicker than a cat's sneeze."

That coaxed a small smile from Penny, which Eli suspected had been Sadie's intent. While they waited for her, Eli eased Penny's shoe off. "Where does it hurt?"

"Right here." She touched her arch. "I stepped on a pointy rock and it hurt something awful."

He examined it closely. The bottom of her foot

appeared tender and bruised but the skin wasn't broken. He'd have Dr. Whitman take a look at it when they got back to town, just in case.

Sadie returned with her wet cloth and began to gently dab at the scratches. As far as Eli could see, they were superficial, as well.

Which meant it was time for him to have that talk with his sister. "You know, I've been very worried about you, Henny-Penny." The nickname, which he hadn't used since she was a toddler, slipped out as if he'd called her that all her life. "I would have been quite lost without you."

Penny's eyes widened. "You would?"

He raised a brow. "Of course I would. You're my sister and I love you." There, that hadn't been so hard to say, after all. In fact, it had felt rather good. He returned the squeeze Sadie gave his hand but didn't take his eyes from his sister. "I'm sorry if I made you so sad that you wanted to leave."

"Oh, no, it wasn't that at all." Penny bit her lip, then bravely squared her shoulders. "I did something terrible, Eli."

"Running away *was* terrible, and you must promise to never, ever do it again. But it all turned out okay, so we will give God thanks and put it behind us."

She shook her head. "That wasn't the terrible thing. I mean, yes, it was terrible and I'm very sorry, but I was talking about…"

He lifted her chin with his fisted hand. "About the night Susan died," he said gently.

She nodded, her eyes filling with tears.

"Sadie told me what you said."

"Don't hate me, Eli, please." Her voice rose to

near-panic. "I didn't mean to do it. I would *never* hurt Susan."

He gave her a fierce hug. "Hush this nonsense. Of course you wouldn't hurt Susan. And I couldn't hate you, not ever. You're my sister, my Henny-Penny. Didn't I just say that I love you?"

She nodded her head against his shoulder.

Eli saw Sadie's tearful approval and it gave him the boost he needed to continue. "Besides, you have it all wrong."

"I do?" She pulled back, rubbing at her tears with her fist. "But I opened the window, Eli. I remember doing it."

He smiled tenderly, silently thanking Sadie for giving him the words he needed. "I went to her room that night, Penny. Her window was open, yes, but it was open all the way to the very tip-top."

Penny wrinkled her nose. "It was? But I can't reach that high."

He tapped her nose. "Exactly. Susan must have opened it wider herself. Which means it *wasn't your fault.*"

He could almost see the moment she believed his words, could almost see the shadow of the burden she'd been carrying lift itself from her shoulders. She gave him another hug, then turned to Sadie.

"Did you hear what Eli said? It wasn't my fault?"

"Of course it wasn't, princess. Now, are you ready to come home? There's lots of people who are going to be very happy to see you."

Sadie came down the stairs to find most of the crowd of searchers and well-wishers had dispersed. But there were still a number of folks in her parlor keeping Eli company—Griff and Ry were there, as were Josie and Viola, Sheriff Hammond and Cora Beth.

"She's sleeping," Sadie announced. "Poor little thing is plumb tuckered out."

Sheriff Hammond stood. "Well, guess I'll be heading off to my place. I'm glad it all turned out okay."

Eli stood, as well. "Thank you, sheriff. We appreciate all you did to get the search parties organized."

The sheriff smiled. "Not much to it. Most folks around here will drop everything to help a neighbor in trouble, especially when there's a child involved." He smiled. "Besides, your missus did most of the organizing."

Cora Beth stood. "I'd best be getting on, as well. I left Uncle Grover in charge and I'm sure he's ready for me to relieve him by now."

Once Sadie had escorted the two of them to the door, she returned to her parlor. "Griff, Ry, I don't think you'll ever know how much it meant to me to look up and see my two big brothers striding through my door today."

"You know we'll be here for you, Sadie girl, any time you need us," Ry said. "All you gotta do is send word."

"We Lassiters take care of each other," Griff added. "All for one and one for all."

Sadie smiled at the reminder of their childhood battle cry. The she turned to Josie. "You, too. Thanks for all your help today."

Josie smiled. "Glad to help. But it seems to me you did most of the hard work." She turned to Ry. "I think these folks probably need some time to themselves. And I have a hankering to sleep in my own bed tonight."

"Yes ma'am." Ry put one arm around Josie, and held out his other to shake his brother's hand. "Good seeing you again, Griff. Maybe next time we'll have more time to visit."

Then he planted a kiss on Sadie's cheek, shook Eli's hand and lifted Viola. With a chorus of good-byes, they were gone.

Griff reached for his hat next.

"We have an extra bed if you need one tonight," Sadie offered.

"I already talked to Cora Beth about spending the night at the boardinghouse." He glanced Eli's way. "Like Josie said, you folks need some time to yourselves right now."

He gave Sadie a hug, then a peck on the cheek. "I'm glad everything worked out all right for you, Sadie girl."

Once they had the house to themselves, Sadie turned to Eli. She had to say this now, before her courage failed her.

"I'm sorry, Eli, I should have listened to you."

His lips curled up into a quizzical smile. "While those are edifying words to hear, you'll have to be a little more specific."

"It's my fault Penny ran away. My stories are what put all those notions about grand adventures in her head. She would have never gone off if I had listened to you and quit writing them."

"Sadie—"

She ignored his interruption, unable to stop now that she'd started. "I threw my new story in the stove this morning. I'll talk to Mr. Chalmers tomorrow and tell him that there will be no more stories from me. And I promise to stop filling her head with my nonsense. If anything had happened to her—" Sadie buried her face in her hands, unable to finish that sentence.

A second later she felt Eli gently tug her hands away. "Sadie, this is not your fault."

He was just being kind. She almost wished he would rail at her, would give her the chewing out she deserved. "I read her letter, remember. She ran away because she wanted to be like Annabel Adams. And I taught her how to ride a horse, and brought her to that place, so it's my fault she got so far, hid so well. I know you'll find it hard to forgive me, but I hope you'll try. From here on out, I'll try to be the perfect wife you'd hoped to find when you came here, to care for Penny just the way you want me to." She took a deep breath. "You two would have been better off if I hadn't—"

"Stop it."

His sharp command brought her up short.

"Don't you dare finish that sentence. I've been thanking God all day for bringing you into our lives."

Her breath caught in her throat. Thanking God?

His lips quirked up again, but there was no mirth in his expression. "That's right. I stopped on the side of the road and got down on my knees and prayed like I haven't prayed in years, like I never truly prayed before in my life. I not only begged God to help me find Penny, but I asked for forgiveness for being such a stubborn, mule-headed fool. For hurting you and Penny the way I have."

"But—"

He placed a finger on her lips. "You may have read Penny's letter but you obviously missed the most important part. She didn't leave because she wanted to be like Annabel Adams, she left because she was afraid I would be mad at her when I discovered her secret. I let my sister believe my love was contingent on her good behavior, let her believe she had a hand in her sister's death, all because I was too worried about fixing things, too worried about keeping everything under control, that I couldn't bother myself to spend time giving her what she needed most."

His self-recrimination tore at her. "You were just doing what you thought best."

"Best for appearances's sake you mean, not best for Penny." He stroked her cheek with the back of his hand. "No, if there is any blame to be cast here, it is all on me. What you brought her was the skill to survive out there, the protection of your loyal pet, and the knowledge that *someone* cared for her. It's why this day had a happy ending."

"Oh Eli, thank you for that. From here on out, I'll try to be the perfect wife you'd hoped to find when you came here, to keep your house in perfect order, to teach Penny to be a lady, to—"

Again he put a finger to her lips. "Sadie, all I really want is for you to be yourself. Because today I realized that, by God's grace, I ended up married to the absolute perfect wife for me."

Sadie was afraid to read too much into his words. After all, he'd had a long, highly charged day. Maybe he was just feeling euphoric. "Do you really mean that? Because you don't have to feel—"

"Mean it? I not only mean it, I'll shout it to the world if you want me to. I've felt this way for a long time but have just been too thickheaded to admit it, even to myself. I'm sorry I couldn't say it before, but I'll say it now. I love you, Sadie Elizabeth Lassiter Reynolds, just the way you are. I wouldn't change one tiny thing about you."

Sadie launched herself into his arms. "Oh Eli, I love you too, so very, very much."

* * *

Eli wrapped his arms around his perfect wife, savoring the just-right feel of her, the wildflowers and sunshine scent of her, the generous, joyous spirit of her. And he silently vowed to spend the rest of his life making certain she never had reason to question his love again.

* * * * *

Dear Reader,

Thank you so much for picking up this book and I hope you enjoyed Sadie and Eli's story. It was fun to revisit the town of Knotty Pine and some of the same characters from my earlier book, *The Christmas Journey.* Eli and Sadie were fun characters to write about—they both had such strong visions of what they wanted from a marriage and were both certain they were 'making the best of a bad situation' going into this one. And of course they eventually discover it was part of God's perfect plan, after all.

Similarly, when I started *The Proper Wife,* I had a clear idea of the kind of path it would take and the lessons these two characters would have to learn. But before I'd gone very far, the story began unfolding quite differently and I found myself both surprised and delighted by the eventual outcome. I hope you will be, too.

I truly enjoy hearing from readers. If you've a mind to comment or just say hi, please contact me via e-mail at winnie@winniegriggs.com or you can write to me at PO Box 14, Plain Dealing, LA 71064.

Wishing you love and blessings,

Winnie

QUESTIONS FOR DISCUSSION

1. Sadie felt that her brothers tended to 'baby' her. Do you think they did and how did you feel about this?

2. Did Eli's fear of snakes make him seem less heroic to you?

3. Sadie's initial reaction to Eli's proposal was quite strong. What emotions did you sense from her?

4. Was the community's reaction to Sadie's and Eli's misadventure realistic for the times?

5. Sadie fought to hold onto her writing—why do you think that was?

6. What did you think of the items Sadie selected to have shipped from Hawk's Creek to her new home? How did you feel about Eli's reaction to them?

7. Were Sadie's and Eli's reactions to being assigned the same room when they visited Hawk's Creek believable?

8. How did you feel about Eli when you learned he never had a more than superficial discussion with Penny about Susan's death?

9. Sadie's talents seemed to be more along the lines of people skills than the domestic arts. Do you

think one set of skills is more important than the other?

10. At what part of the story, if at all, did you begin to understand Eli's dislike of Sadie's stories?

11. By the end of the book, did you believe that Sadie and Eli could truly enjoy a 'happily ever after'? Why or why not?

Love Inspired. HISTORICAL

TITLES AVAILABLE NEXT MONTH

Available April 12, 2011

REQUEST YOUR FREE BOOKS!

2 FREE INSPIRATIONAL NOVELS
PLUS 2
FREE
MYSTERY GIFTS

Love Inspired
HISTORICAL
INSPIRATIONAL HISTORICAL ROMANCE